PRAISE FOR *THIS WRET...*

"If you love wilderness horror, *This Wretched Valley* is a must-read. But be forewarned: after reading this chilling debut, you may never want to set foot in the great outdoors again."—**ALMA KATSU**, author of *The Hunger* and *The Fervor*

"Despite being the author's debut novel, *This Wretched Valley* is a glittering contender for Best Horror of 2024. . . . This book is unshakable."—**CEMETERY DANCE**

"A terrifying debut, rendered with the intensity and skill of Scott Smith's cult favorite *The Ruins* and touches of *The Hunger* by Alma Katsu and *Echo* by Thomas Olde Heuvelt. The novel announces Kiefer's intentions to boldly begin her climb to the top of the genre."—**LIBRARY JOURNAL**, starred review

"Kiefer's debut heralds the arrival of a major new horror talent. Through vivid descriptions of the creepy setting and thoughtful character portraits, Kiefer maintains a feeling of unease and nail-biting tension throughout. Devotees of daylight horror will be entranced."—**PUBLISHERS WEEKLY**, starred review

"Kiefer's gory and intense debut centers on a doomed rock-climbing expedition beset by horrors both human and supernatural. Kiefer, a climber herself, utilizes her knowledge of the sport to deliver an evocative and pulse-pounding survival horror novel inspired by the Dyatlov Pass incident. This disturbing outing marks her as a writer to watch and will appeal to fans of Scott Smith's *The Ruins* (2006) and the Showtime series *Yellowjackets*."—**BOOKLIST**

"Twisty and brutal, Jenny Kiefer's debut unfolds like your favorite creepy new horror flick. Welcome to *This Wretched Valley*, where everything bleeds."
—**CHRISTOPHER GOLDEN**, *New York Times* best-selling author of *All Hallows* and *Road of Bones*

"*This Wretched Valley* is a reality-warping, body-horror, don't-go-into-the-woods nightmare which grips from its very first sentence. Kiefer deftly weaves something Dyatlov Pass–shaped from her characters' hubris and pain, leading them to a ghastly and inevitable end sure to delight fans of *The Troop* or *Blair Witch*. A truly unforgettable debut."—**ALLY WILKES**, Bram Stoker Award–nominated author of *All the White Spaces*

THIS WRETCHED VALLEY

JENNY KIEFER

QUIRK BOOKS
PHILADELPHIA

Library of Congress Cataloging-in-Publication Data
Names: Kiefer, Jenny, author.
Title: This wretched valley / Jenny Kiefer.
Description: Philadelphia : Quirk Books, [2023] | Summary: "Four climbers hike into the Kentucky wilderness to climb a newly discovered cliff face. But things start going wrong as soon as their expedition begins, suggesting something sinister may be present in the valley with them"— Provided by publisher.
Identifiers: LCCN 2023021687 (print) | LCCN 2023021688 (ebook) | ISBN 9781683693680 (paperback) | ISBN 9781683693697 (ebook)
Subjects: LCGFT: Horror fiction. | Novels.
Classification: LCC PS3611.I396 45 2023 (print) | LCC PS3611.I396 (ebook) | DDC 813/.6—dc23/eng/20230526
LC record available at https://lccn.loc.gov/2023021687
LC ebook record available at https://lccn.loc.gov/2023021688

ISBN: 978-1-68369-368-0

Printed in the United States of America

Typeset in Sabon

Designed by Andie Reid
Cover art by rdonar/Shutterstock.com, pryzmat/Shutterstock.com
Production management by John J. McGurk

Quirk Books
215 Church Street
Philadelphia, PA 19106
quirkbooks.com

10 9 8 7 6 5 4 3 2

To R., R., and R.

America is not a young land:
it is old and dirty and evil
before the settlers,
before the Indians.
The evil is there
waiting.

—WILLIAM S. BURROUGHS,
NAKED LUNCH (1959)

OCTOBER 2019

What baffled them was the skeleton.

The other bodies were weird, but they couldn't figure out the fucking skeleton. Just bones, no soft tissue: Not one scrap of skin left. No sinews, no rotting brain, no *nothing*. The bones were arranged together, each one of the two hundred six in its place, a kneecap hidden by new fall leaves. Had the group resorted to cannibalism? It was one of the early guesses. But even that did not seem to fit. The bones wouldn't be so clean, arranged perfectly, as if they belonged to a knocked-over classroom display, sans bolts. There were no scorch marks, no scratches or other signs of instruments, and surely any form of cannibalism that left such a pristine skeleton behind would have required at the very least a blade to peel the flesh. And besides, the group had been experienced hikers.

The coroners and first responders could make guesses about the state of the other bodies—animals, perhaps, though they had not observed wildlife in the area, had not even heard the flap of wings overhead or the crunching of leaves beneath a swift mammal's paw—but this fucking set of bones. It was wrong to move them, the investigators thought, even as they placed them into the evidence bags, each bone lifting away like gravel, no tendons or fat to hold them together; like putting a complicated puzzle back in the box after hours spent piecing the cardboard together.

Was the skeleton from a decades-old death, some hunter who shot himself in the woods? That had been the second guess, that the dried bones belonged to another of the numerous missing persons from the surrounding area, but dental records confirmed that the immaculate set of bones belonged to Sylvia Burnett, a graduate student studying native plants and geology at the University of Kentucky. She'd been part of a research trip with another student, Clay Foster, and two climbers.

She had last been seen at a diner in Livingston, Kentucky, seven months prior with the other two hikers whose bodies they'd found, both bizarrely well preserved, and, like Sylvia's skeleton, odd enough to keep the first responders who had packed them into vans and the coroners who autopsied them conjuring theory after theory.

Had a squirrel plucked out Luke Woodhaven's eyes, thinking them a rare breed of nut? But how had his tongue been removed, they wondered, staring into his decaying mouth, inhaling the worst case of halitosis. Their sense of wonder overrode their sense of smell as they examined, once again, the entirely too-straight line that was the end of his tongue, terminating just beyond his last set of molars.

Had a coyote feasted on the intestines of Clay? But how had his rib cage come to be folded outward like cabinet doors, as if a set of hinges existed on either side of his body? And why was his blood missing? Had it evaporated? Why was he naked?

And where was the fourth hiker? Was she roaming the woods? Or had they simply not pressed far enough into the trees to discover her? All they had recovered of Dylan Prescott was a set of blood-soaked clothing at the abandoned campsite that raised further questions. The largest stains came back from forensics as unidentified and belonging to none of the four campers.

Their theorizing continued long after the morticians had pushed the bodies into the crematorium and placed the resulting cremains in boxes. Each spare moment at work no longer spent idly scrolling their phones, but puzzling over the detailed logs and the thousands of photographs. It was not uncommon for the coroners to become so engrossed in this work that they would stay past their shifts, alerted to the passing time only by a buzzing in their pockets from spouses waiting at home with cold dinner plates.

But still they had zero plausible theories as to how Sylvia Burnett had entered the area in March and lost all of her skin, muscles, and organs by October of the same year. In their obsession, they'd even scoured the theories touted online, the lights of their phones burning their retinas late at night: drugs, cults, poisonous plant matter, wild animals. Cryptids. Cannibals. Murder.

Another odd piece of the puzzle was that one of the bodies had been found just one hundred yards from the road, nestled in autumn brush. How had the camper not heard the rush of trucks loaded to the brim with cargo roaring down the highway every forty seconds? Another coroner guess: delirium, brought on by exposure and dehydration.

Vloggers and content creators thought darker, theorizing that Dylan, the missing camper, had murdered the rest of them and was hiding out in the woods. This theory was pushed to its limits when skeptics asked, *How would she have removed all of Sylvia's flesh? How did she preserve Clay's and her boyfriend*

Luke's body? Why? Too many odd pieces that didn't fit, more discovered every few nights as a detective or coroner or first responder sprang upright in bed, struck by another revelation.

But, above all, that *fucking* skeleton.

In the morgue, they had dubbed her Sylvia Skeleton. Sylvia Skeleton became legend. Forever tied to every medical oddity, every spooky anomaly, every story told in hushed tones around the campfire. She would become the subject of nearly seventy dissertations, at least eight medical journal publications, and several textbook chapters. Thousands of online conspiracies. Museums of medical oddities sent letters to the morgue, the police station, her nearly alma mater, and, once or twice, her poor parents, offering increasingly large sums for the bones, hoping to string them together, to make Sylvia Skeleton forever a sideshow display inside a glass cage. Wanting to find some utility in her death, her parents donated the bones to a university, which did, in fact, bolt them together inside a display case, taking them out only for special seminars.

The Livingston police department had received many reports of the missing party. Suspicion was not raised in friends or family for some weeks, as they knew that the group had trekked into a remote forest for research purposes with limited to no cellular service. The first reports came from Instagram users who detailed a peculiar livestream posted on the account of Dylan Prescott, a popular rock-climbing influencer with upwards of 50,000 followers. Users described it as showing her pensive face in the foreground and a pursuant man in a dark coat behind her. Authorities were not able to recover the video, and it remained a missing piece of cardboard to the coroner's puzzle. The cell phones recovered from the scene either refused to boot or seemed to have been restored to factory settings. When Dylan had not posted in many days, multiple reports were submitted to local and national hotlines, all from users of the app, and eventually from sports reporters who wanted to know what had happened to the up-and-coming climber.

Though these reports had been made as early as April, a major search for the group was not launched until the two students— Clay Foster and Sylvia Burnett—missed their check-in deadline to update their advisor at the University of Kentucky. There was a day's wait as the mentor of the project scoured his overstuffed inbox and understuffed mailbox for updates, requests for an extension, or notification of a delay. Only after he had made sure any communication hadn't errantly made its way to his spam folder or other digital nooks and crannies did he reach out to their families, who also had not heard from the campers since they had begun their trip a few weeks prior. When both parties realized there had not been a peep since they left, they contacted the authorities in Rockcastle County.

And so the search began. Their cell phones must have been dead or out of range, as the closest cell towers had not received a single ping from them. In fact, the final pings from their phones were triangulated to the diner where the four had last been sighted, buying fried chicken and beer, another jagged, oblong puzzle piece that would wedge in the minds of investigators and remain there long after the case had been abandoned. How had the diner been the last ping when hundreds of users recalled Dylan livestreaming and posting to social media in the days afterward, when they were in the woods? An amateur scientist explained it away online, detailing how a strong magnetic field could interrupt cell towers' signals as well as interfere with camera stabilization.

But then how had her posts changed, appearing to differ from those described by confused followers, who swore that she had posted images of herself climbing rock walls, and not the five photographs of leafy ground that appeared in the feed now—all dated March 12 or earlier? And how were more posts appearing on her feed when her phone had been discovered on the scene, battery long dead and the device reset to factory settings like the others?

After 185 days of fruitless searching, a stranded motorist discovered the hikers' vehicle, brush tickling its belly. All the electronics in his own car had inexplicably gone dark, the crooning radio singer pulled off stage mid-note, the clock blinking out, even the gas gauge and speedometer becoming blank circles on the dashboard. He pulled over, his car dying almost as soon as he crossed onto the shoulder. The tow truck would take an hour to arrive at such a rural location. In the passing time, the motorist's bladder filled, and he went into the trees to piss, where his golden stream grazed the Jeep Cherokee's bumper, cleaning it of dirt. Its rust-colored paint was camouflaged by brush, dirt, and autumn leaves.

He peered into the windows. A crinkled receipt sat on the backseat. Long neck bottles of Ale-8 filled the cup holders. The shine of greasy foil winked on the floor. Then something underneath the seat twitched, like a finger, he later told authorities, and as he pressed his forehead against the window, as he squinted deeper, the Jeep's exhaust pipe sputtered. That should be impossible, he said. He knew it should be impossible, but he had heard it, he had felt the vehicle shimmy on its shocks, smelled the sulfurous emissions. He reeled, like a cartoon skeleton jumping out of a skin suit, pacing backward into the woods. He picked a direction, aiming for the road but in fact heading farther into the trees, where he swore he saw a woman matching the description of Dylan Prescott, the still-missing climber, darting deeper into the woods. He called out to her, nearly tripping over a low-hanging chain bearing a NO TRESPASSING sign, before she vanished.

Had his ankle caught on the links, he would have fallen into a soft bed of leaves, his eyes parallel with a swollen foot. Instead, he skidded to a stop just in time, gagged at the sight of the body, and backtracked to the road. He dialed the local police, who arrived precisely thirteen minutes before the tow truck driver, who found the motorist's vehicle functioning perfectly.

The foot belonged to Clay Foster, the leader of the study, now a dehydrated husk of leathery skin enfolding shriveled muscle, the guts rotted or eaten from the opened rib cage. A marvel of science that baffled the coroners nearly as much as Sylvia Skeleton, that his corpse was so fresh. The same was true of Luke Woodhaven, found deeper in the woods, the tongueless fellow, who was also missing his eyes, ears, fingers, and toes. Besides the missing digits, the body was undisturbed—too undisturbed. The skin was still smooth and pink, the nubs of his fingers and toes dried like jerky. Preserved. Both bodies were in similar states, as if the campers had succumbed in the freezing preserves of Mount Everest and not the humid summer and wet fall of Kentucky. Yet forensics determined they had, indeed, died closer to the start of summer than to the end of it.

Clay was the first to be discovered and catalogued, the closest to the car. Next was Luke, deeper into the woods, and finally Sylvia Skeleton, near the campsite. The first responders strung yellow plastic tape across the trees next to the road and parked their flashing lights at the shoulder, drawing more attention than if they had done nothing at all. They placed their little yellow plastic markers around the scenes, miles apart, one for every stray fiber that had made its way into the dirt, one for each quickdraw found nestled in the drying leaves, for each of the still-pitched, pristine tents surrounded by destroyed food canisters and an explosion of clothing and supplies, and one for the dribbles of dried urine on the bumper of the Jeep.

They took one million photographs. There were so many photographs that the high-resolution files filled up three terabyte drives. There were so many photographs that the forensic investigators had an ongoing project to mesh them together, to create a unified, 3D reconstruction of the grisly landscape. There were so many photographs that they wondered what would happen if they leaked one or two to the conspiracy nuts who managed to out-theorize them with no photographs at all.

And after they had taken their photographs and mulled around the corpses, assessing, smoking, constantly feeling a small hand tugging at their pant leg as if asking them to leave, they zipped the corpses into bags and stacked their little numbered markers back together and stuffed the tents and backpacks and dirty clothing into evidence bags and wheeled the bags to the van and checked one last time to see if they had missed anything, any tiny part of Sylvia Skeleton or a bloody blade or even a detailed journal that would make the puzzle whole, something other than the waterlogged notebooks at the campsite that had turned to pulp. Satisfied, they shut the doors of the van.

Then they left that wretched place forever.

FEBRUARY 2019

Fucking finally.

Clay shoved his hands into his pockets. The inside of the hangar was only a few degrees warmer than outside, which was a tropical beach compared to the subzero temperatures of the sky. Tabitha, his faithful pilot friend, walked around the tiny plane, checking the wheels for air, the propellers for cracks, the wings for a disaster in the making. Though they'd discover something of the sort at three thousand feet, still she ticked all clear on her clipboard.

They'd been flying over the Kentucky wilderness looking for some climbable rock for weeks. They hadn't found anything yet, but Clay had a good feeling about today.

They climbed into the plane. Clay clamped his jaw shut and tapped his gloved fingers on his knee while Tabitha checked another host of plane things, blinking red lights, scratchy radios, levers and dials and monitors. Clay jiggled his legs, trying to keep the circulation going. He clicked through coordinates and maps on his laptop, reminding himself over which patch of Kentucky nowhere they were flying: Rockcastle County. There had to be some rock there, right?

"Almost ready for takeoff," Tabitha said. She radioed the control tower and started the engine, a roar echoing through the hangar. "Got everything you need?"

"Roger that," Clay responded. He wished they were in the air already.

Clay and Tabitha had known each other since middle school, when Clay moved to Lexington. Tabitha's father had been a pilot and she'd been able to log enough flight hours as a teenager that she had her license now at twenty-nine. She'd made his life a hell of a lot easier, too. His parents could have bankrolled a private plane for this, but as a family friend, Tabitha could be ready at a moment's notice. Clay only needed to pay for the gas.

With few pilots masochistic enough to take to the air in February, they were primed on the runway within a few minutes. The plane pressed into the sky, the rubber wheels lifting away from the pavement, their bodies pinned back against the seats. The plane tilted and plunged, *up*.

Clay's pulse thumped in his ears, a knot rising in his throat, even though he'd done this plenty of times. He and Tabitha had spent the winter logging hours in this same plane, with the same expensive LiDAR box borrowed from the university mounted to its undercarriage, scanning endless swaths of trees that might be hiding the next hot climbing spot—and he wanted to be the one to find it.

He'd thought of the possibilities of using LiDAR for just this purpose when he was a freshman in a geography class whose professor had lectured on the tech, showing various slides with photos mapped by it, rainbow stripes showing the different levels of pinging made by the lasers. Like sonar, but with light instead of sound, his professor had explained. It was the only lecture of the semester to perk his ears instead of lower his eyelids.

He'd become hooked on climbing that same year, spending his early Saturday mornings in the back of a beater crusted with dirt, the trunk heaped with rope and metal clips and stinky rubber. Introduced to the sport by his roommate, he would crack his knees and shred the skin of his fingers on rock until it was too dark to see the bolts. He'd only managed to become a slightly above-average climber, never having the skills or luck or guts to climb the hard shit, the routes that got you noticed by brands, the routes that could get you money. After tearing his ACL, he'd slowed down on the weekend treks. He couldn't stand to see his buddies sending harsher and harder routes while he scowled from the ground, his neck sore from gazing upward. But he'd always kept the LiDAR project in his back pocket, finally pulling it out for his geology PhD dissertation.

If he couldn't become a famous climber, maybe he could become famous for finding new rock.

So he'd spent the fall inside this cramped, cold-as-fuck single-engine plane, sending lasers down to Muir Valley in Red River Gorge to map existing rock walls, cataloging their nooks and crannies—all those routes he'd never climb. Every other week, as long as the temperature hovered above freezing, Clay and Tabitha would be on the tarmac, setting their course, bundled in layers of wool, down, thick-knit hats and scarves. Winter meant a clear path to rock faces unobstructed by leaves, the trees' naked limbs like a network of veins. It also meant thermoses full of steaming coffee, tiny heat packs in their socks and pockets and even under their hats, cracked before takeoff. Miserable, but necessary—at least, he hoped, it would be worth it in the end.

If he could find something.

By January they finally headed to sites unknown, charting the Kentucky wilderness—starting with other sectors of the gorge in Daniel Boone National Forest and stretching out across the state. But the obvious spots had turned up no nuggets of gold. Clay scanned through mile after mile of pure garbage, his jaw aching after each session from his clenched teeth. If they didn't find something before the trees filled in, he'd have to wait another ten months.

Now they headed toward the wilds of Rockcastle County, a promising area he'd noticed while studying a map of the state.

Something about this trip felt different. It was like the plane was being pulled to the site, like his back was pressed a little bit harder into the seat during takeoff. The pressure in his ears swelled as they reached full altitude.

"We're like pioneers," he said, shouting over the roar of the propellers. "We better find something good, or else my dissertation will fall apart right before I'm supposed to get this PhD."

"But you'll still graduate even if you don't find anything, right?" Tabitha asked.

"Yeah, I'd still graduate, but my thesis wouldn't be as interesting," he said. "And it wouldn't be as likely to land me a job afterward."

"What job would that be?"

"Something of my own design. If I'm fucking lucky, some rube will pay me to do just this—travel around the world looking for new climbing spots. Can you imagine that? Being paid to travel around the world?"

"You really think there's people out there who'd pay for that?"

The radio buzzed with control tower notes. Clay's feet, like a broken oven, soaked sweat through his toes into his socks from the heating square, yet his legs jiggled underneath the computer on his lap to stave off the chill from the rest of his body. He clicked around his screen to turn on the equipment under the plane, and his insides buzzed in anticipation.

"Oh, definitely," he said. "Climbing is a billion-dollar industry. Companies sponsor climbers just to go outside and climb, right? My friend Dylan just got signed by Petzl. So why wouldn't they want me to find new spots? It would be a great tourism opportunity. Imagine you're a struggling, rural little middle-of-nowhere shit town, and you hire me, and I discover that the best rock walls in the world are in your backyard. Suddenly, you have a million visitors each year, all needing food and equipment and things to do when they're sore."

"So your dream job is traveling around to these tiny towns to find rock walls? Traveling the world but seeing only the shitholes?"

"Well, no, I wouldn't be staying in those fucking towns, just flying over them," he said, checking the coordinates. "I'd be staying at the places that have the airports. You know, civilization."

"But on the dime of these shit towns?"

He shrugged. "On someone's dime."

"We're nearly to the coordinates you gave me," Tabitha said. "Fingers crossed."

His pulse screamed against his temple.

The plane twitched. A shudder ran through the cabin that felt unlike turbulence—subtler, almost like a shiver. The computer jittered in Clay's lap. The sweat pulsing out of his pores coated him like a layer of ice. His head felt swollen, his heart pounding. To his untrained eye, the dashboard seemed to flicker with one million warning signs. The red eyes of the blinking lights picked up their pace. The arms on the dials waved.

The nose dipped.

Oh fuck, oh fuck, oh fuck.

Through the windshield, the pointy tips of trees charged toward them, like hundreds of arrows slicing through the air. He lost his breath, the oxygen deflating from his lungs, his body in free-fall vertigo. Closing his eyes, he braced, waiting for the impact. *What a stupid fucking way to die—so close to the finish line*, he thought, a knot of dread forming in his stomach. For a long moment, silence throbbed, deep and pressing, as if squeezing his eardrums. He floated. Every unattached object hovered, he thought, in the few seconds they plummeted.

But when he heard no crunch of metal, when his torso had not been pierced by pine, when no birds' nests exploded against the nose of the plane, he opened his eyes.

Only harsh winter sky.

"Everything okay?" he asked, loosening the muscles in his jaw. "Are we gonna crash?"

"That was weird, but no," Tabitha said, flipping some switches. "It was like a power surge. I'll have to have the electronics looked at."

"What happened? Why did we dip?"

"What do you mean?" she asked.

"The nose dipped for a moment, right?"

"I don't think so," she said. "We hit a bit of turbulence and the electronics flickered, but we've been pretty steady. Are you okay? Breathing kind of heavy over there."

Clay exhaled. "Yeah, I'm good."

"Is your laptop okay?"

Clay had forgotten about the computer clenched between his gloved hands. Relaxing the muscles in his fingers was a deliberate process of releasing each tendon and knobby joint. The screen continued to scroll data received from the laser light pinging beneath the plane to the ground below.

"Fuck," he said. "Seems to be. It's still connected to the LiDAR box, so I guess that's all good too."

"Do you think we got anything? I spied some rock beneath the plane."

"I fucking hope so," he said. He couldn't erase the image from his mind, the stabbing treetops flying up at him like a thousand arrows. Each glimpse out the windshield made his chest hitch.

What emerged, days later, from the laser-drawn image seemed too good to be real. Their seventh trip to the untouched corners of Kentucky wilderness, and they'd found something. At least, it looked like something.

You were right, Clay texted Tabitha.

Success?

I think so.

The images created a rainbow display, with the quickest-returning light waves at the top showing as red and the ground as blue. It looked straight out of a guidebook: tall slabs of rock ridged with cracks and pockets and ledges. From the data, perfect heights for climbing, ranging from sixty feet to one hundred fifty. Goosebumps raised the hairs along Clay's arms as he clicked through the scans, his hands shaking. No more cold-ass flights across random, uncharted expanses of wilderness.

He'd found his needle.

He wouldn't know truly know what he'd found—A whole new gorge? A mere roadside attraction?—until he could assess the site in person. But still, he dreamed of headlines in blogs and magazines, his face plastered on the pages, a ripple through the climbing world. He conjured plane rides to Spain, over pristine stretches of South Africa or Thailand, seeking pimpled rock; a dissertation that gained him not just his doctorate or a seat behind a dusty research desk at a university, but a globe-trotting career. What else could he do with a geology degree? He'd learned by the end of his first year in the PhD program that a career in academia was not for him.

Clay didn't know that this future would never materialize, and not because of the normal causes of failure—lack of resources, of connections or money, all of which he had—nor simply because no journal would publish his findings, because nobody in the climbing industry would think that what he offered was a valuable service worth the money and hassle. He didn't know that his research would never be read or reviewed by a single person other than his dissertation advisor, Dr. Berry, who in the fall would attempt to examine the scans, trying and failing to recover a corrupted file. For now, Clay reveled in his ignorance, in the future he wanted to manifest, one brimming with fame and fortune and all the gleaming things that accompanied them.

———————————

Later, in his advisor's office, he compared these scans with the ones he'd captured in Muir Valley, the new site on the left screen and the established on the right. Clay and his advisor pored over them for hours, stopping only when one or the other had to attend class.

"There's definitely something here," Professor Berry said. "Sometimes it's almost like I'm looking at a carbon copy. What you found looks almost identical to Muir Valley. It's odd. Are you sure you've got the right data pulled up?"

"I'm pretty sure," Clay said. "Look at the file properties."

Professor Berry clicked around the left screen, opening it. As expected, the file had been created that month.

"It's just so strange," the professor said. "Look here. It even looks like they share the same foliage."

Sure enough, at the bottom of the screen were twin sets of trunks, both leaning left, both with a nub toward the middle from a broken limb. Clay's heart stopped beating for a second. *Fuck*. Had he accidentally written over the most recent data? Had he merely been looking at Muir Valley under a new file name?

Clay leaned in toward the screens, looking for even a single variation. There wasn't one. He'd have to go back up in that fucking plane again, chilled to the bone. *Fuck, fuck, fuck.*

Professor Berry checked his watch. "I have to get to class, but we can look over these later," he said, exiting the office.

Clay stayed in his advisor's office, the room suddenly sweltering. How could the two spots possibly have identical rock faces? The more he searched the new image, the more it became a mirror of the old. The same pocket at the top right, the same asymmetrical crack in the middle, the same spidery shrubs spilling over the top ledge, the same elevation. He placed a bookmark on both files and noted the coordinates of each location in his journal, seemingly the only difference between the two images. He gave up on his spot-the-difference game, clicking around to bookmark other areas of interest from the unexplored region.

The more he digitally hiked, the more bookmarks he accrued, to the point of uselessness: by the time his advisor returned, he had at least seventy flags around the file.

"There's a lot of good stuff here," Clay said.

"What did you find?"

"There's a lot of similar features to other walls we've studied. I'd like to start planning a field test. Actually go there."

"Can you bring up that spot we were looking at earlier?" Professor Berry said. "The one that seemed to be a carbon copy of Muir?"

The Muir scan was still open. Clay clicked through the left screen again, searching for the first bookmark he'd made. But the twin trunks had vanished. Instead of pockets, the limestone was cracked all over, a series of miniature fissures spreading across it, as if it had been smashed with a sledgehammer. The ground lay bare.

"Huh," he said.

"This is what we were looking at earlier?" Professor Berry said.

The coordinates matched.

"Must have been a weird glitch," Clay said, grinning.

"I guess so," his advisor said. "Old university computers."

"Is there any chance I can get started on the fieldwork?"

"Let me review the files a little bit more, but I think you should be able to get out there as soon as next month."

Clay couldn't believe that his idea would actually produce a field excursion and not just a bunch of useless maps and data to extrapolate. And not only had he found something, he'd found a sparkling fucking diamond, one that didn't even need polishing. It had just been hiding.

The screen seemed to pulse. Clay assumed it was another glitch, another trick of old university computers when that same troublesome stretch of wall had yet another face for a brief moment, another new set of features, as though it were crumbling.

——— ———

Clay recruited his friend and fellow student Sylvia to accompany him and help with notation. He'd known her since undergrad. She was more into the botany side of geology, studying how geography and climate change affect native plant life. She readily accepted his invitation—provided she was granted coauthor credit on any publications.

He needed a climber. Clay typed, deleted, and retyped his message into the tiny screen of his phone. He needed to get this message right—he needed *her* to be the one to go on this trip: Dylan Prescott, a just-signed pro climber with fifty thousand followers. He'd known her since his climbing days, and they'd kept in touch here and there. But he'd never asked her to help him with something so important, and he wasn't sure if her brand would let her go. Maybe a phone call would be better.

Hey, call me when you get a second.

He sent the message and scrolled through her Instagram photos, square after square of her body contorted into pretzels against tawny granite. An occasional pop of color dotted the rows of images: the rare occasions when she posted from climbing gyms. If her face wasn't hidden behind a tight, dark ponytail, it was grimaced in determination. Her latest post, just a week old: *So excited to announce I'm officially a #Petzl athlete! I've always used their gear on my trips, and I can't wait to grow our partnership!*

A few hours later, his phone rang.

"Hey," Clay said.

"Hey, what's up?" Dylan replied. "Everything okay?"

"Yeah, I actually wanted to talk to you about a climbing opportunity. I found a new, undiscovered wall."

"That's amazing. How did you find it?"

"It's part of my PhD dissertation," he said. "I'm studying LiDAR tech. Let me email you some things real quick."

On Dylan's end, he heard only the clicking of her laptop as she looked through the LiDAR scans.

"If you're available for a trip, I'd love to have you join to climb. Make some first ascents."

"This looks just like Muir Valley," she said. "Where is this?"

"South, a bit. About an hour away from Lexington."

"Oh my god," she said. "I'm just, like, itching to get on this rock. When would we leave? What are the details?"

"I'm still working on some details, like trying to find out who owns the land, if anyone, and if they're okay with us going there. We're hoping to head out next month if everything goes well. It'll be me, another graduate student named Sylvia, you, and I assume your boyfriend—Luke, right?"

"He can come too?"

"I imagine you'll need a belayer," Clay said. "I'll be busy documenting stuff, so I can't help there. I'm sure you won't want to free solo."

"I hope you're okay with a crag dog, too," she said. "Where Luke goes, Slade goes."

"Maybe he'll protect us from monsters," Clay joked.

"I'll have to ask my brand team," she said. "Maybe they can sponsor me. I'm so new. It's weird to be signed."

"Congrats, by the way."

"It just seems like—I don't know," she said. The clacking of her keyboard ceased. "Like a dream. Like it was made for this. For us."

Dylan's knees already ached, trapped between the driver's seat and the backpack on the floorboard. Her muscles tensed in anticipation of scaling the walls.

"The coordinates are about three miles from the road," Clay said, navigating south from Lexington, spouting this information for the third time since they'd piled into the car half an hour ago. "So we should be able to get back to the car reasonably quickly if we need to. But it'll be a hike—there's no path to follow."

"Venturing into the unknown," Luke said. "Where no one can hear us scream."

Laughter filled the cramped Jeep. They'd jammed everything they might even possibly need in the car: sleeping bags and tents and clothes and climbing gear created a mountain so high that the rearview mirror became useless, reflecting back the polyester mound. A small cooler sloshed underneath the mountain like an underground stream. All stuff they'd have to lug three miles into the woods. Dylan was used to packing much lighter, but this was more than a simple backpacking trip; she assumed Clay and Sylvia needed special equipment for their research. Clay certainly wasn't acting like it was one of their old, easygoing trips to the Gorge. His shoulders were nearly up to his ears.

The polyester of Dylan's leggings chirped against the leather seat as she bounced her legs, all of her exhilarated anticipation channeled into them at the thought of getting the chance to make a first ascent. She could leave her legacy on that wall. She could name the routes, make sure Petzl wouldn't regret signing her, would make her their top athlete, even. Who else gets to develop new rock these days? That would surely put her at the top of the brand's list for funds and ads. She imagined not needing to have a day job; imagined even more brands clawing at each other to give her money.

When Clay sent her a message out of the blue, she'd assumed he either was getting married or had suffered some terrible accident. It had been a few years since they'd hung out, though they texted and kept up with each other online. She never imagined he'd be reaching out with such an amazing opportunity—lucky they'd bonded years ago at the bottom of a crag at the Gorge. Still, something nagged at her, a tiny voice whispering that this must be too good to be true. Maybe it was just the stressed vibes Clay emanated, his knuckles nearly ghost-white along the steering wheel.

She'd been working her ass off for years to get signed. She'd scaled half of the 5.13 routes at Red River Gorge and had made headway on her second 5.14, worried her first was a fluke, almost too easy and fluid. She hadn't been quite able to replicate that climb. But it was enough. And now that a brand had signed her, she couldn't let them down, not after they'd given her some money for this trip. Everything had to go right. It had to be perfect—it had to create buzz. Maybe then they'd send her somewhere amazing, fly her halfway across the world, to Albarracín in Spain or Waterval Boven in South Africa. Plaster her face on their ads.

Something deep inside her worried that the signing was a fluke, too. What if she never climbed anything greater than that one 5.14? What if nothing came from this trip? What if Petzl cut her loose, thinking her a waste of time and money?

In the backseat, Dylan scrolled through Instagram, scraps of phrases pouring through her head as she thought about what she might post as her official announcement of the trip. She'd shared some teasers—*more exciting news coming soon, be sure to follow and check this space!*—but was saving the reveal for the moment she laid eyes on the rock.

Slade sat in the back between her and Luke, panting so much his drool poured out of his mouth like a fountain. Stepping in her lap, he rained slobber down on her phone, blurring the image on the screen.

The first time Dylan had met Luke it was because Slade, then a puppy, had managed to escape his harness and run over to her table at Miguel's Pizza. He'd leapt onto the table, nearly stealing her slice of pepperoni.

"Sorry," Luke had said, pulling Slade away. "Oh, hey, you're Dylan, right? I follow you on Instagram. You've done some really impressive climbs!"

"Yeah," she'd replied. At that point, she only had a measly one thousand followers and had finished a handful of 5.13s. "Cute dog."

They'd exchanged phone numbers, discovered they both lived in Louisville—a couple of miles apart—and had been dating ever since.

Now, the dog pressed the entirety of his weight into her lap, drawing archaic symbols along the windowpane in wet nose. A sudden bark followed, all four passengers jumping at the shrill sound, the car slithering in its lane.

"What is he even barking at?" Clay asked, righting the car.

"I don't know," Luke said. "Probably sees a deer or something. Or thinks he does."

"He barks at everything," Dylan said. "Bud, it's okay." She petted his back and scratched behind his ears, shushing him. But Slade would not be deterred. He began to yip, his paws dancing on Dylan's lap. Pounding little bruises into her already-tender thighs. She wished Luke would have done some better training with Slade.

Slade's yelping transformed turned into little *boof*s when Luke pulled the dog into his lap. "It's okay, bud. There's nothing out there."

There never was, Dylan thought.

In the front seat, Sylvia unfolded a paper map.

"Why did you bring that ancient thing?" Clay asked, laughing. "Where did you even get it?"

"You don't think it'll be useful? My mom gave it to me." She unfolded and refolded the map as she scanned it, never letting its wings spread fully, careful not to encroach past the center console. Sylvia had been quiet most of the trip, scribbling in a notebook or staring out the window.

"We have a brand-new GPS tracker that will tell us exactly where we are at any moment," Clay continued. "Why would we need that? You can't even tell where anything is besides the roads."

Sylvia continued her origami, creasing rivers and highways, until she settled on a section composed of mostly green, the words ROCKCASTLE COUNTY sprawled across the paper.

"This is a topographical map," Sylvia said. "But it doesn't show any rock faces. Just trees."

"Must be out-of-date or something," Clay said.

"Maps like this can't be out-of-date," she said. "Not unless there's a new road added or something. Topography doesn't change that fast."

"I don't know," Clay said, squeezing the steering wheel tighter, his voice strained. "Must be a mistake."

"You don't think that's weird?" she said, tracing a finger along a crease. "That there's this huge crag but it's never been found or documented—or even seen from the road?"

"What do you think is going to happen?" Clay asked, forcing a laugh. "Do you think the LiDAR just made it all up? That a huge pillar of rock just popped out of the ground? We're going to get there and it'll just be a bunch of trees?"

"It's just interesting," she said.

Dylan's leg bounced against the floor, the pack at her feet reverberating in time. It might be *just interesting* to Sylvia in the front seat, but Dylan needed this trip. She needed that rock to exist. This wasn't course credit for her; it was her life.

This trip could erase all fears of inferiority, could silence that little whining voice deep within her that whispered at every quiet moment that she was a fraud; that Petzl had made a grave mistake in signing her. She hadn't won any competitions, hadn't climbed anywhere outside of Red River Gorge. But if this trip went well, she could prove to herself—and everybody else—that she was worthy. Nobody, not even the men who dominated the climbing industry, got to develop a whole crag. This trip was special. Under no circumstances could she fuck it up.

She wanted to scream, just to release the tension of her anxious mind.

As Clay pulled off the highway, turning onto a single-lane road, Slade did it for her.

———————

The acrid stench of cigarettes slapped Dylan's nostrils as they entered the diner that Luke had spotted, a dingy, run-down hole-in-the-wall with a sun-bleached sign. A final meal, Luke had suggested. Her stomach growled at the prospect of a plate of real food, a last indulgence before rehydrated meals cooked over a tiny gas canister stove and endless energy bars. The four sat at a smooth laminate table, the only party in the restaurant for lunch. A waitress slid plastic-covered menus in front of them. Slade was trapped in the car, windows cracked, vocalizing his displeasure.

"That your dog out there?" she asked.

"Yeah—sorry," Luke said, his arm around Dylan. "He'd rather be in here getting a hot meal."

Dylan scoured the menu, washed-out photos of pancake stacks and burger clip art beneath the sticky plastic.

"You guys here to do some kayaking on Rockcastle River?" the waitress asked, seemingly putting the puzzle pieces of their appearance together: new faces, thick-ankled hiking boots, fancy brands stitched onto the breasts of their jackets. "Isn't it a little early in the season for that?"

"We're here to do some exploring off Route 490," Clay said.

The waitress paused, her pen and pad hovering in midair, like a buffering video.

"Oh, so this is like a last meal," she said.

Luke laughed. "That's what I said!"

"Where off Route 490?"

"Just a few miles from here," Clay said. "Just a little south, right by the river, but on the other side. Why?"

"Why do you want to go there? Nothing there but trees and deer shit. Better off on one of the trails farther north."

"We're students at UK studying the topography," Sylvia said.

"A lot of people who go into the woods on that side of the road don't come back out," the waitress said, scratching the tip of her pencil across the pad as if she were striking out tally marks, one for each of them. The sound made Dylan shudder. "Or, if they do, they're really weird after. Won't talk about it, or talk about seeing all kinds of weird shit. Haunted shit."

"What do you mean?" Dylan asked.

"Well, you hear stories," the waitress replied. "My uncle said when he was in high school in the eighties, some kids in the grade above him went into the woods right after school let out and never came back out. Later the sheriff found them, and they'd all killed themselves."

The four sitting ducks stared at each other, their palms sweating onto the menus, cutting through the caked-on grime of ancient ketchup. The moment would have descended into heavy silence without Slade's constant baying and the percolating of the coffee maker, gurgling and dripping, slowly releasing its stale smell into the air to create a toxic cologne.

"So, what'll it be?"

The Jeep's doors clicked closed.

"Well," Clay said, "that was weird."

The group burst into nervous laughter.

"Oh my god, that waitress was so weird," Dylan said. "She must be bored out of her mind. Making shit up to pass the time. She probably just watched some horror movie last night."

"What? You don't think the woods of Rockcastle County are filled with ghosts?" Luke joked, wiggling his fingers at her.

"She was probably right the first time," Clay said, "about the trees and deer shit."

He turned on the car and pulled onto the main road.

"I mean, don't get me wrong," he continued. "Deer can fuck you up."

"Good thing we've got Slade to scare them off," Luke replied.

"That dog would bark at them, and then run at the first sign of danger." Dylan laughed. "He runs away from squirrels if they act feisty, don't you, buddy?"

In the front, Clay input the coordinates into his phone at a stoplight. The cool, female voice of the phone's GPS told him to take a left up ahead.

"Wait a minute," Sylvia said. Her phone's screen shone bright white. From the backseat, Dylan could see a snippet of a headline: LOCAL HUNTER. "Some people have actually gone missing here. Some of these are pretty recent."

"People go missing all the time," Clay said, his voice clipped. He angled the car around a curve.

"Rockcastle County only has a population of 17,000," Sylvia said. "That's super tiny for the amount of reports I'm seeing. Livingston alone has had at least five residents go missing in the past two years. Hunters searching for deer, mostly."

Dylan's stomach churned, the grease from the meal turning rancid. They had a GPS tracker and their phones, she rationalized—the hunters probably just got lost and couldn't find the road and starved to death. No way were there actually ghosts or some weird death cult hiding in the woods. Stupid.

"Maybe they just left," Clay said. "Maybe they were just tired of this town and its one restaurant with its one creepy waitress."

At that exact moment, they sped past the restaurant again. The wheels on the Jeep screeched across the pavement as Clay braked, Slade thumping against the back of Sylvia's seat. The creepy waitress in question leaned against the building with a cigarette, smirking at them with a *back so soon* smile.

"Y'all get lost?" she called. "Decided against going into the fucked-up woods?"

"What the fuck?" Clay said, examining his phone, ignoring the waitress. "I followed the directions. One left and one right. So how are we back where we started?"

Sylvia's laughter sliced through the car, almost as startling as Slade's outburst on the highway—the most noise she'd made since Dylan met her a few hours ago. "So much for your precious technology," she said, punching Clay's arm.

"User error," Clay grumbled.

This time, the GPS voice led them onward to their destination, a patch of trees off Route 490 that was indistinguishable from the rest of the forest. Still no rock that Dylan could see— shouldn't it be towering over the trees?

Clay wove the Jeep through the trees, the bumper grazing bark, somehow always finding enough space between the crowded trunks, until he finally pulled off the road just enough to conceal the car from thieves or teenagers bored enough for malice.

"Nice parking job, but will we be able to get out?" Dylan asked, not sure whether she meant back onto the road or out of the vehicle itself. A tree trunk stood just outside her window.

"That's a problem for later," Clay said, hopping out of the car.

Dylan's door *thunk*ed against the tree, leaving mere inches for her to escape through. To her right, Luke had clearance enough. Slade leapt out of the car, barking.

Clay and Sylvia began unpacking the mountain of supplies from the trunk, eroding the layers of polyester and cotton they'd have to carry into the woods. Dylan hoisted her pack onto her back, clipping the strap across her chest. She took the leash from Luke, and Slade pulled at it as he lunged forward, throwing Dylan off-balance and nearly knocking her into Sylvia.

"What's going on with Slade?" Sylvia asked.

"He probably just smells that deer shit," Dylan said, tugging him back. Sometimes she wished they didn't drag Slade everywhere. She was nervous enough without having to keep track of him and manage Luke's worrying. The air held a static electricity that raised goosebumps against her skin.

Once everyone had loaded their shoulders like pack horses, Dylan's backpack heavy with metal carabiners and rope, they started their hike. Luke had to practically drag a whimpering Slade along behind him. Ahead, Sylvia carted a miniature cooler full of beer, and Clay fiddled with his GPS gizmo, a red plastic thing with oversized buttons and an undersized screen, like a prehistoric Nokia cell phone. He input the string of numbers that would lead them right to the crag.

Dylan looked ahead. Again she wondered, shouldn't they be able to see the rock? Shouldn't it be towering over them, stark through the naked branches? Maybe Sylvia was right—maybe there was nothing here. Maybe they'd been led here by some glitch, Clay too reliant on his tech to notice that it had failed.

Dylan would be a disappointment before she even got started.

Or maybe Clay was luring them into the woods to kill them. He was always obsessed with trying to get her to watch some scary movie or another when they hung out years ago, and this whole trip he'd been coiled up as tight as a rattlesnake. But the thought of Clay wielding a machete and chasing them through the woods made Dylan chuckle. Knowing him, he'd probably stumble before he could make the first slash.

Too late to turn back now. She headed deeper into the forest with the rest of the group, picking her way between nettles and brush.

Tacked to a nearby tree, rusting, nearly swallowed by the bark as though it were viscous lava, hung a sign: NO TRESPASSING. A relic of the developers who'd abandoned the land long ago but held on to the deed.

Soon, the sign would be swallowed entirely.

1700s

It was a place they knew to avoid.

The Cherokee and Shawnee knew its ways.

The only plants that survived its soil were those not meant to be ingested, were those that lapped up its poisons. Black elderberry with blood-red stalks poked up, drops of dew clinging to the succulent fruit. Misplaced manchineel grew near the creek, a suspicious, enticing yellow fruit dangling on its blistering branches, the oil so potent it could take your sight. Pokeweed, snakeroot, spiny jimsonweed. The beady eyeballs of white baneberry. A cornucopia of all the pretty flowers and plump fruits known in their communities to cause hallucinations, heart palpitations, roiling stomachs, and vomiting.

All before death.

Any other plant languished, the seeds never sprouting more than a few inches before rotting, or becoming brittle, yellow husks. They could raise tomatoes, but the fruit would turn from green to black on the vine, the flesh deflating into a wrinkled sack of blood.

The place never appeared the same twice, but it couldn't hide itself entirely from those who knew to look for it: thickets of poison ivy twined around poison oak; shimmering sunlight; an inert sense of calm, of longing, of deep, ravenous hunger that could be satiated only by the berries and fruits that grew there.

When this patch of earth was hungry, it would glitter all the more.

And so the message spread: *do not touch this ground*.

But if a passing group of colonizers—their horses overloaded with furniture and bags of flour—came down the path blazed by Daniel Boone, if this weary, sickly group headed right for it, then they were welcome to forge right on ahead.

MARCH 8, 2019
2:15 P.M.

Luke tugged on Slade's leash, the harness carving a line into his brindle fur. His nails scratched into the dirt, his fox-like ears perked and alert. The Australian cattle dog stared into the trees, his hackles raised along his back, a cautionary mohawk. His growl, low and long, bounced off the trees of the forest. Slade would not budge, like he'd had a sudden change of heart.

"Slade, what is it?" Luke asked, bending to level his eyes with Slade's, his own taut, clenched jaw in line with Slade's sneer. He peered along the same sight line as his dog but saw nothing that might spook him or activate the hunting instincts he'd never shown on their previous trips to the Gorge: no wild birds dissecting a carrion meal, no half-snapped tree limb swaying like a waving arm, no fox or coyote challenging him to a duel, licking its teeth in preparation.

Luke bit his lip. Could Slade be sick?

"What do you see, bud?" Dylan crouched down too, peering in the same direction. She ruffled his fur.

"Do you think he's okay?"

"Yeah, he probably just saw a deer zip by or he's just

overwhelmed by all the smells," Dylan replied. "Or maybe he just needs a break. We've been hiking for about an hour. You worry too much about him."

That was probably true, Luke thought, but Dylan didn't understand. Slade was his first dog, the first living thing besides himself he'd ever been responsible for. As a puppy he'd had parvo—and quickly recovered—but ever since that week in the hospital, Luke jumped at every unusual behavior, every incident of vomiting or coughing. He'd search symptoms on his phone while Dylan chided, her eyes in a book, "Sometimes dogs just throw up."

The group sat on a moss-covered log, taking a breather, weeds up to their ankles. They'd have to check for ticks once they made camp—the last thing Luke wanted was for Slade to catch some tick-borne disease, the little bugger burrowing beneath his long, bristly fur until it was bloated to five times its size. Dylan pulled out a small bowl and poured water into it, encouraging Slade to drink.

Luke unzipped his jacket. The air had been cold enough to nibble at his skin when he had first left the Jeep, but after trekking with forty pounds on his back, sweat pooled in the crooks of his joints and slipped from his scalp, cooling as it slid down his neck. His tongue rolled around in his mouth, dry and bitter. He took a swig from Dylan's water bottle.

Slade, now hydrated, again pulled at the leash, barking into the woods at some invisible monster.

"Is Slade okay?" Clay asked.

"It's like he sees something, but I don't know what," Luke said.

He tugged on the leash, trying to pull Slade back to the water bowl. He waved a hand in front of Slade's line of vision. Only when Dylan produced a small morsel, a corner of a peanut butter trail bar, did the dog let his nose lead him away from the apparent danger in the distance.

Slade was never this excitable. Luke's gut screamed at him to trust his dog, to go back to the car and back to Louisville and maybe even to the vet. He exhaled. He was overthinking things, like he always did with Slade, who was probably just overwhelmed by smells, like Dylan said. They'd never been hiking off trail, where animal scents were probably amplified.

After their break, Luke followed behind Clay, who still had his nose buried in his handheld GPS unit. With no trail to follow, the group was simply a dot on the screen, moving ever so slowly closer to the wall.

They encroached into the wilderness. The ground was rough beneath their feet, full of brambles and twisting roots and thorny vines. They tottered under the weight of their oversized packs, placing each foot with tender care, as if the leaves were lined with bear traps.

But they discovered that they had not been the first to wander out into these particular woods—the waitress had been right about that, at least. Cradled within the organic matter rotting on the forest floor were remnants of those other humans: Budweiser cans with rusted edges; a T-shirt drowned in the dirt and twigs, the previously white fibers forever stained; yellow, waxy hamburger wrappers; the chipped and cracked handle of a hatchet.

These markers of humanity brought Luke some comfort, small reminders that they were not the only ones to push out into the woods with no trail to follow back, that humans had shared this space with wildlife for decades.

"Must not be too far off the beaten path," Dylan said, poking at the soggy T-shirt with her toe.

Slade sniffed at it, still taut at the end of his leash, Luke's bone-white knuckles gripping the loop. Slade jumped back and growled. A pit formed in Luke's throat. He wanted to turn back—to return to their cluttered apartment and call his boss and take back his resignation, the open-ended trip too inconvenient for his work to keep him on. They said he could reapply once he got back, but he knew they wouldn't keep the role open for him. And he knew how much this trip meant to Dylan. He didn't want to be the one to cut it short. And for what—Slade growling at a soggy T-shirt? It would be worth it, surely, for Dylan to develop this place. He couldn't take that away from her.

"I guess they didn't know what treasures these here woods hold," Clay said, dipping his voice into a cartoonish drawl. "I hope we find gold in these here hills, in that there wall."

"Clay, how far have we hiked?" Sylvia asked, craning her neck to look back at him.

"About a half mile according to the GPS," he responded, smacking the device between his hands. "Ugh, what the fuck? This thing is brand-new and the screen just flickered. We'll need to switch out the batteries when we get there."

"Shouldn't we still be able to hear the road?" Sylvia asked.

Luke craned his neck like a deer who'd just heard the telltale twig-snapping sign of a hunter. She was right. Not only could he not discern the noise of trucks barreling down the service road, but he couldn't distinguish any other sounds either: no whipping wind, no early spring birds chirping. Only dead, flat silence. Goosebumps pushed their way onto the skin of his arms, a shuddering jolt running through his bones. How had he not noticed until now? Suddenly Slade's behavior didn't seem that odd.

"Maybe there's no traffic right now," Clay said.

"There's always traffic," Sylvia replied. A thorny plant caught her pant leg, tugging like a pleading child. She unplucked its tiny fist. "How many semi trucks did we get stuck behind once we got off the expressway? How many did we see going past when we were getting all our gear out of the car?"

They plodded on, now all too aware that the only noises were their own: their feet crunching dry leaves, Slade's low and constant sniffing, their exaggerated, exhausted exhales.

"You don't think it's weird?" she asked. "It's like we're in a soundproof bubble."

"I don't know," Clay said, nearly tumbling over a downed trunk. "The woods are always quiet. Maybe a truck got stalled and everything's backed up. Maybe the animals haven't returned yet, haven't woken up. Maybe all the deer got hit by trucks or killed by all the hunters who have nothing better to do out here."

"Or maybe they were scared away by the ghosts of that waitress's uncle's past!" Dylan interjected, waggling her fingers. Sylvia rolled her eyes while Clay laughed.

———————

Luke groaned when Dylan pulled out her phone. He braced himself for her fake, chipper personality.

"Hey, guys," Dylan said, holding her phone at arm's length, the screen reflecting her and, behind her, Luke. He stepped to the side as much as he could, dodging the camera's gaze. He hated being on camera. He admired Dylan for being able to throw on this persona at a moment's notice, to not shrink away from the lens, but at the same time, her Instagram voice scratched his ears like shrieking slate.

"We're heading into the woods here in Kentucky to find a new climbing spot. I can't say exactly where, but it's a little south of Lexington. We'll be here for a few weeks to develop the area, and I'll get to set some routes. Hardly anyone gets to be the first on a rock wall! I'm so excited for my first Petzl outing! I'll be sure to keep you guys updated on what we find and what we're doing, depending on the cell coverage we have out there."

Slade nuzzled his snout into the dirt and started digging. He let out a bark. Luke pulled at his leash, trying to move him away from the spot and whatever had attracted him.

"Slade's here with us, too, and very excited about all the smells," she continued, panting in the gaps between the words. "This is an undeveloped spot, so there's not even a trail here—I don't know if you can tell that we're just walking through brush. Our faithful guide, Clay, an old friend of mine, is leading us there with GPS coordinates. At least, if anyone else has climbed it, they haven't told anyone about it!"

They pushed deeper into the woods. The trunks began to look identical to Luke, like a repeating pattern, but they followed Clay and his gadget, all faith in the GPS machine. Even Slade walked with a loose leash now, calm, no longer tugging and pulling away trying to sniff something or other. What was behind the change of heart?

Luke glanced down. In Slade's mouth sat a huge bone. He trotted with it between his teeth, drool raining down, plopping onto the dirt.

"Oh my god," Luke said, slapping his hand over his mouth.

The bone, smooth and bleached, jostled with Slade's jovial bounce. It was the length of a human shin, and Luke thought he even spied the head of the bone, worn but still there, that would have connected to the knee. His stomach somersaulted inside him, churning acid up into the back of his throat.

"Ew," Dylan said, turning. "Where the fuck did he find that?"

"I don't know," Luke said, swallowing the bitter bile. "Slade, drop it."

Slade tilted his head up and over at the curious request. He pretended he didn't hear. He clamped his teeth tighter, clicking them around the bone.

"It's probably just a deer leg or something," Clay said.

"It looks too big to be a deer," Luke replied.

"What do you think, then?"

"I mean—it looks like a tibia. Didn't Sylvia say a lot of people have gone missing here?"

"That's absurd," Dylan replied. "Slade's been on a short leash the whole time. We would have noticed if he'd stumbled upon a whole skeleton. It's probably just some animal."

"I don't want him to get sick," Luke said. "Who knows how old it is—or what kind of bacteria or parasites are on it."

Luke commanded Slade to drop it, and again Slade played his game of selective hearing. While Luke and Slade engaged in their battle of wills, Dylan sighed, slipped a knife from her pocket—a gift from Luke she carried on every trip—and cut a sliver of duct tape from a roll hanging off her pack. Wrapping it around the end of the bone, not wanting to touch it with her bare hands, she pulled. Slade's teeth did not budge, maintaining his death grip.

"Slade," she said, staring directly into his eyes. "Come on, bud. No. Let go."

She wiggled the bone, rattling it against his teeth. The contents of Luke's stomach vibrated in sync. But Dylan persisted, and, slick with drool, the bone finally slid through Slade's teeth. He snapped at the air in an attempt to grab it again. Dylan flung it into the woods like a boomerang. Slade tried to follow, snapping the leash taut. He howled after it, as if he could summon it back.

"Come on," Clay said impatiently. "We should reach the rock soon."

"Cool," Dylan said. "I'm itching to get on the walls."

"How much longer, do you think?" Luke asked.

They'd been hiking into the belly of this forest for three hours. The early spring sun, its reach not yet extended by daylight saving, had begun its descent, the yellow light twinging orange. It would be dark soon.

"Um," Clay said, again spanking the GPS between his hands, "maybe another thirty minutes."

They picked up their pace, Luke's pack feeling like pallets of bricks. Slade moved in tandem with him.

He cast a final glance at the bone Dylan had chucked into the brush, gleaming white against the wet leaves, a beacon on the dim forest floor.

"So weird," he muttered.

MARCH 8, 2019

4:55 P.M.

The woods remained soundless.

The quiet raised the hairs on Sylvia's neck, her heaving breath loud in her ears when Luke wasn't cracking jokes, or when she, Dylan, and Clay weren't discussing the climbing and the research ahead. She was still learning all the terms, but she'd done a deep dive after Clay had invited her on the trip, watching climbing competitions online and reading whatever she could about the sport. Whenever there was a lull in the conversation, the silence pressed against her eardrums.

Maybe she was paying too much attention, perking her ears so much in these in-between moments that she missed the nuanced noises: the light breeze knocking branches into each other, hooves pushing against worn deer paths in the distance. Slade had found a bone, so obviously animals did live—and die—here. She relaxed her ears, widened her eyes. Took a deep breath and moved her focus to the plant matter around her.

But that only revealed another disturbance. Were they walking in circles? Either little patterns seemed to be repeating or they were passing the same spot. Every few yards, the scene seemed to replicate: On the left, there was a little white-capped mushroom that stood at the base of a tree, right between the split of two roots on a bed of moss, either a puffball or a destroying angel—she'd have to examine it to know for sure. On the right, there was an oblong node sticking out of a trunk, smooth like a worn doorknob and at about the same height. Next to the trunk was a tree plagued by vines, all stretching up in the same precise pattern, all hosting the same pronged leaves.

Beyond, she continued to see overgrown tangles of poison ivy and oak and the white tops of hemlock. Further into the trees, were bright, dark berries—nightshade?—and the purple flowers of foxglove.

"Guys, be careful," she said. "I'm seeing some poison ivy, so we'll want to change when we get to camp and be careful about what we touch. And we'll have to clean Slade's paws and muzzle really well with Dawn to get off any oils. Make sure he doesn't eat any plants. I'm seeing some other toxic things—weird how they're all congregated together. How much longer do we need to hike?"

"Just a few more minutes," Clay said. "Do you need to take a break? We're really almost there."

"Doesn't it seem like we keep passing the same spots? I keep seeing the same markers."

"The GPS is working—the battery's a little low, but it's working," Clay said.

"Everything looks the same in the woods," Dylan said. "Especially when there's no trail."

"That's true," Sylvia admitted.

Sweat trickled along the skin of her back, soaking into her shirt. The straps of her backpack weighed heavy on her collarbones, so much pressure she feared they would snap.

"I'll be right back," she said. If she had to pass that black elderberry stalk one more time, she might be tempted to pluck it and examine it.

She set her backpack in the dirt, her shoulders already sore, a blooming bruise on each one. Though she'd known Clay since undergrad, this was her first camping trip with him. She had never gone with him on his climbing excursions, preferring to head to the botanical garden or grab pizza between classes. But when Clay had asked her to join him, to help document the findings and agreed to coauthor any eventual publications, she jumped at the chance. She wanted to do her dissertation on how native plants interact with geological features, so the trip could do double duty. She'd thought she was fairly fit, but the others—all with extensive hiking and climbing experience—definitely had more stamina than her.

She plodded away from the group down the slope into the trees, in a straight line so she could find her way back without having to play some awkward game of Marco Polo. She stepped purposefully, avoiding the curling vines of poison ivy. Her backpack a small purple blip against the landscape, she squatted, the stream flowing before she could fully move her pants out of the way.

"Shit," she said, trying to direct it away.

A crunch echoed behind her. Her muscles tensed at the sudden influx of sound, the snapping twigs like a gunshot in the silence. Did someone follow her down here?

"Guys, I'm okay," she called. "You don't need to follow me."

Craning her head over her shoulder, still peeing, she saw only trunks upon trunks in the distance, duplicating like a mirror reflecting another mirror. At the top of the hill, her pack waited, a bright purple beacon. A singular laugh bounced through the forest. Another one of Luke's jokes, probably. Guess this one was actually funny.

She heard it again, the crush of leaves, almost directly in front of her this time, she was sure, but no movement crossed her path. Surrounding her was more poison, stinging nettles and the bulbous doll's eyes of white baneberry. As she scanned for the source of the noise, she spied a glimmer, something that wasn't dead leaves or sticks or dirt or even a beetle. Something smooth and glossy.

A toenail.

The sight of it cut her bladder dry. She inched closer, still squatting, moving like a strategic crab. It was a smooth nail bed: yellow instead of pink, still attached to a greenish-purple toe, the rest of the foot buried in loam. The ridges of skin were pock-marked with dirt. Her breath caught inside her throat.

Her hand hovered above the foot, ready to move the leaves aside. She tipped forward, nearly landed headfirst in the grue-some thing, ass up with her pants around her ankles, but caught herself on her knees. At the last moment, she turned her head away, plunging her hand into pure wetness that she was sure was rotten flesh. The greasy chicken from the diner inched up her esophagus. The ooze of slimy bloat curled around her fingers and she swallowed to keep from vomiting.

She took a deep breath, inhaling the musty scent of wet leaves and dirt. She'd have to look at some point—she couldn't stay crouched wrist-deep in a corpse forever. When she finally un-twisted her head, the foot was gone.

Her hand sat wrist-deep in plain old muck, not flesh soft like pudding. She spotted the glimmer again, the thing that seemed out of place before. What she'd thought was a toe was actually the edge of a curious fungus called dead man's toes, an elongated purple mushroom with a little cap at the end like a nail.

She released a tepid laugh, her tense muscles relaxing, and stood, pulling her pants back to her waist.

How could she, the self-appointed botanical expert, have mistaken this for a foot? How could her mind have created that lifelike image—the yellowing, chipped nail bed, the dirt-coated skin? She stared at the mushroom, inching closer as if the foot would suddenly reappear. She wished she'd brought her camera down with her—she'd only ever seen pictures of dead man's toes in books.

"Are you okay down there?" Clay called. "We'll be hiking in the dark if you take much longer."

"Sorry," she replied, picking her way back up the incline.

"What happened to you?" Clay asked, laughing. "Was the hill that steep? Fall into a mud pit?"

"Distracted by plants," she replied.

"Of course." Clay chuckled, fidgeting with his device, smacking it to jolt the batteries.

Sylvia swung her pack firmly onto her shoulders and shivered, the adrenaline waning, feeling the cold, wet mud soaking into the knees of her jeans.

"Are you okay?" Luke asked while Slade tugged him in the opposite direction. "We can rest a bit longer if you need to."

"No, I'm okay," she said, another shiver curling through her, the image of the rotten toe etched into her mind. "I thought I saw a foot down there! But it was just *Xylaria polymorpha*."

"It was—what?" Dylan asked.

"Oh, some plant or another," Clay said, chuckling.

"It's this mushroom that looks like toes," Sylvia said.

"Creepy," Dylan said.

"Are we good?" Clay asked. "Ready to continue?"

MARCH 8, 2019
5:46 P.M.

The trees opened up into a valley, like a hole scooped out of the earth by a hungry god or a divot left by a meteor. Dylan stood at the precipice, just before the forest floor tipped down, a severe angle lined with trees until it leveled off after about one hundred feet. Lush, green grass, knee height, swayed at the base of the valley in front of the rock, a perfect bed for their tents. The rock stood like a pillar in the center, and sunlight glinted off a stream curling around the back side of it. In the late afternoon light, it seemed to glow.

The rock beckoned to Dylan. The hairs on her arms pulled taut, toward the wall, every part of her being drawn to it like a magnet to metal. Even the sweat running down her back and beneath her arms seemed to be drawn to it, trickling sideways along her torso. She had to stop herself from speeding ahead, down the steep ravine, rushing through the trees like a midnight shopper at the gates of Walmart on Black Friday.

The rock glittered, the lowering sun's rays glinting off mica or quartz or some other precious substance. The walls' pockmarks and cracks and crags made her fingers itch. Her pulse picked up and strummed against her wrist. Her endless train of anxious thoughts derailed, fell sidelong off the track in a fiery explosion that warmed her insides. In that moment, it did not matter if she was a woman trying to prove herself, if she wasn't skilled enough to send every route on the wall. She needed to touch it, to scale it.

"Holy shit," Dylan whispered. "It's perfect."

"Almost too good to be true," Clay said.

As they started down the lip of the valley, Slade stiffened at the end of his leash. He would not budge.

Luke tugged, and the dog dug his paws into the ground. Immoveable, Slade stared down the incline, his haunches raised along with the ridge of hair on his back, a cautionary mohawk. His growl, low and long, bounced into the valley.

A flash of unease crept up Dylan's spine. She'd never seen Slade act like this—even when they'd encountered racoons and possums during trips to the Gorge, he'd never so much as sniffed in their direction.

He tugged on the leash again, elongating the scratch marks in the dirt. Daring the revenge of Slade's teeth, Luke fed him another corner of the trail bar.

The four moved down into the valley, the ground soft, the air warm when they left the surrounding trees, Dylan leading Slade by the nose with more treats. Dylan and Luke pitched their tent in the grass, the movements easy and automatic, having performed each step so many times that paint had worn away from the poles. Clay helped Sylvia with her tent once he had erected his own. The trees lining the edge of the valley seemed to inch away from them as they pushed the stakes into the ground.

"Dylan, check this out," Luke called. He tapped the bark of a nearby tree, where the scabbed shapes of an *S* and a *T* resided inside of a heart. "Want to?"

Dylan pulled her knife from her pocket and started scraping their initials into the bark.

"Hey, hey!" Sylvia said, dropping a stack of wood. "What are you doing?"

They were nearly done. "We're just leaving our mark," Dylan said. She finished scraping the *L* and folded her knife.

"You can't just scar the trees," Sylvia said. "This is a research mission. We need to leave everything just like we found it, as much as we possibly can. Ecosystems are fragile, especially in areas where people don't normally go."

"People have been here already," Luke said, pointing at the other set of initials.

Sylvia sighed. She ran her fingers through the fresh lines, and Dylan noticed that the tips came back sticky and dark red.

"That's weird," Sylvia said, touching her fingertips to the sap again. "I'm not sure what species of trees has sap like this— especially ones that would be native to Kentucky." She snapped a picture and pulled out her notebook, scribbling notes.

"Already hard at work?" Dylan asked her, peering over her shoulder.

"Yeah, Sylv, the work starts tomorrow!" Clay called, working to build the fire, using foraged bark and twigs for kindling. "Tonight is for ghost stories and beer."

"I think we've had enough ghost stories from that waitress," Sylvia joked.

With a little effort, the fire roared to life, licking each added piece of kindling, boiling that unusual red sap.

MARCH 9, 2019

8:23 A.M.

The morning air was bright and cold against her skin as Dylan stepped out of the tent, and silent as ever. Behind her, the tents rippled as if they were breathing. The trees staggered like auditorium seats up the side of the valley's bowl, which was marred by mossy trunks felled by some storm. Dew glistened on the grass. The granite wall seemed to expand before her, looming and stretching.

It glittered, little specks of sunlight flickering as the morning light crept up the rock face. The light exposed its acne, all of the messy pockmarks and cracks and jagged little pieces she'd been hoping for, more glorious in person than on Clay's scans. Deep in Dylan's bones, it pulsed through her, the magic draw of the rock, like something had wrapped its hand around her wrist and pulled.

Entrancing her so deeply that she left the tent unzipped behind her.

Her body hummed with electricity, every atom of her being jittering, the static in her ears growing louder with each step closer to the wall. Every step away from the rock pained her—even moving in a parabola to avoid the firepit. The pain ebbed when she reached the rock, but the magnetism in her fingers became a physical pull. She struggled to keep them at her sides, to stop them from reaching for it and climbing with no rope or harness or any sort of safety net. She had to remind herself to breathe.

But she touched the rock anyway. Damp-feeling in the way cold things usually were, the rough rock zipped a brief electric jolt through her fingers as she clutched a ridge caked in dirt.

Her other hand clenched a crack, and she lifted her feet off the valley floor, set them against the rock in her hiking boots—nowhere near as sensitive as the sleek, rubber-soled climbing shoes whose leather had molded to her feet, little concave buttons for each toe. But she was good at this, even with the constant doubt, and she knew how to position the pressure in her foot to utilize the edge of the bulky boot, gripping even the tiny crevices inset in the stone. She pulsed up to the next spot her fingers could shoot out to and clasp.

She reminded herself with each inch upward to keep an eye out, to not climb too high with no rope and no crash pad. Each time she looked down, trying to discern the distance between her body and the ground, the electricity inside her sparked up again. Her entire being urged her *up*.

Keep going, whispered a small voice, *just one more move*.

But another part of her—the part that had seen compound ankle fractures from a three-foot drop and snapped humerus bones and had read about worse, all from climbers much more experienced than her—forced her to stop. Already ten feet off the ground, she moved in reverse. Her feet felt around sightlessly on the rock for a place that would hold her weight, like wading into a murky pool where electric eels lurked.

She was careful, but still—her thick boots found a loose scrap of slate. Putting her weight on it was all it took for her tension to break, for her to fall. It was like dropping into an endless void. Her heart clamped inside her chest, her muscles bracing for impact.

Shit. This whole trip would be over before it even began, all because she couldn't wait two hours to get climbing.

Her boots hit the ground and she bent her knees, rolled onto her back, an automatic reaction after many failed routes.

Leaning up on her elbows, she marveled at the granite, her pupils widening, her breath returning to its normal pace. She wished she could really make her mark permanent, make herself famous—no mistaking that she climbed these walls first and set the routes. Make something no one could take from her. She could have placed bolts and anchors permanently into the wall if she'd brought a drill down into the valley to bore into the rock.

But this rock bled.

"Are you okay?" Clay called.

A twitch ran through Dylan. She blinked and turned to face Clay, who had come up behind her and was looking at her with concern.

"Yeah," she replied. "I woke up early and couldn't fall back asleep."

She stood up, against her body's urges, and returned to the firepit with Clay. She started boiling water for coffee.

For a quick moment, she had an intrusive thought, an image of the little canister stove tipping over, right into the cache of dry, brittle wood beside it. Setting the whole valley ablaze. The image expanded, even as she turned down the flame and moved the wood farther away. But still there remained the mental image, superimposed on top of reality: the flames caught a patch of dry grass, which tunneled a neat little line of fire into the trees, like someone had carefully dowsed a precise sprinkle of lighter fluid for it to follow. Then the whole basin was ablaze, instantly. As if it had spontaneously erupted.

Her overactive imagination must be a symptom of her insomnia. Reality shifted back into place.

"Are you sure you're okay?"

"Yeah," she said. "I think I need the coffee. I was studying the routes. You've found a really good spot."

"Do you remember that one summer when we basically lived at the Gorge?" he asked. "We camped at Miguel's for weeks on end."

"We ate so much pizza. I can't believe we were even able to get up any walls with all that cheese in our stomachs."

Clay laughed.

"It's nice to be back to something like that," Dylan said. "I miss that summer—going climbing every day, hanging out, not worrying about jobs or rent or anything." Or needing to prove herself worthy. Just being able to enjoy the climb without all the pressure.

"Getting grimy as hell with only a tiny shower stall," Clay said.

"And we don't even have that here. We're going to get stinky for sure."

———

Dylan's coffee had grown tepid by the time Luke crawled out of the tent, yawning.

"Why didn't you wake me up?" he asked, sitting next to her

by the firepit.

"I don't know," Dylan said. "You were snoring and curled up so cute with Slade, so I thought I'd let you sleep."

"Where is Slade?"

"Isn't he with you?" she asked. "Do you want some coffee?"

"He wasn't in the tent when I got up. And the tent was unzipped."

"Oh, shit," Dylan said, her stomach plummeting. "He can't have gone far—probably just needed to pee. We'll find him."

The four searched the campsite, in and around the tents and all of their supplies. They screamed Slade's name into the trees, the sound echoing against the heavy silence. They walked in wider and wider circles, calling out to the dog, Sylvia and Clay glancing more longingly at the wall and their research gear with each revolution.

Dylan didn't remember doing it, but she knew she was the one to leave the tent open. It wasn't like Slade to go far, but why hadn't he come when they called? He could be anywhere by now. She should have worked harder to convince Luke to leave Slade with a friend for the trip, but Luke said he'd be too worried about him to focus on anything else. Now Slade was gone and holding up the work. And it was her fault.

Once more, Dylan ducked her head into the still-unzipped tent, hoping against the leaden ball in her stomach that Slade would be in there, snoozing in the corner, obscured by their packs.

But she only found the buzzing of wayward flies.

MARCH 9, 2019
9:46 A.M.

Luke's eyelids were heavy and hot with impending tears. Why had Slade run off? Why hadn't Dylan just zipped the tent back up? He withheld a scream, clamping his teeth together until the turbulence of his rage slowed, like the settling sediment in a snow globe. It was an accident. But now Slade was gone.

"He can't have gone far," Dylan said.

The pair trudged up the hill in the direction they had come from, armed with Slade's leash and a handful of smelly treats. By the time they reached the top of the ridge, sweat had pooled on the back of his neck. There was no sign of Slade—the mud revealed no paw prints or tiny tufts of hair or even a pile of shit. The air was so still that not even a single branch shifted from its place. Luke wanted to fall into the dirt and let the leaves cover him until he, too, could not be found.

"I don't think he went this way," Luke said, wiping his eyes.

They scrambled back down the steep hill into the valley where Sylvia and Clay were busy documenting and setting up equipment. Luke caught their sidelong pitying glances while they snapped photos of the wall and scribbled in notebooks.

Back up the hill he and Dylan went, this time directly behind the tents. Their voices vibrated through the forest as they whistled, called out Slade's name. Every few moments, they stopped, like spooked creatures, the only movement being their eyes inside their sockets. They listened for Slade, their ears alert for snapping twigs or rustling leaves or low whimpers. Luke inhaled, deep, as though he could track Slade if only he could get a whiff of his pungent, musty fur.

He couldn't have gone far. They had to find him.

They pushed further into the woods, repeating these steps like a dance routine, turning up nothing but silence.

"I'm sorry, Luke, but I think we should head back," Dylan said. Somehow, they were still at the edge of the valley's bowl, their tents in sight. They must have been walking in circles.

"He has to be here somewhere," Luke said, his voice hoarse from screaming. "Maybe if we go just a little farther—"

Dylan sat down on a log. "I'm sorry. I don't think we're going to find him. We don't want to get lost ourselves."

"We have to find him."

"We should get to climbing soon," Dylan said. Her knee bounced like a piston, the motion so heavy that it seemed to rock the earth, brittle leaves crackling and dancing beneath her shoe.

"The wall's not going anywhere, Dylan," he said. "We can take a day or two to look for him."

"How will we find him?" she replied, gesturing to the vast forest. She stared at the dirt, unable to meet his face. "We've been looking and calling his name for over an hour. He could be anywhere by now."

Luke could not produce an answer. He seethed, his body filling with fire. How could she be so callous about this? Didn't she love Slade? He'd given up his job for this. They'd packed all of their possessions into a storage unit for this trip—no point paying the rent for an apartment no one's going to live in, Dylan had said. Now she wanted him to give up on Slade, too?

"And how would we find our way back?" she posed.

"We could borrow the GPS thing," Luke said. "I mean, we should at least fucking try. What if he's just a little farther and we miss him?"

"We can set a bowl of his food out and the clothes we were wearing yesterday," Dylan said. She still couldn't meet his eye. "I heard that dogs can smell that stuff for miles. That's how people lure their missing dogs back home."

"This is important," Luke said. "We can delay climbing for a single day."

"This isn't just a fun weekend to the Gorge," she snapped. "This is like a job for me. I came here for a purpose, to be a vital part of Clay's research and to start developing this area. I quit my day job. There's a lot riding on this—Petzl expects a lot from me."

"I quit my job too," he said through gritted teeth. "I did that for you, and you act like you don't give a shit about Slade."

"That's not fair," she spat, finally meeting his eye. "I just don't think that there's much we can do right now. He could have run off in any direction. He could be all the way to Lexington by now. What's your game plan? How do you propose we search the entire forest for him? I know you're worried, but the best thing we can do right now is try to help lead him to us and not get lost ourselves."

Tears burned against Luke's corneas. He'd failed. And Dylan would no longer help him.

They turned back, heading toward the tents in a straight line. Neither spoke it, but Luke suspected they both felt it: the trees seemed to open up to form a broad path pointing straight down the hill, leading back to the fire blooming at the campsite.

Luke glanced once more up into the forest, toward Slade and his freedom, the spaces between the trees glowing beneath the rising sun. Going after Slade could mean getting lost himself. He had no choice but to plunge back into the valley, a tightness worming its way into his chest while they climbed down.

"No luck?" Sylvia asked when the pair reached the fire. Her camera now sat on a tripod facing the rock.

The tinny sound of the empty leash crashing to the ground like a meteor was her answer. Luke sat heavily on one of the tiny camp chairs they'd brought. He wiped at his eyes, staring into the fire.

"He'll come back," Dylan said, fiddling with a small gas canister. When she reached out to rub Luke's back, he recoiled, curling away from her touch. "He's a smart dog. Relax."

"How can I relax when he's lost in the middle of the woods?" Luke said, his hands shielding his wet face, absorbing the sting of the smoke.

Dylan continued to rub his back. If she really cared this much, they'd still be looking, Luke thought bitterly. The blaze reached its orange-yellow arms out in a yawn. Clay placed new kindling into its outstretched hands, and it licked and smacked at its new meal.

"Dogs have good hearing," Dylan said. "And this valley is like a giant echo chamber. He'll hear us and smell our food and clothes and find his way back."

"We didn't hear anything from down here when we were

looking."

"They weren't really making any noise down here," Dylan continued, unfolding a tiny grate and snapping it onto the gas canister. "And you were probably paying too much attention to trying to hear Slade."

Luke dragged his hand across his face. He stared into the flames, unconvinced. Every dark scenario projected into his mind—Slade hungry and cold, a little shivering doughnut of fur; Slade's ribs broken, kicked inward by a rogue frightened deer; Slade flattened by a big rig barreling down the road; hungry Slade eating something he shouldn't, his hunger pangs replaced by death pangs. But what could he do? Dylan was right—Luke couldn't risk getting lost himself, risk freezing and starving his own body. Slade could be anywhere by now.

It was just as likely Slade had made it back to the road, that he was safe and warm in a stranger's kitchen, eating scraps from their frying pan.

Right?

———————

There was crunching in the trees. Luke swiveled, half his body bent inside his tent to retrieve his gear. He dropped his climbing harness and tried to catch the low sound again, the noise muffled by the laughter and chatter of the other three preparing for Dylan's first ascent.

He wished they would shut the hell up.

He had definitely heard something. The group didn't notice as he ducked out of his tent and crept into the trees lining the basin of the valley. Shadows hung beneath the spring canopy, the sun freckling the forest floor.

"Slade?" he called, his voice cracking.

He paused, listening for a response. Placing his hand against the warm bark of a nearby tree, he perked his ears, listening, hard, beyond the campfire chatter for Slade's whimper or growl, for the patter of paws.

Something chittered just to the left, scratching in the leaves, like the crinkle of tissue paper.

"Slade?" he called again. "Is that you? Come here, buddy. I have a treat for you."

He scanned the forest floor, little tendrils of green poking out of the blanket of rotting fall leaves. There was no movement. But the crunch crackled once more at the moment he turned his back, the moment he again abandoned the search. When he returned his gaze to the trees, a dark silhouette hovered in the periphery of his vision.

It emerged from between the trees, and his breath caught in his throat. A dog-shaped thing crouched ahead, its head bobbing near the ground. Luke edged closer. The smacking sounds of its teeth ripping flesh from bone twisted his stomach into knots, sloshed and foamed the bitter coffee inside him.

"Slade?" Luke whispered, stepping closer, nearly touching the fur of the thing's back. His pulse pounded against his rib cage. "Is that you? What do you have?"

The beast abandoned its meal and turned its head. A pair of yellow eyes glowed, like a werewolf in all those pulp horror stories Luke had read in middle school. It raised its haunches, long tufts of fur lifting along its spine. It had brindled fur like Slade, but its rib cage showed beneath its skin. Flecks of white polka-dotted its back.

If this was a dog, it wasn't Slade. At least, not the Slade Luke knew.

They played their game of chicken, there in the dark shade of the trees, neither even blinking, let alone breathing.

Luke took an experimental step backward, wondering if it would pounce at the movement. The brush crackled beneath his shoe in slow motion. The eyes did not move. Neither did the thing attached to them. He took another step back, keeping his eyes matched with the beast's, with its impossible yellow orbs. In the next moment, the beast lifted its jowls. Fangs appeared inside the thing's mouth, dripping wet, with miniature reflections of the fire inside each drop.

Then it vaulted toward him, its teeth snapping together with a ferocious click that echoed through the trees. Had Luke not turned and ran, sliding down the hill, had he taken that first step just moments later, the thing's teeth would have closed around his wrist, tearing through sinew and shattering bone.

That telltale tissue-paper crinkle of paws on leaves followed him as he exited the trees into the valley, panting and sweating, his feet slipping down the steep incline. The beastly thing did not follow him past the tree line.

In fact, when he chanced a glance behind him, he saw nothing at all.

The valley returned to its soundlessness—a thick and pressing quiet. When he was certain the thing wasn't going to pass through the trees, he turned around to meet more eyes, Dylan's this time.

"You okay?" she asked, halfway into her harness.

"No. I just saw something weird," Luke said.

"Did you go into the woods?" she asked. Her eyes grew wide as she took in his dirty pants and shoes, his heaving chest.

"What's wrong?"

"I thought I heard Slade," he said, still out of breath. "I had to check. But it wasn't Slade, it was something else, a rabid dog or—I don't know. Are there bobcats or coyotes or something out here? It seemed hungry—or angry."

She peered into the trees behind him. "I don't see anything," she said. "Are you sure?"

"Do you think I'm hallucinating? It probably just ran off."

"No, sorry," she replied. "I just don't see anything. Are you ready to get started?"

"What?"

"Climbing—you know, the thing we came here to do?"

"I think we should go look for Slade again. What if that thing, whatever it was, finds him?"

What if it already had? He hadn't gotten a close look at what the thing had been eating. He dug his fingernails into his palm, trying to scratch away the mental images of a mauled Slade, of blood-matted fur and a final whimpering cry before that thing stripped the meat from Slade's bones. He itched to go back into the trees, armed with Dylan's knife, to scour the woods until they either slayed the beast or rescued Slade.

"It's probably just a deer or something that's not used to humans," Dylan said. "It's not going to get Slade. He's a smart dog."

The yellow eyes hovered behind Luke's own eyelids, lying in wait each time he blinked. He glanced toward the trees. He wasn't sure how he'd get to sleep with the knowledge of that thing prowling, teeth sharp enough to tear flesh.

"It definitely wasn't a deer. It really looked like a dog, but like, rabid or feral. And it was eating something, like raw meat. What if it hurts him?"

"I'm worried too," Dylan said. She squeezed his hands with hers, her tone soothing, as though Luke was a child who was worried over his stuffed toy in the washing machine. "But he'll be okay. He's smart. It's best to stay put—what if we go looking for him and he comes back and we're not here? He doesn't know Clay or Sylvia. And we're so close to civilization. He'll probably end up on a road where someone will find him."

Luke gave her a half smile. Dylan was probably right. Slade would be okay. He had to be.

But again, Luke saw the lightbulb eyes of that thing, now without even the aid of shutting his eyes. He bit the inside of his cheek. Slade was out there, alone in the vast, untamed woods of rural Kentucky, and there was nothing he could do about it. What if that thing sniffed him out before Slade found his way back? Luke should have left him with a friend for the duration of the trip. A sharp pang pierced his chest when he realized he'd probably never see Slade again.

Thick silence permeated their camp, the air stifling.

As if they were trapped in a bubble.

MARCH 9, 2019
11:01 A.M.

Dylan uncoiled the rope. Almost ready to climb.

The rock radiated its magnetism, its charm. The air grew warmer, and each minute she unzipped her jacket a bit more, the little teeth like tick marks counting down to her time on the wall. Her pulse thumped a rapid tempo against her temple. The sun lit the area she'd climb—*soon, soon, soon*—like a spotlight, meaning she wouldn't be squinting as she searched for the next hold. The rock would be baked, the perfect temperature for fingers.

"Hey, guys," Dylan prattled in a cool, transformed tone. She held her phone at arm's length. "I somehow have some signal, so I thought I'd do a live! We're here at the crag I told you about a couple days ago, brand-new rock and my first trip with Petzl." She pivoted to point the phone toward the wall. "Clay and Sylvia are two grad students studying this for their PhDs—as you can see, they are very serious. They'll be cataloging everything we do here, taking lots of notes and pictures.

"We're going to start climbing in just a bit—on the first route and first ascent ever in this area. The walls are gorgeous and I'm excited to get up there. We're going to start on this one here."

She scanned the camera up the rock before turning it back on her face. "I won't really be able to tell until I get up there, but I've been mapping the moves and it seems a lot like The Offering at Bruise Brothers in Muir Valley. So it should be a good warm-up route."

Her arm grew heavy, her elbow locked in place. The muscles in her cheeks ached inside of this persona she adopted whenever a lens captured her. Hopefully she wouldn't have to do it much longer—just the occasional update for Petzl. It had been fun at first to see how many people cared about her climbing, but it quickly became a job—something to maintain, always the pressure to produce new content, having to remember to take pictures and videos instead of just enjoying the climb.

From the bottom left of the screen, faceless usernames with questions bubbled up, stacking on top of one another so fast she could barely read them before they disappeared under the weight of new ones. She caught one—*Will u be bolting?*

"No, we won't be putting up any bolts this time around, unfortunately," she replied. "That's where you literally drill into the rock to put permanent anchors that other climbers can clip their rope to. I would love to set up some sport routes and put that safety gear into the rock, but this is just a sort of fact-finding mission. We need to leave this space the way we found it. Maybe later we can come back—" She glanced at the wall.

For a moment, she forgot about her thousands of followers, about her current stream. She could not have even produced her mother's name or her own address in that split second, her whole being eclipsed by the lure of the rock. Her arm lowered, her forehead framed by fat clouds on the screen.

"Uh, sorry," she said, slipping her perky mask back on. "We

hope some better development will come later, but for now I'll be naming some of the routes as I make those first ascents. Hopefully they're not too hard! I'll be posting here with updates, so be sure to follow so you don't miss out. I'm going to go get ready and do some climbing now! Talk to you guys soon!" She clicked her phone's screen off, the mess of emojis and jumbled messages disappearing.

She hadn't expected to have signal by the rock wall. Part of her wished it would go away, so she could just enjoy the climbs and worry about her following later.

Back at the firepit, Luke sat in his harness, staring into the trees, sipping coffee.

"Are you ready to belay?" she asked.

"Did you pump up all your little followers?" he said when she sat next to him.

"I have to do that," she said, following his line of sight into the trees. Nothing moved, the scenery so static it looked more like a photograph than a three dimensional forest. "You know that. Someday I won't have to do that shit anymore, but I'm new at Petzl and have to maintain my audience. I know you find it annoying."

Luke grunted. "You're so fake on there."

"I don't know what to tell you, Luke," she replied. "I'm not going to keep my sponsorship if nobody knows who I am. I thought you understood that."

"You act like that's all that matters," he said.

"You know that's not true," she said. "Look, I'm sorry about Slade. Really. And I'm sorry if I came off as insensitive. But you don't have to get snippy with me or act like it's some slight against you. I really do see this as a job—one I can't do without you."

She leaned her head against his shoulder, that corner of him sharp, pinching her cheek against her teeth. Reaching around behind him, she rubbed his other shoulder with her callused hand.

"Are you ready to get to climbing?"

———————

"Everything good to go?" Dylan asked.

"I'm ready," Sylvia said, adjusting her notebook.

"Yeah, we're good to go," Clay replied, standing behind his fancy camera.

Next to the wall electricity hung in the air, a force that tugged on the little hairs on Dylan's arms and the base of her neck. She had heard that sort of thing could happen right before a bolt of lightning struck in the exact spot you occupied, but the sky remained a clear, bright blue.

She examined the granite in front of her. She knew precisely where she would place her hands to begin, where she would lift her weight to hoist her feet. She had even spotted the places where she'd insert the safety gear, the little metal nuts and winged cams that would settle into the rock and connect to the rope tied at her waist, so that if she fell, she'd have a shorter drop and wouldn't plummet to the ground in a mangled heap.

She took a breath. She'd been training for a moment like this since her freshman year of high school when a friend had dragged her to the local climbing gym. She'd only managed to climb for about an hour before her muscles swelled and the skin of her fingertips revolted, sent shockwaves of sharp pain up her tired arms when she tried to grip the rough plastic holds of just one more route. That hour was all it had taken—she was hooked. But the weekend trips to the Gorge cemented it for her. This is what she wanted to do, get paid to climb. And now she'd been given her chance. She couldn't fuck this up. She wouldn't.

"Climb on," Luke said, holding the free end of the rope loose in his hands, ready to feed it up to her and ready to pull it taut should she fall.

And she climbed. She moved up the rock, smooth and easy. The warmth of the day's light pressed against the back of her neck. The rock was dry, full of sand and sticky cobwebs, and she shoved the metal cams into the wall, each piece fitting smoothly and snugly into the grooves of the stone. It was like she'd done this exact climb before, almost like International Route of Pancakes in Muir Valley—more akin to rote memory than a brand-new wall. Most new routes meant fussing thirty feet in the air, trying to position an inch-wide square of metal to touch as much of the rock as possible so that it would hold her if she fell, the muscles in her opposing arm cramped and locked in place, keeping her on the wall until she finished fiddling with the gear. But this wall? No strained, twitching muscles screaming to let go while she clipped the quickdraw, no scrabbling above her head for an unseen hold. Pure magic.

The trend continued for the rest of the morning. Luke fed her rope as she pressed upward, each movement captured by Clay's camera. By their late lunch, she'd completed ascents on four routes.

Around the fire, between bites of trail mix and flame-toasted bagel, they huddled over the screen of Clay's iPad, probably the worst gadget he could have lugged out into the woods. Clay edited the photos he'd taken of each route, snaking his finger along the path Dylan climbed to chart a red line. Sylvia scribbled in her notebook, asking Dylan questions about the quality of the climb—the texture of the rock, the firmness of it, the difficulty rating she might give each route. What name she would bestow upon it, letters forever associated with this valley.

Dylan clicked open her phone, watched herself crawl up the wall, tiny, more like a spider than a person, often out of focus or barely in frame. For all his shiny gadgets, Clay wasn't much of a cinematographer. She found a one-minute chunk in the middle where she flowed smooth and silky, and posted it to Instagram, the signal—fortunately and unfortunately—holding strong: *Here's a little preview of what we found today. It's gorgeous here. My first #FirstAscent!*

MARCH 9, 2019
1:49 P.M.

Sylvia jotted down the coordinates of each route from the GPS tracker, scribbling in a nearly illegible scrawl. She'd been tasked with the busywork, with the actual writing-it-down part—not too stressful, but still, she noticed Clay wasn't doing anything but manning the camera.

"Where are your notes?" she asked.

He tapped his finger against his temple. "All up here," he said. "I'm going to write it all down later."

She slid the notebook underneath her armpit and balanced his camera, spinning the lens to bring the crags and jagged rock into focus just beyond Dylan, who was warming up at the base of the rock for her second session.

"Fixed that for you," she teased. "Can't even manage your own equipment."

Standing behind her, Clay leaned in, his hot breath condensing on her shoulder while she clicked around in the settings. Though the camera stood only twenty feet, give or take, from the wall, the digital display framed Dylan as if a science fiction machine had shrunk her. On her hips dangled wires and cords, little metal chunks and spring-loaded cams swinging by her thighs. In miniature, she tied a figure-eight knot with the rope and looped it through her harness.

"Got everything set up, o camerawoman extraordinaire?" Clay asked, shoving his hands in his pockets.

"Sure do." She focused on the camera, adjusting one last setting, teeth gritted.

"Good," he said. He gulped the last of an energy drink before crushing the can and throwing it across camp toward the firepit. It clanged against a tree trunk and ricocheted into the thick plant matter beyond.

"Hey, not cool," Sylvia said. "We need to leave this place clean. There's a really interesting and old ecosystem here, untouched by humans. If we're going to be here, we need to respect the land. Leave it like we found it."

"Chill," he replied. "I'll clean it up later."

Sylvia grumbled. Clay handed her a beat-up cell phone. "What's that?" she asked.

"Dylan asked if we could film it on her phone."

"Okay?" she replied. "What am I supposed to do with it? I'm taking notes. Why don't you film with it?"

"I need to pay more attention to this camera," he said, "so we have an accurate record. Besides, Dylan asked you to do it this time. She said I sucked. Why don't you just find some place to lean it and record?"

Grumbling again, Sylvia opened the camera app and stomped away from Clay. This was unlike him to pawn his work off on others. He usually wanted to be in control of every little thing. Maybe he was really stressing out about this field study and his dissertation.

The tiny screen of Dylan's phone captured only a fraction of the wall. Sylvia moved backward, past the firepit, past the tents, until her back pressed against bark. The whole route still did not quite fit into the screen's tiny real estate, but it would have to do. She scanned the tree for knobby knots, low-hanging limbs, anything to hold the phone in place. She found no ledges—only smooth trunk. She dropped her head lower, scanning for another support, considering some creative piling of rocks or using vines as rope. Beyond the trees lay thickets of poison ivy, clumps of hemlock. Dark fruit of baneberry. All matter of poisonous treachery. She jotted their names in her notebook—*Lots of poisonous plants surrounding camp in clumps. Wonder if there is something in the soil quality? Or the terrain?*

She found no good way to prop up the phone. Instead, at the base of the tree, just steps from their tents, she spotted deep scratches in the dirt. A set of four. Like claws.

A shudder vibrated through her. The silence of the valley pressed upon her while she listened for something prowling between the trees. Nothing stirred. Was this left by the creature Luke had seen?

Whatever it was, it was long gone, the soil beneath the slashes dry and flaky.

She found a spot for the phone, hit RECORD, and hurried back to the wall.

———————

In her notebook, Sylvia scribbled Dylan's frustrations into ink. *Seems to be struggling, Rte. 6, midway. Canvassed up the first third, then moved left before downclimbing and trying moves on the right. Top of the rock appears smooth from the ground.*

Perhaps some tiny spots for her hand?

On the wall, Dylan fiddled with one of the cams, a metal gadget that would allow her to connect the rope to the wall. This one flapped like wings, two curved and notched pieces unfolding from pinching little wires in the middle of the thing. Sylvia checked her watch. Dylan had been meddling with the cam, trying to wedge it into the wall, for more than three minutes. The muscles on her left arm, the one holding her body upright—no rope yet to hold her—twitched, the tension of her tendons visible even from the ground.

Struggling to place safety equip. Needs to get it positioned correctly so she can attach the rope to catch her if she falls. Already too much space between the last safety clip—she can't go higher.

It took a singular *Fuck* ringing through the bowl of the valley to get the thing shoved into the wall in just the right way. Dylan clipped the rope just in time to yell another word: *Falling!*

Sylvia gasped when Dylan's body plummeted, her pen scratching a deep line of ink across the page, scoring through the notes she'd just taken. The rope stretched and deposited Dylan just a few short feet below the clip, now pushed further into place by the drop, by her weight. Luke stood on tiptoe, the other end of the human pulley heaving upward in response.

Dylan shook out her left arm, flexing the tight muscle, the movement reflected in the tiny camera screen. Sylvia's own arm ached, her tendons pulled taut from scribbling. Even with the camera recording everything, she scratched each movement Dylan made into the log, needing to get everything precisely transcribed. She doubted Clay would really hold all the details in his head. Her head bobbing between the scene and her page,

Sylvia charted in her notebook: *Falls after placing cam, Rte. 6, midway—maybe 40 ft. up. No visible injuries, muscles seem sore. Clips remain in wall.*

She didn't realize she'd been biting her lip until blood sprang like a well, the river running between her teeth. She'd watched climbers fall on video as she was doing her research, but seeing it in real time made her chest constrict.

"Are you okay?" Luke called up to Dylan. Luke released slack, his feet lowering to the dirt.

"Yeah," Dylan yelled down. "I don't know if I'm going to be able to finish this one today."

"Are you ready to come down?"

Even from the ground, Sylvia could see Dylan deliberating, her gaze pinging from her shaky forearm to her scuffed shoes to the sun diving behind the rock face, pouring blinding light into her eyes while leaving the rock dark. Sylvia hesitated, her pen hovering above the page, waiting for the decision. Still dangling from the wall, Dylan shook her left hand again, trying to reset the knotted tendons. Her toes slithered along the rock, kicking off showers of dust.

"Bring me down," she called. Luke pulled the arm of the belay device on his harness, and the rope twitched through the hook. Dylan lowered.

Sylvia scrawled: *Took a fall, uninjured. Did not complete, attempt #3, Rte. 6, midway.*

"Fuck," Dylan said when her feet touched the ground.

"Rough one?" Luke asked. Dylan struggled to undo the tight knot still connecting her to the rock.

"Mostly just that it's the end of the day," she said. "I'm wiped. It sucks that the gear is left in. If I'd have known I'd have to bail, I would have used one of the cheapo things we brought to sacrifice to the gods of safety."

"You'll get it tomorrow," Luke said, relieving her useless hands of their task. He pulled the rope. It slipped out of the abandoned clip and snapped to the ground like a whip. "Let's go see if those remaining beers are still cold."

Finished climbing for the day. Gear still in rock, Sylvia scribbled, then snapped her notebook shut.

As Dylan took a step toward the campsite, her feet slid on the dirt as if it were an iced-over sidewalk. Sylvia processed the oddness—why was that lone patch of dirt dry enough to skid on when every other inch of this valley was caked in mud? Sylvia bent down, brushing the dirt with her ink-stained fingers.

"What is it?" Dylan asked.

"Not sure," she replied.

"I almost slipped," Dylan said. "It felt like loose sand on smooth concrete or something."

"Maybe it's just part of the rock," Clay offered, crouching down with the others.

"Maybe," Dylan said. "Sometimes the ground is rocky underneath the wall."

They swept the dirt away. What they uncovered was a thick, rectangular mass that extended away from the rock wall, the edges smooth and pin straight, as though it were planned, as if someone had placed it there. They unearthed about three feet of this slick substance before it turned at a sharp right angle and continued straight once more, parallel to the wall.

Sylvia dipped her head lower, ran her fingers across it. "Oh my god," she said. "This is petrified wood."

It glittered with hues of deep red and white, slick crystals within the logs forming an *L* jutting away from the rock.

"That's so strange," Sylvia continued. "It looks like the foundation of a building that recessed into the ground at some point. There must have been a house or shack here, or at least someone started to build one."

"Why would someone build so close to the wall?" Dylan asked, running her fingers over the crystallization in the wood, the cracked quartz inlaid like veins. "And who would have built it? The only signs that anyone's been back here were those initials in the tree trunk. Everything else we found was over a mile away."

"Who knows," Clay says. "Maybe it was a lean-to a long time ago. Maybe like a hunter's shack?"

"Look at the join. This is definitely the foundation of a house," Sylvia said. "It almost looks like it goes *under* the rock face." Her hands itched to record this. She went to unscrew the camera from the tripod.

"Optical illusion," Clay said. "Maybe as the wood got pushed into the ground, it shifted and got pushed under the rock, into a crevice or something."

Sylvia rolled her eyes. "And maybe it's just trees that were cut by lightning and fell this way, entirely square, doorway and all," she clipped, returning with the camera. "Petrified wood takes millions of years to form—it must have already been petrified when they built it. What a cool find!"

Sylvia snapped photos of the human-made structure, zooming in where it seemed to cut underneath the tower of rock.

They squatted, each one of them marveling at the old wood, at the space at the front wide enough for a door. Sylvia let the camera drop on the lanyard around her neck and scribbled: *Found*

*man-made structure near the wall. The wood is petrified—must
be millions of yrs old. Looks like the foundation of an old house,
maybe a lean-to or log cabin. Rest of the structure is gone, so
probably at least a hundred years old. The foundation goes beneath the rock somehow. Puzzling find this far into the woods w/
no trail to lead here. Maybe trail grew over? Could flooding have
pushed structure under rock—maybe caves beneath?*

Sylvia lamented that the rest of the structure had been demol-
ished, by time or natural disaster or human hands—everything
but this glittering, quartz monument.

MARCH 10, 2019
1:43 A.M.

Late that night, pained howls reverberated out among the trees.

Luke couldn't be sure the pangs and yelps ringing through the valley, hour by hour, weren't Slade somewhere in the woods, hungry and crying. Cold. His paws caked with clumped mud. There was a whimper so low he couldn't be sure it was there at all. A tiny little pang, a just-there cry for help. Were those the sounds a dog made? Was it just cruel wind? Or was it that horrible *thing* he had seen in the trees earlier that day?

He could only imagine the worst. Perhaps Slade had made it back to the road just to be sideswiped by one of the giant trucks barreling down the narrow lanes. Maybe he'd found his way to another part of the forest populated with hunters that mistook him for a deer. Or maybe he found a coyote and the thing mauled him for being too close to its baby.

As much as he wanted to unzip the tent and lunge into the dark forest—an agonizing thought bumped through his head that perhaps Slade was waiting for him just beyond the tree line—he knew he'd just get lost as well.

Every once in a while, the moaning would start again, jolting him awake in the night. A cycle formed: as soon as his eyes fluttered closed in sleep, the sound resumed.

Nothing to be done but lie awake and listen.

MARCH 10, 2019

9:12 A.M.

The fire snapped at the bitter morning air. The remnants of the previous night's dinner littered the pit: the pinched aluminum corpses of the last of the tepid beer, the crumpled foil pouches of ready meals. Dylan had hardly slept—dreaming of shadows outside her tent, silhouettes with hands holding knives, pacing back and forth. Exhaustion hung heavy against her shoulders, her skin still pimpled by the fear that the figures weren't dreams at all—that she had been as wide awake as she felt.

But once she got a glimpse of the wall, she forgot the night's imagined intruders, the shadow people that lined the interim space between sleep and wakefulness. She planned her movements by miming in the air at the base of the rock. She gulped her coffee and started warmup stretches, bouldering and traversing across the bottom five feet of granite. Her skin electrified as she climbed, little jolts of static jostling through her fingertips like she was touching ungrounded metal and not solid rock. The sun warmed her neck, its bright fingers working out the soreness of the prior day, easing her tendons, stretching them like soft taffy.

Luke uncoiled the rope underneath the troublesome route,

mute and sullen. He threw the cams and quickdraws into a pile, the metal clanging like an out-of-tune orchestra. In the pile, Dylan spied a carabiner whose clip had come undone.

"Hey, babe, can you be a bit more careful?" she said. "This gear isn't exactly brand-new. And we don't have any extras if things break."

Luke grunted.

"What's wrong?" Dylan asked, knowing Luke would balloon with rage until he exploded if she did not coax the hot air out of him.

"Nothing," he replied. He kicked at some gravel.

"Is it something to do with Slade?" Dylan sighed. Of course—how could she have forgotten? A pang of guilt twinged through her body as she said the dog's name. She was the reason he'd escaped and she was the reason they had stopped looking for him. But what were they supposed to do? Cancel the trip and form a search party? Let themselves get lost in the woods? Besides, it wasn't her trip to dictate—it was Clay's.

"I thought I heard him last night," Luke said, biting his lip.

"I didn't hear anything last night." She didn't mention what she had dreamed. It struck her only now that the entire scene had been utterly soundless.

"Something was out there," he replied. "It sounded like something in pain, like it was hungry or crying, or cold."

"I doubt that was Slade," she said, trying to reassure herself as much as Luke. "Maybe it was just a bad dream. I had one too."

"I'm so mad at myself for letting it happen."

"It's not your fault," Dylan said, hoping he wouldn't counter with the truth—that it was *her* fault. She needed a clear mind to climb, and she needed him to belay, to be alert to her movements on the wall and not craning his head trying to hear imaginary howls. So she sat with him, letting him drain snot and tears into her collar until he was a dried husk, all the while the wall beckoning, pulling taut the hairs on her skin.

———————

Dylan fiddled with her harness, pulling the straps to tighten around her legs.

"Ready to get started?" Clay asked. He'd left her and Luke alone before, huddled together at the base of the rock next to their mound of tangled equipment, though he made his annoyance no secret by pacing a short distance behind them, grumbling to himself.

"Yeah, sorry," Dylan replied. "Luke's having a hard time with Slade gone."

"Have you thought of any route names?"

"Good question," she said. She pointed at the far end of the wall, the first route she climbed, the one with no other name than *Rte. 1* in Sylvia's copious notes. "Maybe 'A Later One' for that. 'Pure Kentucky Adrenaline' for this one I'm trying to conquer." She coated her hands in chalk, the calluses from the prior day's climbs stinging already. She rubbed excess chalk from her fingers onto her ankle, the imprint like a skeleton hand. "Are you all set up?"

"Been ready for an hour," Clay said.

The electricity sizzled into Dylan, shivering her bones. She jumped, shook out her hands to release the charge. With a grimace still plastered to his mouth, Luke snapped pictures of her on the wall, bouldering just above the ground, cropping to make it look like she was climbing much higher. She selected the three best photos to post—a task she completed with dull eyes and quick swipes. Her face smiled back at her, all teeth.

Pure Kentucky Adrenaline on these walls #Climbing #FirstAscent

Once Dylan touched the wall, she was off. No kinks this time. It was as if she had snuck out at night to memorize the movements. She reached the deserted clip in just a couple of minutes, held up by all her safety measures, taking mere seconds to shove each metal cam into the crevices and clip the rope.

Dylan climbed for hours in this way, fluid and easy, giddy. The rock anticipated her needs—a gap for her hands, right where she wanted to place it. None of the flailing fingers searching for a grip from yesterday. None of the *pray to whatever deity might be out there* from previous attempts while trusting her rubber-tipped shoes to hold fast to the tiniest prick of granite.

Dylan's arms should have been sore. One thirty-minute rest break between routes and a stomach full of coffee and sticky oats should certainly *not* have sufficed as a muscle-smoothing balm. But the muscles of her forearms weren't tight. They hadn't woven into the hard knots that could only be undone by time or some noxious-smelling ointment or rough fingers. They remained as light and primed and ready as they were at the start of the day, after she had gotten over the funk of the previous night.

Halfway up a new route, the rock provided a deep pocket, a welcome reprieve for her fingers from all its tiny, crimpy holds. She shook her free hand behind her, an automatic movement, the tendons loose already. She could hang out in this spot all day. The rubber of her shoes clung to the wall as if by glue. She probably could have leaned against the wall, hands free, and napped.

She placed another cam while she remained steady. The metal fit into the wall with ease, and she clipped the rope through the carabiner.

The rest of the route above her looked much harder. Lots of tiny grips, cracks half the size of her fingertips.

"Climbing!" she called down to Luke.

The rope went limp at her waist and she pushed upward, her hands curling again around tiny pieces of granite. She set her foot into the deep pocket, the one good hold, and hoisted upward again.

Her hand fell into another big pocket.

The same pocket.

The clip she'd last put in place sat right in front of her, though she had just now climbed above it. The rope even looped through the clip and back to her harness. She stared at it for what felt like an eternity. How could she be back down here? She'd felt her foot move into the pocket where her hand now gripped, sweat smearing onto the rock.

She shook it off and pushed upward once more. But the loop continued again—and again. Sweat poured through her shirt from her scalp, dripping into her eyes. She repeated the same three movements, always circling back to the same damned clip and pocket. She climbed the loop until her muscles grew taut and sore, until the sweat on her palms worked its way to her fingertips, and she slipped off the wall. Luke caught her, locking the rope in place with the belay device, stopping her fall just a few feet below the clip.

"You'll get that one easily," Luke said once she was on the ground. "Must have been a fluke—it seemed like you had it."

"I kept climbing in circles."

"What do you mean?"

"I would go up and somehow keep ending up under the clip I'd just placed. It was so weird—you didn't see anything?"

"No, nothing like that," he replied, his face scrunched in confusion. "I mean, I guess it looked like you were sitting in that one spot for longer than usual, but I thought you just needed a break."

"I really felt like I was just climbing and climbing and climbing—but not going anywhere."

"Sylvia and Clay were recording. Maybe you could watch the video and see what happened."

The camera felt heavy in Dylan's hands. In the tiny screen, she watched herself scramble up the wall like a spider. Luke was right—she hesitated by the clip before she fell, but that was all. Just hesitation.

***

They took a quick break for lunch, just enough time to stuff granola and Clif bars into their mouths, to quell their stomachs' pestering. Dylan gulped water, bumping her knee like a metronome. Her body itched to get back onto the rock. She checked her phone to see how her post was faring—already more than two hundred likes and a handful of comments. She scrolled through the notifications tab and thought she spied a comment from Petzl. But when she clicked to view it, she received an error message, the page unable to load due to low signal.

Clay's coffee breath shuddered over her shoulder. "Got a lot of hits?" he asked.

"Yeah," she said, clicking around the screen. She clamped her jaw tight around her tongue. "I suddenly lost connection, though."

"We *are* out in the woods," Clay said, laughing.

"Yeah, I'm aware," she quipped. "But I've had great signal so far and I haven't moved at all. It just suddenly disappeared."

"What are you going to do?" Clay shrugged his shoulders and moved behind Sylvia to peek at her scrawled notes.

"Fair enough," Dylan said, standing and stretching. The wall loomed, treacherous yet golden. "Honestly, it might be a welcome reprieve from the grind of it. I feel like I can't ever take a break."

"Yeah, no signal will force you to take one," Clay said. "Are you ready to keep going?"

Luke ground his knuckles into the buttons of his spine lining his neck. "You don't need a longer rest?"

"Nope," she said, ignoring the knot forming in her chest, the sudden, fleeting feeling of doom. The sun hung at the top of the wall, almost as if it had settled into the rock, like a fiery prize she could reach up and grab. It blinded her.

"Give me a minute longer," Luke said. "My neck is still sore just from looking up at you."

Dylan's body thrummed, a cauldron of anxiety and eagerness. Every one of the little hairs lining her arms raised, all beckoning her back to the rock.

———

She was nearly at the top when it happened.

Perhaps it happened because the sun shot directly onto her face as she searched for a handhold, leaving ghostly imprints across her vision when she tried to find that good beak she'd grabbed previously, somewhere to place her foot. Perhaps the sudden cold breeze froze her buttery muscles or her earned exhaustion was finally setting in. Perhaps the little flashback to the previous night, that jolt of fear at those stark legs hovering outside of her tent in her dream, pricked right through her amygdala, the split second of enveloping dread making the ground seem much farther away than it ever had before.

She managed to fit the cam into a jagged crevice. But when Luke fed the slack through the belay device, when she reached below her to try to grab the rope to clip it in, her foot slipped. Her scream rang out across the valley, sharp and piercing. Dylan's left arm was locked in a harsh *L*, the muscles of her forearm taut and distinct beneath the skin like the coil of rope at Luke's feet. Her fingers gripped the wall with just a centimeter of skin.

She knew it would happen before it did. She yelled a harsh *Fuck* as her left foot unhooked from the wall, popped away like a firecracker had exploded beneath it. She dug her fingertips in deeper, the sharp granite ripping through skin, a last-ditch effort to stay on the wall. With two opposing limbs already free, the other two couldn't hang on, couldn't right the balance, and they, too, popped away from the wall.

The fall felt long. Her body floated down, weightless, the sun searing her retinas. But she didn't reach the ground, didn't leave a cloud of dirt to settle onto a body mangled with new elbows and knees. It ended with a sharp jerk at her waist, the harness catching her—but only for a moment. The last clip Dylan had placed in the wall, the thing that was supposed to be her safety, ripped out of the rock and took a chunk with it. It triggered a chain reaction, each clip she'd set snug into the wall also pulled loose by her sudden dropping weight, all in a fraction of a second before she came to a stop—thirty feet down.

One clip did hold, and what she collided with wasn't the ground, but Luke's head, which had been hoisted skyward as their human pulley righted itself. Her feet kicked his poor unhelmeted head, a jerk reflex. Luke pulled clips out of the wall, too, on his way up, and ricocheted back to smash the other side of his skull into the wall. Stuck between a foot and a hard place, both rattling his brain.

"Are you okay?" Dylan yelled.

Luke spun on the other end of the rope. His fingers fumbled near his crotch, trying to work the belay. They moved like an injured spider crawling over unfamiliar terrain. It seemed to take every ounce of effort for him to work the muscles in his neck, to pull his head upright. If the belay didn't have a locking mechanism to clamp onto the rope, they'd both be splayed on the ground right now.

Fuck, Dylan thought. *He must really be injured if he can't work his fingers.*

"Luke, talk to me," she said. "Please!"

He opened his mouth, but instead of words, instead of a pleasant *Yes, I am fine, just a little bump on the head, let me lower us now*, a tongue lacerated by his own teeth drooled out blood. He groaned.

"Fuck," she whispered. Below them, Clay and Sylvia stood, too short to reach them. Sylvia touched the dangling length of rope with trembling trepidation, as if her touch would be the thing to make everything go wrong. As if that bit of rope tracing loops in the dirt was the load-bearing wall of this accident.

Above them, the last clip still in the wall, a tiny inch-long hunk of metal, sat pinned against the rock.

Was it shaking?

Dylan followed the path of the rope, casting her eyes above the clip, the thing she had thought was holding their weight. The rope snaked up to a jagged point jutting from the wall—how had she missed that giant hold?—where it had caught. It looped around the sharp point of granite and led back down to her harness. But there, at the peak of the loop—did she spy fraying? Was she imagining those little fibers poking out of the rope?

"Shit," she said.

Of course Dylan's first major fall would be on day two of what was supposed to be her big breakout expedition. They hung only ten feet from the ground, but she'd seen some nasty injuries from shorter heights. One of her first climbing buddies, the one who'd taken her on her first trip to Red River Gorge, had shattered her ankle rappelling down, *after* finishing all the hard work of a 5.11—she'd let the rope out too fast and slipped on a patch of loose debris at the base of the wall.

Dylan was so caught up in the terror of their inevitable drop, scanning the ground below them, waiting for the rope's split, that she did not glance farther up to the spot where the top clip had pulled free. If she had not been calling to Sylvia and Clay to gather every soft item in camp to spread across the fall zone, she might have seen that the clip had taken a chunk of rock with it, and that the fissure was marred by a sticky, deep-red substance.

As if bleeding.

Sylvia and Clay moved as directed, like little dolls below her, hauling camping pads and sleeping bags and even loose armfuls of clothing to the base of the wall. Fibers of the rope groaned, like a creaky door, and then snapped in two. Each sent a jolt through Dylan, hanging helpless. The untethered pair moved below the two climbers, spreading the stuffing around, kicking away the clips that had rained down from the wall, little metal daggers lying in wait to wedge themselves into the spaces between Dylan's vertebrae or jump up into the iris of a wide eye. Maiming her to the point of never being able to climb again, ruining not only the trip but her entire career. The last thread of the rope snapped in two at the moment that Sylvia slapped her own sleeping bag onto the ground, the edges soaking up the persistent mud.

Dylan and Luke dropped like stones. The rope slithered out of the remaining clips, thumping to the ground and across Luke's poor, battered, unhelmeted head. He whimpered. His hand found his head, rubbing a spot to the left of where the rope had slapped him. Dylan prayed he was just in shock.

She sat up, assessed. She could recall her name. She counted exactly ten fingers on her hands, three with brown-red blood crusted around the nail beds. Her head did not pound. Her ankles and wrists had not snapped beneath her, had not bent into some shape they were not designed to make. No ache blossomed between her ears. She had survived the drop with only light scrapes along her knees and elbows and blooming purple swaths on her thighs and waist where her harness had dug in. She exhaled in relief. Had they dropped six inches to the right, they would have cracked their bones on stones pushing out of the dirt. She unclasped her helmet and cursed their lack of forethought to bring a second one for Luke.

She crawled to Luke, who was still lying down, apparently unable to lift his head or any other part of his body. His knee bent at an odd angle, the bottom half of his leg pinned beneath his body.

"Oh my god, Luke," she said, voice quivering. But even as her chest tightened at the sight of him, limp like a rag doll, the magnetism of the wall still pulled at her, even now, and a little pang of sorrow stabbed inside her at her now-spoiled ambitions.

Luke whispered something, too low to hear or understand. His eyes glazed but wide, he seemed to be looking at something over her shoulder. A chill seeped into the adrenaline pulsing through Dylan's veins. Like an ice cube sliding down her spine. Clay stood at Luke's head and Sylvia was running to her tent to gather her first aid kit—there could be no one behind her. Still, Dylan turned and followed the line of his sight, just to be sure.

No monsters.

Only trees.

They carted Luke over to the firepit, Dylan and Clay each scooping a shoulder underneath one of his armpits, moving slowly. They poured him into a canvas seat like a scarecrow stuffed with rocks, limp and heavy, a picture of how Dylan's insides felt. They placed his swollen ankle into the dregs of the cooler, empty aluminum husks bobbing around in the water.

"Luke, how are you feeling?" Dylan asked. "Can you say something?"

"Dizzy. My head hurts and my vision is blurry," he said, the words running together.

"Is he going to be okay?" Dylan asked Sylvia. She twisted her hands in her lap, picking at the dried blood lining her cuticles. Luke's head lolled on his shoulders, his gaze cloudy.

"He definitely took the brunt of the fall," Sylvia said. She wrapped his wrist with a stretchy beige band, trapping a stiff stick inside. His already-puffy wrist disappeared beneath the brace. "I have a little bit of medical training—just an emergency first aid course. I think his wrist and ankle are fractured, if not broken—we'll need to elevate them. He definitely has a concussion, and he'll probably go in and out of lucidity. Luckily there's only small scrapes on his scalp, so hopefully it's a minor one."

Hopefully his brain isn't swelling up in there, Dylan thought, not daring to say this part aloud lest she speak it into existence.

Dylan sat in a chair across from Luke. She lifted his ankle and set it on her knee to elevate it so Sylvia could attend to it. He squealed as if her touch was fire.

"So what's the plan?" she asked. She pinched the muscles of her thigh to stop herself from bouncing it.

"We should get him to a hospital as soon as we can," Sylvia said.

If we can, Dylan thought, trying to piece together the puzzle of getting him back to the Jeep—up the steep hill, through the miles of undeveloped forest. They'd probably have to get a helicopter to cart him out, with neither his ankle nor his brain being able to support his weight for the journey. If any of their phones worked—Dylan hadn't checked whether she had a signal again—they could call for help. They had the coordinates and everything. They'd be okay, Dylan told herself, trying to believe it.

Sylvia handed two iron-colored pills and a bottle of water to Luke. "I need you to focus on staying awake," Sylvia said, in full nurse mode. "That's all. We're going to work to get you to a hospital."

"Okay," he said. "How—" He tensed in the middle of his

thought, his body straightening like a board, nearly kicking the cooler over, spilling the pond inside. Dylan placed a hesitant hand on his shoulder. His eyes—gazing off into the trees—widened.

As if he could see something she couldn't.

———

Dylan's heart beat in her chest at double its normal speed. While Sylvia played makeshift doctor, Dylan and Clay tested their cell phones, clicking on the screens and wandering around the basin of the valley hoping for a signal. Nothing. Clay's face snarled and he sighed deeply, his lips pushing quiet words under his breath. Probably thinking the same guilty thoughts that swam through Dylan's mind: *Of course an injury occurs during such an important trip. Of course. Now everything is delayed and ruined.*

While she hoisted her phone, moving to the same spot where she'd held her first livestream, Dylan craned her neck to look up the wall at her lost and ruined gear—mourning the expensive clips still stuck in the rock, too high to retrieve; the two useless, compromised halves of the rope; the winged cam destroyed, the metal mangled, along with the chunk of rock it removed. The wall pulsed into her, radiating heat as if it were a mirror redirecting the sunlight.

She suddenly wanted nothing more than to touch it, to scramble up and pluck out the cams. They'd just bought that damn rope right before this trip—brand-new. Two hundred dollars of the stipend from Petzl. And they hadn't brought a backup. Who could have foreseen a brand-new rope ripping in half? But they should have prepared for it anyway—though Dylan had never heard of a rope breaking like that, not unless it was extremely old or the core had deteriorated. Now the trip was ruined—she couldn't climb anymore.

Not that Luke could belay her at any rate, she thought, her chest tightening again, suddenly remembering her broken boyfriend—he kept fluttering out of her mind. But Sylvia or Clay could do it, couldn't they? Clay knew how to belay, and all he was doing was standing there behind a camera and watching while she climbed. Sylvia was the one taking the notes, and she could make sure the camera was recording. She didn't think Clay would want to halt the research, and—

Once Luke was taken care of.

How did she keep forgetting about him?

Her brain fogged, her train of thought wearing a headlight that only pointed down one track. It was like the rock was the only thing that could push up above the fog in her head.

She glanced over at Luke. His bandaged arm hung against his chest inside a makeshift sling—a pair of Dylan's leggings tied into a loop—and his leg was similarly wrapped and propped up on a chair. His head sat upright on his neck. He'd be fine. She'd seen worse injuries at Red River Gorge—plenty of snapped bones, a fractured skull, blood oozing from an ear—and every single one of those people had recovered. And if they already had to leave to go to a hospital, it couldn't be that much farther to backtrack to Lexington to buy a new rope.

After Luke got settled at the hospital. Of course.

She clicked the screen open once more on her phone. And it remained consistent—zero bars. She clicked the emergency call option anyway. Three dots bounced in the center of her screen, sending out an invisible SOS. But the call dropped before it connected. This same scenario repeated numerous times, on all of the other phones.

As a last-ditch attempt, something futile to try, Clay even pushed the SOS button on the side of the GPS device. But the damned thing must have been broken—pushing the button did precisely nothing at all.

"Cheap piece of shit," Clay said, smacking it with his palm.

Dylan's chest tightened. They had no choice but to try to heave Luke up the hill and get back to the car. There would be no helicopter rescue.

Next to her, the rock throbbed: *climb, climb, climb*. Like a heartbeat, it thumped into her ears. When she put her hand against it, a pulse tapped against her skin, not from her body but from within the rock. Her fingers wrapped over a beak as if trying to contain this beating, but as they did, a shadow fell across her hand, forming a curious optical illusion, as if each digit had melted into the rock, becoming gray, speckled granite. Like stalagmites, little fangs of granite pushed up out of the spots where her fingers should be.

She marveled at her wrist ending in stone.

"Hey," Sylvia called. "We can't get any signal, so we need to get back to the car to get Luke to the hospital."

It was not until Sylvia spoke that the trance broke, that the rock over her hand dissolved. That she was free to let go.

MARCH 10, 2019

4:47 P.M.

Sylvia searched the edges of the woods for sticks to tape into a crutch, careful to avoid the thick patches of poison ivy. She'd instructed Clay to stuff excess food back into the bear-proof canister. He'd needed something to do—in the wake of the accident, he'd just paced back and forth, grumbling to himself about his spoiled dissertation. And the last thing they needed was animals running wild, destroying their shit all for a taste of peanut butter. He smashed the food back into the canister, bread turning into gummy balls, Clif bars transforming into hourglasses.

At this rate, they wouldn't make it back to camp until tomorrow morning at the earliest, and Sylvia knew that a part of Clay—a part she didn't recognize—was itching to drop Luke off at the doorway of the nearest ER and speed back to the research site as soon as a nurse exited with a wheelchair to get Luke. Dragged from some deep part of her consciousness, Sylvia could imagine his callous words, something he might say while they drove off, only once out of range of Luke's ears—"What are we going to do? The doctors will take care of him." And she knew he'd expect her to join him.

That wasn't the Clay she'd known all these years, but it was the Clay who'd been showing his face here in the valley, stomping around in the mud, griping about his dissertation being ruined.

Clay joined Sylvia by the trees, her arms filled with long, spindly branches. She dropped them when she spotted a better choice, thick and hefty.

"What are the chances we can actually get him up that hill?" Clay asked, kicking a crushed aluminum can into the brush. He looked back at the rock, at his camera still mounted on the tripod.

"I don't know," Sylvia said. "But we have to try."

"What if we can't?"

"Let's cross that bridge when we get there. Help me carry this."

Clay and Sylvia carried the branch back toward camp, and then he and Dylan worked to fashion a crutch that might support Luke's weight, assuming he could manage to balance his body up the steep hill. While Clay and Dylan sliced at it with camp knives and taped pieces back together, Sylvia rewrapped Luke's ankle, trying to contain the ballooning skin that now barely resembled a foot.

"I'm so sorry, guys," Luke said. "I should have made sure to pack our other helmet. I should have been paying more—" Then his mouth moved as though he were still speaking, but no sound came out. The hand strapped to his chest trembled. The twitches transmitted to Sylvia, crawling up her spine like a nest of spiders.

Luke swayed in his seat, his oversized and glassy eyes pointed at the tree line. She waved her hand in front of his face, slicing through his line of sight. Nothing—not even a blink. Was he getting worse? They might not even make it to the hospital until morning.

"Luke, are you okay? Still with us?"

He swallowed and blinked. "Yes," he said.

But Luke wasn't lucid or stable enough to stay upright, even with the crutch. He pitched forward almost immediately, teetering on his uninjured ankle before Clay helped him back into the seat.

They would have to carry him. Sylvia looked up the steep hillside, rubbing her thumb against the fingers of her opposite hand. She wasn't sure they'd be able to. Was it even possible?

Dylan draped Luke's free arm around her shoulders and Clay hooked his hands under Luke's damp armpits. Luke's good foot shifted, the ankle rolling, and for a moment Sylvia's heart stopped, thinking it, too, would snap, that they'd be left at the bottom of this treacherous hill trying to make some sort of stretcher out of sleeping bags and twigs. But the ankle righted itself and found solid ground.

———————

The hill loomed mountainous ahead of Sylvia. The trees stretched to the sky, already darkening, the bright blue fading into orange, the warm spring air shifting to cold spring night. While Clay and Dylan readied themselves for the hike, smothering the fire, Sylvia flipped through her notebooks. She heaved a loaded breath when she uncovered it—the coordinates of the Jeep. Clay had nearly trekked off ahead of her with the GPS tracker before she could jot them down. Now, she input them into the device and threw the notebook back in her tent, zipping it up for good measure.

"I guess we're ready," she said, throwing a backpack of necessities over her shoulders.

Sylvia carried the homemade crutch they'd built from duct tape and sticks behind the five-legged racers. She didn't speak it aloud, didn't want Dylan's heart to pound with anxiety, but Luke was severely injured—she was no nurse, but she knew enough to know that going in and out of lucidity midsentence was bad news. She gritted her teeth to keep quiet. Dylan and Clay took most of Luke's weight, nearly dragging him despite his one working foot, grunting with the effort. After just four slow, heaving steps, not even out of the campsite, they had to stop to engineer a backward sling for Luke's purpling leg, the bruise already inking up above the bandages.

Sylvia scanned the campsite for a way to build the brace, creating a complex puzzle out of each item around the campsite until she spotted the destroyed rope, coiled at the base of the cliff. Dylan winced as Sylvia sliced through a length of it, as if mourning its loss.

"It's got no other use to us now," Sylvia said.

Clay stabilized Luke as Sylvia and Dylan draped the loop over his shoulder and hooked the opposing, offending foot into the other end, behind him. Wadded T-shirts created a layer of cushion against his shoulder and ankle to absorb the harsh tension. His face remained vacant, a blank slate contrasting the tense, wrinkled expressions on the rest of the group. Could he really not feel anything in that leg, Sylvia wondered? Perhaps he could not yet distinguish pain—perhaps the synapses and nerves and signals had become jumbled and rerouted when he hit his head, because he had not made any yelps or winces, had not even gritted his teeth as his swollen foot traced a heavy line through the mud. He'd only cocked his head like a confused puppy.

They started up the hill with slow, deliberate steps, the steep incline rising like Everest. Sylvia followed the five-legged monstrosity her friends had become. She watched them anxiously. Each laborious placement of their feet determined whether they would topple. The hillside was damp and slick, and Dylan and Clay stomped into this muck, used its wetness in their favor by agitating it enough to become sticky.

Only halfway up the perilous hill, the sky had already lost its blue. Sylvia struggled to see between the tree trunks, the budding canopy obscuring any remaining sunlight. Even in the dusk, Sylvia spied the trembling of Dylan's unsteady, exhausted legs. Dylan shoved her boot into the next spot of mud ahead, grounding her already-caked sole before shifting her and Luke's weight. With nowhere to rest and no way to unload Luke's weight without his bound-up body simply skidding back down into the valley like he was on a Slip 'N Slide, they hiked on.

The little dot on the GPS tracker in Sylvia's hand seemed stationary. *Muddy ascent up valley hill—why so wet? No record of recent rain*, she thought, tucking away the thought to write in her notebook later.

After another few yards, the stomping trick no longer worked for Dylan—her boots had accumulated too much soil to gain any sticky traction. Like walking on well-oiled glass, her feet skated backward toward Sylvia.

"Shit!" Dylan yelled.

One foot popped upward and her knee crashed down into the muck. Sylvia, her own lungs screaming with sharp needles even without Luke's weight on her shoulders, waited for the rest of the bodies to topple along with Dylan, for a tangle of connected limbs to slam into her on their way down, for all four to find themselves back at the bottom of the hill, each with matching bruises and swollen ankles and wrists and brains.

What she did not expect was for Luke's working foot to stamp down into the dirt, holding his weight.

"Are you okay?" Luke asked Dylan. He shifted his weight, one incorrectly tensed muscle away from Dylan's fate. "Last thing we need is a broken kneecap to go with my leg."

"Yeah," she panted. "Let's just get up this damn hill."

Dylan smacked her boots against a trunk one at a time, knocking off the mud. When she took Luke's hand to drape his arm over her neck, he squeezed her fingers. Tight. Behind them, Sylvia could see his knuckles go white.

Luke leaned as far forward as his marionette straps and strings would allow. Then he vomited, chunks of half-digested Clif bar splattering on the toes of Dylan's boot. Clay turned his head away. The wet barf-slick slithered down the steep hill toward Sylvia.

"S-sorry," he stammered, vomit-spittle dripping from the corner of his mouth. "Sudden wave of nausea."

"It's okay," Dylan replied.

The starchy, sharp scent of bile slammed the back of Sylvia's throat, and she swallowed spit to stop an uprising of her own stomach's contents. She stepped around the trail of barf.

Luke cleared his throat and spat. On Dylan's shoulder, his fingers twitched like spider's legs, as if he were trying to reach for something, for his pounding head or maybe to wipe the dregs of vomit from his mouth, but couldn't connect the correct sequence of synapses.

Sylvia checked her watch and took a mental note of the time, wishing she had some way to record, some way to be useful. 6:32. *Luke lucid but still exhibiting concussive symptoms—vomiting, grabbing at air, unable to correctly position fingers.*

"Are you okay now?" Dylan asked. "Do you feel any pain?"

"Yes," Luke said. "My head."

"We need to get you to a hospital. Are you good to keep going?"

"I'll try."

The trio resumed their laborious, lurching steps. Luke's ebbing lucidity didn't help much—he kept setting his foot down on top of Dylan's, or directly into various roots, brambles, and other obstacles.

Luke having trouble coordinating, Sylvia jotted in her mental notebook.

By the time they finally made it to the top of the hill, heaving and sweating, full darkness enveloped the sky.

———————

Now, Sylvia led the pack, GPS tracker in one hand and flashlight in the other, its light like a beacon through fog. Darkness seeped between the tree trunks around them. It wrapped around Sylvia's chest and squeezed. The beam of her flashlight scanned the forest floor, revealing more patches of poison ivy, thick hemlock, and rotting leaves from the previous fall. She even thought she saw a patch of stinking carrion plants, with their five fuzzy leaves like starfish, surrounded by buzzing flies, though that should be impossible. Carrion plants aren't native to the Western hemisphere, let alone Kentucky. How did they get here? She wanted to stop and document—there was no way she'd find this spot again—but Luke came first.

An insane thought wormed into her brain: that there was a repeating pattern to the vegetation, some sort of tessellation in the plant matter. But she dismissed the idea. She must be imagining things.

The group progressed slowly, covering so little ground that Sylvia often stopped to wait for the other three to catch up to her, shining the flashlight back to light their path. In the shadows, their bodies blended together, their limbs lurching and flailing like a monstrous centipede. Each time Sylvia turned around to watch, the hairs on the nape of her neck raised in alarm and she resisted each urge, each invisible hand pulling at her sleeve, each goosebump sprouting up on her arms, telling her to turn tail and run.

It was just a trick of the light, she told herself.

Still, she couldn't suppress a shiver.

They advanced in this way, slinking, for an hour. She took more notes in her mind—7:45, *making slow progress. Many rest breaks. Hoping we're almost to the car, can't tell on GPS. Starting to feel heavy sensation in my chest—unsure if stress, anxiety, or strain. Dylan and Clay seem ready to collapse.*

At least they'd crested the hill. They should reach the Jeep soon. The moon hung in the sky now, just a slice, and stars twinkled between the branches overhead.

"I need to take another break," Dylan said between strained breaths.

They stopped. Sylvia slid the backpack from her shoulders and set it at the base of a tree. Clay and Dylan sat Luke on top of the pack before swiveling their heads and pinching their necks, trying to work out the knots.

"How much farther?" Dylan asked. She sank down, collapsing into the dirt.

"I'm not sure," Sylvia said. "We've been following the

guideline on the GPS, but I don't know how to tell how much farther we've got to go."

"What do you mean?" Clay asked, his voice rising. "It should say right on the bottom of the screen."

"I just see the map and a green line," Sylvia replied, handing over the device. "Maybe a setting got turned off?"

Clay clicked buttons on the device. His brow furrowed. He smacked it against his palm, and the screen flickered.

"What the fuck?" he whispered. He stood and flicked his flashlight on, swinging the beam of light around in quick passes. Then the light settled. It pointed downward.

It illuminated something bright. Something orange.

Their tents.

They were back at the top of the hill. "What the fuck," he repeated.

"What? How is that possible?" Dylan said. She leaned her head back, thumping her skull against a tree trunk. Tears escaped from her closed eyelids.

"I'm so sorry, guys," Sylvia said after a hefty silence descended, after she could no longer stand its throbbing against her eardrums. "I don't know what I did wrong." How had she messed up so badly? She'd followed the line just as Clay had showed her. They hadn't taken any turns and had definitely been moving forward. How had they ended up back where they started? It didn't make sense.

"We have to keep going, right?" Dylan asked.

"I don't know," Clay said. "I don't know what's fucking going on."

"We need to get Luke to a hospital," Dylan said. "Can we still get to the car? I still don't have any cell signal."

"It's getting darker," Clay said. He pressed the SOS button, holding it down, still to no effect. He pressed more buttons until the screen darkened. After a few seconds, it lit up again. "I don't want to get lost, but I really don't want to try to go back down that fucking hill," he said. "Sylvia, you help with Luke. I'll work the GPS."

"Yeah," she said, handing over the emergency pack. "Lead the way."

———————

This time, Sylvia and Dylan supported Luke while Clay forged through the brush and monitored the GPS, the group inching along. Clay kept plodding too far ahead and having to stop, waiting for the five-legged twilight creature to catch up. For an hour they continued this way, Sylvia's shoulder aching with sharp daggers, her shallow breath scraping the inside of her throat. Even her teeth radiated with pain, the cold night air raking over them with each inhale.

Clay followed the little dot as if he had poured all his faith into it. It seemed to Sylvia that he was not even blinking.

The machine was by no means infallible, true, but the way they'd been turned around still didn't make sense. It was a puzzle Sylvia couldn't piece together.

"What could be interfering with it that made us go in a circle?" she asked, panting with exertion. "Did you remember to replace the batteries?"

"Yes, I swapped them when we got to camp," Clay replied, a dark silhouette ahead of them. "Brand-new out of the package."

"Could I have misread the device? How did we backtrack?" They hadn't done anything but move forward after they crested the hill. They hadn't made a single pivot to the left or right, let alone backward, besides sidestepping trees or overgrown brambles that would have snagged Luke's bobbing bashed foot.

"I don't fucking know," Clay growled. "Let's just fucking get to the car."

Something, or *someone*, had messed up and Sylvia knew his grumbling and muttering meant he had settled on her. It couldn't be the machine, he was probably thinking, his brain scrambled by frustration and exhaustion. It had to be user error.

"I feel like we've been hiking forever," Dylan said. "How much longer until we're at the car?"

"I don't know," Clay said. "The GPS still isn't showing the fucking mileage. There must be a software update I didn't catch before we left or something. Fuck."

"Does the dot show that we're closer?" Sylvia asked, a heaving breath splitting the question in two. A stitch carved into her rib cage, the needle threading into her lung.

Clay sighed and examined the tiny screen. He clicked around. The dot sat in the center, a little bowel obstruction on the intestine line snaking across the green background.

"I can't really tell," Clay said. "Fuck. We might be halfway or have a whole fucking while to go."

A heaviness returned to the spot between Sylvia's lungs, like a stone had replaced her heart.

8:25 p.m., still trying to reach the car. No way to know how much ground we've covered.

"I think Luke's getting tired," Dylan said. "He's not responding as much anymore, and he's dragging his foot again."

"Fuck!" Clay screamed, coming to an abrupt stop. The harsh sound scrambled Sylvia's ears. "What do you think we should do?" He addressed the group. "Keep moving forward to the car or turn around and go back to camp for the night? It's going to be at least another hour of hiking either way."

"I don't think we're going to make it to the car tonight," Sylvia said, the words tumbling out before she could stop them. "The campsite is probably closer. Maybe we should turn back and send someone out alone in the morning."

"So this was a huge waste of time, then," Dylan said, her voice thick with tears. She pressed her palms against her eyes.

8:27 p.m., too dark and Luke too tired to continue. Must return to valley.

When they gathered enough strength to pivot, shuffling Luke awkwardly between them, Clay pointed his flashlight back in the direction they had come from.

The halo of light bounced off the tree trunks before revealing the trick. They would not have to hike another hour. They were, once again, at the top of the bowl, their tents sitting like blisters in the dark valley below.

MARCH 11, 2019
10:43 A.M.

Not even halfway through March, and Clay was sweating through his layers. He'd already tied his puffy jacket around his waist, but salty perspiration still leaked through his pores, pooling beneath his arms. A pond formed in the groove of his back, trapped against the daypack with its bladder full of water that he sucked out through a cord looped over his shoulder. When he passed beneath gaps in the tree canopy, in the spaces where the sun poked through its fingers, his whole body swayed, little blotches of darkness jittering in his vision. The blip on the GPS moved, but not steadily. He'd been hiking for a couple hours, but the machine said he'd only moved about half a mile.

At least he was moving. He was certain he'd reach the Jeep, hoping it would be just a little while longer now that he wasn't carting Luke. They should have sent someone out alone last night, should have done whatever they could to speed this process along and get Luke to a hospital so they could get back to the research. And he shouldn't have let Sylvia navigate, although how could he have predicted that she would fuck up so monumentally?

He pressed on. The itchy feeling of déjà vu crept up his arms when he stepped through a briar patch, twisted and gnarled like sleeping snakes, in the exact same configuration as one he'd passed ten minutes before, the same pokey vines forming a figure eight. A section of bark level with his face, the wood beneath white as his own skin, had been carved from three trees along the path so far—the mark so distinctive that he'd puzzled over the first instance, grazing the smooth surface with his fingertips, wondering how the bark had fallen away from the maple. By the second instance, he'd started a tally and snapped a photo. Perhaps it was some type of fungal infection—Sylvia would have known. He'd have to ask her about it once everything was settled. When he noticed the third mark, he clicked open his phone and checked the photo, sure that he had somehow circled back, his pulse gaining speed and the sweat no longer from the day's heat. The pattern matched the photo exactly, down to the mossy lichen around the border and the neighboring trees.

But, according to the GPS, it could not have been the same tree. He had progressed farther into the woods, closer to the road—if only by a few hundred feet. As he continued, even the canopy leaves seemed to replicate themselves, folding over one another in the same formations. The same vines of what he hoped was not poison ivy snaked up the tree trunks. The same snagging, thorny root stuck up where he placed his foot, his toe catching inside the perfect loop twice before he picked up on the pattern.

Pattern? he thought. *How can there be a fucking pattern in the woods?*

He kept his focus on the ground, watching for the loop, eyes flicking back periodically to the screen of the GPS. If he looked up through the branches, if he tried to study the terrain, he dizzied and stumbled, his head throbbing. Somehow, the trees looked like a bad Photoshop job, like someone had cut an image and pasted it several more times to create a full picture.

His vision swayed again. His foot found the repeated root, and he tipped forward onto the ground. Catching himself on his wrists, he unhooked his toe and rolled onto his ass, leaning against the nearest trunk with his eyes closed. He slammed his fist against the dirt. If he opened them and saw the fourth iteration of that barkless dot, he might scream.

When he finally cracked his eyes open, afraid of what he might see, an unexpected shiny glint winked back at him. A little, blinding spark of sunlight reflected from something buried in the loam just beyond his reach, leaving pockmarks in his vision. Surely it was some man-made thing; nature was matte. Some piece of trash, probably. Maybe a rusting can of food. Maybe a map in a bottle that would lead them the fuck out of there.

The glint pulsated as if it were sending out a laser signal—not unlike the box strapped to the bottom of the plane that had tricked him into coming here in the first place. Clay leaned forward and dusted earth away from the thing, gentle as an archaeologist uncovering bone. A green glass bottle, corked. If it ever bore a label, the paper and glue had long ago been destroyed by mud, by snow, by an overflowing creek. Clay pulled it from its bed of earth. The glass shone in his fingers, a clear liquid inside sloshing.

The few minutes of rest had transformed Clay's sweat into icy rivers. Then they dried, sticky and stiff like cold paste coating his sore muscles. Goosebumps sprouted on his skin. His skeleton rattled. Even the puffy jacket pulled back over his torso did not stop his shivering. He nibbled at a Clif bar, the spongy texture somehow bitter and rancid, then threw it down in disgust.

Fuck this. Curious, he uncorked the bottle and took a sniff, recoiled from the harsh fumes. The bottle must be moonshine. The woods of Kentucky had once crawled with moonshiners.

He should be watching Dylan scramble up the wall with Sylvia scribbling notes right now, not shivering, alone, in this dungeon of trees, struggling for hours just to get back to the car.

Fuck it. He brought the bottle to his lips.

He swished the harsh liquor around his palate and swallowed.

The vine that had tripped him curled near his toe like the head of a snake. And then it twitched like one. He shuffled his feet closer to his body, blinked hard, and then the vine solidified into an ordinary bit of foliage. He tapped it with his toe.

Great. Now he was hallucinating.

Wrapping his arms around himself, he tried to hold his shivering bones in place. It was just exhaustion. It had to be. He'd gotten no real sleep the past couple of nights, between the nightmares and hiking up a steep hill while hauling Luke's body. Not to mention stress. No wonder he was seeing shit. That's all it was.

The beginnings of a migraine bloomed at the back of his head. Eating the rest of the Clif bar would help, he decided, biting off another rancid piece. Maybe another swig of the liquor would calm his nerves.

The wet sounds of his own chewing and the sloshing of the liquor against his teeth filled his skull, drowning out the stagnant silence, until his jaw ached.

Suddenly, his own sounds were replaced by the crunch of something flat and smooth against the forest floor. A horse whinnied, the sound so shrill and foreign that Clay's muscles jumped away from his bones.

More noise accompanied: shrieking infants, plodding feet, the creaking of cargo. Then, above the din rose a hymn, the voices cacophonous:

> *Earth, from afar, hath learned thy fame,*
> *And worms have learned to lisp thy name;*
> *But, oh, the glories of thy mind*
> *Leave all our soaring thoughts behind.*

A group of people passed by on a dirt trail twenty feet away: Women in old-fashioned cotton skirts, the hems stained with dirt, bonnets with tight knots beneath their chins. Swaddled babies bounced between what looked like wooden pegs—chair legs?—jutting from huge packs strapped to the sides of the horses. The babes screeched with each bump. Stick-thin boys and men followed behind the horses on foot, some barefoot, their feet callused and bruised, sidestepping horse shit.

Even had Clay's jaw not slackened, any call he might have made to bring attention to himself would not have been heard over the swell of their voices. The synapses of his brain fired all at once, sending signals throughout his entire body like an alarm piercing sleep.

"What the fuck?" he whispered. Was he hallucinating an entire group of people now? He squeezed his eyes shut, rubbed them until white spots flashed. But the vision remained when he opened them.

The hymn continued, bright and happy and loud:

> *Might I enjoy the meanest place*
> *Within thy house, O God of grace,*

Not tents of ease, nor thrones of pow'r
Should tempt my feet to leave thy door.

Clay's arms pimpled with goosebumps. He crept closer to the path on hands and knees, ignoring the thorns that stabbed into his palms, the treacherous tendrils of poison ivy that swiped oils into the creases of his skin. The bottle burned against his side, tucked into his waistband.

One man sang louder than the rest, with more gusto. His trousers were immaculate, unmarred by the slop everyone else had stepped through. His shoes bore gleaming buckles. Where the rest of the party's clothing was worn ragged, with ripped hems and fraying seams, elbows and knees rubbed thin, this man seemed to have stepped out of a tailoring shop. He held a tattered, leather-bound bible aloft, imploring the group to sing louder.

"Sing, for the glory of God," he yelled. "We are almost to the promised land!"

Clay stayed hidden in the trees, every muscle stiff, as if the group would disappear, be startled out of existence, if he moved a single joint out of place.

The company passed along the trail in a seemingly never-ending line of weary, hard-lined faces. The man with the bible stood on the side, between two trees, trying to maintain morale. He soothed a fussing baby with a single touch.

"I know your bones are weary," he said. "But nothing worth doing is easy, and your reward will come soon."

If Clay stood and took a mere five steps, he could reach out and touch this man, feel the woven texture of his clothes.

"I must be fucking going crazy," Clay whispered.

The man radiated. An aura surrounded him, like a bright cloud of pure sunlight. Even under the shade of the tree canopy, Clay's eyes watered, singed at the edges, if he stared too long. His mind still could not make sense of the procession, the migraine pounding harder. It felt like his brain was swelling inside his skull.

It must be some sort of historical reenactment, he decided, some society in Livingston that liked to dress up in old-fashioned garb for some fucking reason—to stave off boredom, for something to do other than watch TV or drive to the Walmart or tip cows, or whatever else people did to fill time out in the sticks.

But where had the trail come from? He consulted the GPS, but there was no sign of any sort of path or even a continuous gap in the trees. Fuck. The machine must really be broken. He might have smashed the fucking thing to plastic confetti if he weren't so engrossed by the passing cavalry.

At last, the final horse trotted past where Clay knelt. The man with the bible patted the broad shoulder of a man at the end of the line.

"I'm going back up ahead," he said. "Be wary of arrows and hatchets from the tree line." Then he scurried on swift feet through the weaving caravan.

Clay hazarded a movement. He released the muscles of the hand holding the rest of his Clif bar, which dropped into the brush, a relic that the first responders would miss months later. He stood, his breath suspended, slipping his backpack on, already sweating inside the jacket. The sweat sizzled into evaporation when it reached the bottle at his hip. He tried to blink as little as possible, some part of him still not convinced by his reenactment explanation—the sores and calluses on the travelers' feet and the patina of their clothing and packs were too real. Keeping his eye on a single rock set into the packed earth, he moved between the trees and stepped out onto the trail, his foot landing directly in horse shit.

Ahead, the final horse bobbed. Its packs shimmied on its back, holding an infant who yelped and whined. The woman sitting on the horse, balancing between the giant packs, leaned over and scooped the baby into her arms.

"Hey!" Clay called. The words scraped through his throat. "Hey, I need help!"

The woman cooed at the baby, lowered her bonnet-covered face to the infant.

"Can you guys help me?" Clay shouted. His lungs stung. "My friend is hurt and needs to get to a hospital. Hello?"

The caboose of the caravan continued down the trail as if Clay were not there screaming at them. Perhaps their singing was too loud. He walked toward them, cupping his hands around his lips.

"Hey! Does this trail lead to the road?"

Then the woman on the horse lifted her head from the infant, which had stopped shrieking, which had stopped squirming, which had stopped doing anything at all. It had gone limp in her hands. Clay halted as her face pivoted toward him.

A darkness, wet and sticky, spread around her mouth. Smears reached her gaunt cheekbones. One dot stood like a freckle on her forehead. Even at this distance, Clay could see a drip plop from her chin onto the unmoving child. She parted her lips, yellow and brown teeth showing beneath webs of the darkness Clay could not make himself identify as blood.

"What the fuck, what the fuck," he muttered, frozen in place.

The woman licked her lips, her tongue like a worm poking out of soil.

She stared, eyes wide, unblinking, with her slick grimace frozen to her face until Clay turned around, his stomach queasy, heading down the trail in the direction from which they had come.

Still, their hymn continued, and the woman's voice echoed down the trail:

> *God is our Sun, he makes our day;*
> *God is our shield, he guards our way,*
> *From all th' assaults of hell and sin,*
> *From foes without and foes within.*

WINTER 1779

At night the trees cracked like pistols.

The summer had brought heat and drought, and the winter brought such lasting cold that the snow piled to grown men's knees and the sap froze solid in the trees, snapping the wood and bark. They'd followed the reverend down the Wilderness Road and through the wild Kentucky frontier to this valley after he'd guaranteed their congregation the promised land, simply because they wanted to take it and they could. For a few months it did seem that way: lush green beneath their feet blistered from miles and miles of walking over rocky mud, through overgrown rivers and creeks; sturdy oak they'd razed to build cabins; wild hay to feed the animals. A little creek, runoff from the river, swam around the edge of the valley, their new homestead.

But their promised land soured.

Whispers spread as the snow piled higher: God had abandoned them.

All of the seeds they poked into the rich-looking soil, dark and glossy, had pushed their heads out and turned bitter, some drying into brittle stalks and others producing fruit that transformed from acerbic and unripe to mushy overripeness overnight, rotting on the vine. They tried plucking the hard, sour fruit and setting it on windowsills and counters to attempt to catch it at freshness, but still they woke to the buzzing of flies and gnats around slushy, stinking pulp and stained, ruined wood. So they ate the bitter fruit.

Now, the creek sat frozen in a solid block all the way to its bed, and they had to melt buckets of snow for water.

Even James and Mary's dog had soured, turned mean, baring and snapping his teeth. When he managed to catch something in them—a child's arm—the task fell upon James to finally set him at ease. He lured the dog away from the cabin with a scrap of meat and stuck his knife in a place that would let the animal go quickly.

They had managed to keep the baby alive with piles of wool, checking every hour for breath if he did not cry for Mary's sparse milk or from his other mysterious ailment, the one that had afflicted the other children, the older ones who had come down the trail. It started with blotchy red rashes and ended beneath a little wooden marker in a plot of land at the edge of the settlement. By the time the snow started to fall, the makeshift cemetery had crept all the way up to the cabins. Now only the tips of the crosses poked above the mountainous white drifts.

The pair woke to the sun's glare reflecting from the new snow and set to work. Mary gathered a bucket full of icy snow and stoked the fire in the stone fireplace while James took the hatchet to chop away a slab of meat from one of those who had frozen to death and been left to preserve in the snowdrifts outside. The ground was too hard to continue with burials, and there was nothing left to do but use the meat to supplement their diminishing stores of the acrid harvest. He did not think of his neighbor as he chopped the flesh, cutting through the cotton covering the stiff calf down to the bone.

Mary peeked beneath the blankets where the baby lay. He cried for her milk, but she was dry. She'd been unable to produce more than a few drops for days. Her once plump baby was now a sack of bones, and his hoarse cries and rumbling stomach pierced her ears. She could not let him suffer another moment. Even if he should survive this winter, somehow, he would just be taken by the same affliction that had put the other children in the earth. He would never leave this rotten valley, this cursed place the devil had made to seem bright and wonderful.

She took the pillow from her bed and pressed it against his little body. His brittle, malnourished bones cracked beneath the down, but she held steady until his cries waned and his squirms ceased. Until he, like everything else, was cold. She plucked his tiny body from the nest and held it to her, cradling it, tears rolling across its head when James returned, his hands and face frozen.

"The Lord has called him home," Mary said.

James responded with a sloppy slap of the leg against the floor, the top of it glazed with ice, the cotton underclothes still stuck to the skin. Something bubbled within him at the sight of his cold child, something brewed from months of the bitter fruit the valley had produced, something it had infused there, something that made him squeeze the hilt of the hatchet.

And lift it.

Still clutching the limp infant, Mary found her way to the door and into the snowbank, the slush soaking her skirts, clutching her ankles. Her husband closed in behind, stepping on her hem. She sloshed forward and disappeared into the bank while he raised the hatchet and brought it down, into her shoulder, into her neck, into wherever the blade landed, hacking away as her screaming mouth was stuffed with snow, the white soaking up the dark, black tar that her blood had become.

MARCH 11, 2019
11:34 A.M.

Dylan sat next to Luke by the fire, three cell phones spread across her lap. It had been a couple of hours since Clay had left alone, hiking up and out of the valley to try to get help. She stared at the screens as if she could will them into having a signal, as if the magic of this place was a benevolent spirit granting wishes and all she had to do was ask—and not some terrible entity that turned them around the night prior. Sylvia said she hadn't had service since they'd left the car and Luke had the same service provider, so it was unlikely that his phone would connect either. Still, Dylan monitored them all for any movement, any sweeping cell signal that might wash down into the bowl.

"What do you think happened last night?" Dylan asked. She'd been turning the question over in her mind all morning.

"I don't know," Sylvia replied.

"None of us ate anything weird," Dylan said. "Like, none of us did any drugs or anything that might make us *think* we were moving in a straight line while we were actually going in circles."

"There are some mushrooms that have hallucinatory effects."

"Could there be spores in the air or something?"

"I mean, that's possible, but I haven't seen any mushrooms—besides a variety called dead man's toes on the way in, but that wouldn't cause us to hallucinate. I'm sure it was just because it was dark," Sylvia said. "Clay will probably find the way now that there's light."

"I hope so."

"Is there anything I can take for my head?" Luke asked between bites of sloshy oatmeal.

For most of the morning, Luke had been lucid. But he'd drift, his gaze pointing into the forest. Always into the trees. Once he asked about Slade, as if he'd forgotten that his dog was gone.

Now, before Sylvia could even pull out the packet of aspirin, it happened again. His eyes widened and his jaw slackened, the rest of his body going rigid like a corpse. Oatmeal spilled from his limp jaw like thick, beige drool. It slopped onto his pants. Dylan wiped it away, reminded of all those movies where a wife has to wipe away her husband's spittle after a terrible accident.

This is just a concussion, she told herself. *It's been less than twenty-four hours. This is normal. It's not forever. He's still talking and alert most of the time.*

Still, she needed to walk away from her broken other half.

"I'm going to go see if I can get a better signal in other spots," she said, nodding at Sylvia, who was trying to coax Luke into taking a pill.

She pocketed the phones and wandered. Every few minutes, she removed the plastic bricks and hoisted them into the air, spinning in a circle. Still nothing. She plunged farther into the woods lining the bottom of the valley, keeping an eye on the campsite, on the three Xs made by their neon tents. Her restless feet led her to the creek that ran around the valley, cloudy water languishing over slate. She walked alongside it, hoping to God or any deity that she'd stumble upon a farm or a trail or a fucking cell tower in the middle of the forest. Time ebbed, slowed down. The scenery repeated, each stretch of greenery an identical twin of the one before it, the way all forests look without markers or paths. Still, this time it really did feel like the scenery was repeating.

A movement in the water caught Dylan's eye. Tendrils curled through it, like little oil slicks, the color of rust. She squatted, leaning her head close to the water. They squiggled like tadpoles, but the tails attached to no little sperm-like heads. She dipped her fingers into the murky stream. When she removed them, their tips were coated in a thin film.

The color of blood, she thought, almost unwillingly, as if a disembodied voice had whispered the words.

The creek curved through the trees, and for a moment she wondered whether she should follow it deeper into the woods, whether it led to civilization. After all, whatever shit was polluting the water was probably runoff from some farm upstream, some pesticide that would eventually make its way into the municipal drinking water.

Hell, it would be *her* drinking water if they didn't get out of this valley soon.

"Yum," she said, wiping the muck across her pants and pulling the three phones out. Still nothing.

To think, just hours ago this was what she'd wished for: no signal so she could focus on climbing.

The rusty tentacles bobbed in the tepid water. They writhed and twisted beneath the surface, but the creek water itself sat eerily still.

She tossed a rock into it, wrinkles rippling across the surface.

When the water flattened again, the tendrils, the runoff shit, whatever the fuck it was, curled around the rock, like they were examining it. Like they had little minds of their own. She knelt down, curiosity tipping her body forward, her nose centimeters from the metallic-scented water, and nearly pitched headfirst into it. She caught herself at the last moment and instead fell on her ass, landing in soft mud. Something hard and blunt jabbed into her thigh. A coiled length of piping, corroded green copper caked in clay. Had she not dropped on top of it, she might have mistaken it for moss or lichen.

She scooped mud away, the darkness of it sticking to the ridges of her fingerprints, uncovering more green copper, the coil connecting to a straight pipe that attached to an enclosed bucket. Wrapping her mud-stained fingers around the pipe, she pulled the thing free. Something resembling purple fingers curled around the base, like preserved frostbitten flesh. Some type of weird plant. Probably that mushroom Sylvia had mentioned. She imagined this was how Green Boots's fingers might have looked if one of the climbers on Mount Everest had dared to peel back his orange parka.

She set the copper contraption upright. It was an old still.

"What the fuck is this doing out here?" she said aloud, her voice jarring in the silence. "Someone trying to make moonshine?"

On its side was a gaping hole, the metal jagged like sharp, crooked teeth. Dylan stuck her finger into the hole, swiping the wet inside. It cleaned her finger of any traces of ingrained dirt, and she held it beneath her nose. It smelled of sharp, fermented corn. The scent was fresh—as if the still had been used just hours ago instead of lying buried long enough to corrode.

For a fleeting moment, she wanted to bring it to her lips, to let any dregs of moonshine drip down her throat, to give her a prohibition buzz that would dull her fear—before remembering why she was traipsing out in these fucking woods, a snap back into focus like she'd been in a trance. The still was probably full of mud.

Her stomach knotted and an ache bloomed in her chest as she thought of Luke, of his limbs tied into makeshift slings softened with sweatshirt pillows, of his broken head, of how she had forgotten about him for even a single second. About his distant eyes, that haunting stare that was *not* glazed—he was looking at something, she knew, she just didn't know what.

She wasn't sure she wanted to know.

Dylan shuddered beneath her jacket. She removed the phones, one by one, from her pocket, clicking the screens on.

"Fuck," she said. Still nothing.

She kicked the stupid old still, denting the base. The thing shouted a sharp twang out into the trees. A more effective SOS than the damn hunks of plastic in her hands. She kept her phone out, the only device that had ever gotten any signal since they'd arrived, and wandered farther, abandoning the copper husk to be discovered by someone else—or simply to be consumed once more by the earth and the rain.

She took eighteen more steps with her phone hoisted in the air before she turned off the screen and squeezed it inside her fist, swallowing the urge to chuck the fucking thing against a trunk or smash it with a rock. Instead, she slipped it back into her pocket.

It wasn't supposed to be like this. She was supposed to come here a fledgling climber with a brand-new deal and leave the next big thing, the it girl of the moment, the next Lynn Hill, Petzl crowning her their star athlete. She had seen it. She had dreamed it in those weeks between Clay's invitation and the drive down, those glorious nights of anticipatory insomnia. Her name was supposed to live forever—in guidebooks, in newspapers, in magazines, on the fucking sign that would sit at the trailhead leading to this site.

But that dream died. Not when Luke got injured—belaying is easy to learn. But last night, when they dipped back down into the bowl of this wretched valley once more, she knew she would not be ascending another route. She knew, at the same time, that Clay could still finish his thesis with the limited data they'd collected, would probably go on to publish that, and then someone else, some rich asshole, would swoop in like a vulture to complete the task—would hack a path through the Kentucky wilderness and take what he thought was his, just because no one had ever said he couldn't take it.

Yet another man would claim all the glory, and her first ascents of the six routes would be a mere footnote to the story, perhaps erased entirely once they drilled permanent bolts into the walls. When they inevitably changed *her* routes, the paths she chose up the rock. And then they'd name them something stupid or, worse, racist. They'd bulldoze an expanse of trees for a gravel parking lot, nested away from the main road. Cheesy gift shops would pop up, and they'd chop down more trees to make fancy, upscale camping sites or maybe even cabins to rent. That shitty little diner would probably resurface as something else, all the grime scrubbed away.

But that was the whole point, right? That's what she wanted. For *herself*.

And who knew what Petzl would think—her first sponsored

trip ending in a severe accident. Did she even know what she was doing? Would they drop her?

Maybe, she thought, her dream could be resurrected once Luke was squared away, once doctors could wrap his bones in a real cast and fix his poor little head. They could buy that new rope and return. She could have Clay belay or teach Sylvia. It would be okay.

But some small, sure inkling wrung her organs dry. The gymnastics routine left her stomach in a tight, pulsing knot. Sweat beaded against her forehead. Somehow, she knew that Luke would not make it to a hospital anytime soon. Clay would not find the car, would not reach the road, would not call for emergency services with the stupid broken GPS. There would be no heroic helicopter swooping in to save the day.

In her distracted wandering, she almost stumbled headfirst into the rock wall, a new stretch of it around the corner from where they had made camp. The thing was like a giant column in the center of the valley. The air around it seemed to palpitate. Her skin buzzed with a magnetism she couldn't name or place. The rock felt cold and dry against her callused fingers. Dylan stepped back, against every instinct of every atom of her body, to take in the full wall, tracing with her eyes the movements she might make on the route—if she were able to climb it. But that would require a whole set of impossible dominoes to fall, and all of those little plastic gravestones were misaligned. Luke's fall was the solitary piece that had upended everything.

Climb it anyway.

The thought whispered through her head as though it was thrust up from the earth itself, like a tendril vining its way up, curling around her legs and piercing her ear. The inner voice was clear and distorted at the same time—like the vocal cords had been worn to thin, taut strings—like it belonged to someone else.

Plenty of people climb without ropes.

That was true—many great climbers did climb without gear, ignoring any and all safety measures, using just their strength and will: their body against the rock. But usually that was on routes they knew, had practiced for hours and hours before they even attempted to ascend without rope. Free solo climbers trained and primed their muscles to be at peak performance, made sure every movement was memorized. Dylan had never been this bold. She'd always been a calculated climber, one who planned out her moves and practiced until she got it right, sometimes getting lucky enough to send something on the first try.

No, not lucky.

The voice inside of her growled. Okay, maybe it wasn't entirely luck, but she'd certainly had her share of bad falls. Why chance it—especially now, when there was already one hopelessly injured camper? They did not need another smashed head. She knew plenty of climbers with smashed heads—and didn't that one famous climber die free soloing? With climbing there was always a chance of fractures and injuries, even with all the gear.

You're good enough to do it.

She scanned the route, mimed where she would place her limbs, mapped out the crux of the problem. A difficult one, she surmised. She backed away from the wall, ready to leave. It looked too hard.

The weight of the phones suddenly pulled at her waistband. She fished them out of her pocket, clicked them on. Still nothing.

You can probably get a signal up there.

That decided it.

On the first two attempts, she fell—her foot sliding, a tiny beak of a handhold just too far away. Wet mud smeared across her ass. She removed her bulky hiking shoes. On the third attempt, her bare feet held, and she caught the tiny piece of rock between her left thumb and fingertips, gripping until her knuckles went ghostly and her body stabilized, her toes flying away from the rock for a second. She climbed on. She stuck her fingers into pockets full of spiderwebs and dust. She jabbed her toes on the sharp, virgin granite. Focusing only on where her hands or feet would go next, she worked the problem, pushing away thoughts about the growing distance between herself and the ground. She did not think about how she would maneuver back down, should that decision not be made for her.

The tendons in her wrists twanged like violin strings, the melody repeating with each crimp she pinched, each hold spanning no more than half a fingertip. Her muscles ached. A cramp squirreled its way up her calf. Clenching her right arm in a constricted *L* she flicked her left hand, shaking out the knots the wall had worked into it, repeating the motion with all four extremities, until her muscles once again became smooth machines that propelled her to the top of the route in just three more swift, easy movements.

Above her, the last five feet of rock was smooth and slick, rounded perhaps by rain, leaving her stranded in her body's tension against the wall, unable to climb farther. She shuffled, trying to position the pocket on her pants away from the wall while also kicking her foot around for a better, wider hold. Her fingers and toes twitching against the rock, she steadied herself to free one hand and pluck out the first phone she could reach—Sylvia's.

The screen flashed on—but there was nothing, not even a blip of LTE when she raised it as high into the air as she could.

She slid it back into her pocket. Her entire left arm cramped, the muscles locked into their tension, her fingers losing feeling. Before she fished out phone number two, she hooked the fingers of her right hand onto the wall to shake the loose the spasm. As her left arm shook like an air-drowned fish, her feet shuffled— enough for them to snap free. Tiny pebbles rained down to the ground. Her toes scraped air.

Fuck.

The distance between her free hand and the wall seemed to span a thousand miles. The weight of her body pulled, heavy, against her remaining attached limb. The tendons inside stretched, ready to snap. It would be a courtesy, she thought— for her mind to have the pain of a swelling, limp hand to ponder instead of her impending, shattering doom. She threw her tired left hand at the rock. Hoping her worn skin could catch it.

Her fingers scratched at it, forming little baby hooks. Crumbled granite filed her nails. The muscles in her other arm faltered, twitched, begged to be released from duty. She squeezed them tighter, pulsed blood into them, her left hand still scrabbling for a hold. She scrunched her eyes closed, waiting for the drop, praying to all the gods she didn't believe in and, somehow, her left hand found a miniscule scrap of stone and clung—for literal, dear, precious life.

Her feet continued their arc outward, flying through open air, and she crushed her fingers into the wall, no room in the holds for more than the very tips of her fingers, until her legs completed the pendulum, swinging back to the rock. Her toes grabbed on. She exhaled, nearly loosening her grip in that moment of near miss, of sheer relief.

When she regained her breath and control of her body, she gingerly pulled out the second phone. Her own. At waist level, even at this altitude, the phone registered no invisible cellular waves. An EMERGENCY CALLS ONLY banner mocked her from the screen. She knew it wouldn't connect, that even a call to that three-digit number would not be able to ping another tower. Still, she lifted this hunk of plastic into the air, too, watching as absolutely nothing changed on the screen. She swallowed a deep bite of air, set her limbs in place, and then slid the phone back into her pocket.

One last chance.

The third phone—Luke's—had one single bar.

The thing nearly dropped from her hand when she tried to open the screen, to get to the number pad, as if she'd never clicked around a cell phone with a single hand before. She held her breath at the thought of losing it. Though the phone slithered less than a centimeter down her palm, that was all that it needed to drop the signal.

If she had been smart—if her entire focus had not been on maintaining her hold with swollen, sore, exhausted muscles, if her heart had not been beating so fast and cruel in her chest, racing blood through her veins, if she could retain any wits at such an altitude, she would have dialed a number—any number—before her hand shot automatically upward to chase the fleeting signal. But she did not, and the signal could only be maintained if she hoisted the phone up, pushing herself higher with pointed toes. Her left hand, still locked in place, throbbed, the blood rushing around her white-hot joints.

With the speed of frozen molasses, she clicked around the screen with her thumb. Should she just call a standard emergency operator? Would it be better to try to dial the Livingston police? Or should she make a call to a relative, to someone else who could fret and prod the authorities and make sure something actually got done? She didn't have the damn coordinates, either. Would an emergency operator be able to triangulate her location? Could she even stay up here long enough for that to happen?

Her body trembled, twitched. Her thumb input three digits, then moved down to the green call icon, then to the speaker button as the phone tried to connect with two miniscule bars.

A ghostly wail reverberated up from the ground, piercing the thin air at the top of the route.

"Slade?" she said, barely audible, even to herself.

She turned her head, another automatic reaction, her body moving without her input. At this height, the tops of the trees swayed beneath her. Beyond them, the hills of Kentucky rolled, and she could even spy the highway, the trucks smaller than toys. Maybe she should have brought a fucking flare gun up here instead of these cell phones—humanity was so fucking close.

She looked back at the phone. The call still had not connected.

The little beak of rock that supported all of her weight, that her left hand had melded to—she could no longer distinguish the end of her hand and the start of the stone—cracked. It splintered inside of her stranglehold, sharp pieces like broken bones jutting into the pad of her thumb, ripping her skin. Wet blood dribbled out, staining the rock. The phone dropped from her grip as she threw her hand back at the wall. Muscle memory and sheer dumb luck guided her fingers into place. Once more, she breathed, shallow, sucking air in and out, in and out.

Two strikes—she didn't want to chance a third. She started

the treacherous descent.

Below her, Luke's phone ricocheted against the rock, spinning away before smashing, face-first, on the ground.

Sweat oozed from Dylan's palms, the rock growing slick. Her fingers, greasy now with blood and sweat, slipped as she looked down toward the ground swaying beneath her. The distance between her and the safety of the earth below made her dizzy. She squeezed her eyes shut and counted the length of each slowed breath, trying to push away all of the racing thoughts reminding her that she was at least fifty feet in the air with no rope, no spotter, nothing to save her should she press her weight down on a sandy hold or a chipping piece of granite, causing her feet to slip off and pull her whole body off the wall, or if her hands became too clammy and wet to hold on to the little crimps on the way down, or—

She exhaled, disturbing the dust on the shelf of rock in front of her face. Her breath shook, caught in her throat, never reaching her lungs. She was suddenly aware of every inch of her body, from her toes engulfed in staticky numbness to the cramp beneath her rib cage where the bones pressed into her abs, to her heart, seemingly pounding a hole through her chest. Little bits of granite had punctured the delicate skin at the edges of her foot.

If only she could go up and over the top of the wall, she might be able to find some way to hike back down or else find an easier route to downclimb, one of the ones closer to camp with oversized pockets that fit all of her fingers. Or maybe she'd be able to flag down a plane or helicopter. But she couldn't go over the top, and she couldn't climb sideways—the rock was smooth to her left and right. The only way down was the way she'd come.

She shifted her weight away from her left foot, the movement of every muscle and tendon and bone choreographed. Her forearms tensed, taking all the weight. She repeated this dance with her hands, transferring her weight to the least sweaty, least bloody palm. Unhooking her fingers, she wiped them on her pants and gripped a piece of the rock close to her waist. At the pace of thick, dripping sap she moved down the face of the stone, one careful limb at a time. Each movement could result in a painful, prolonged death by shattered skull and bone-punctured lungs, leaving her an explosion of unrecognizable flesh at the base of this pockmarked rock, left to choke on her own blood and wait for the end.

Maybe Sylvia would find me like that, she thought, moving in a downward rhythm until her foot slid on loose dirt. Her entire body froze in place, every single muscle a knot. She held her breath for a whole minute before her fingers tingled for want of oxygen and she started moving again. Going up had been smooth, but backtracking left her shaking. Was the rock slicker and wetter now? Was that her own blood coating it, or her imagination run amok?

Twice her feet popped away from the wall, sliding on gravel or dew, and she squeezed her fingers into the rock, lucky her hands were so strong, that her body was an adrenaline factory. No other choice but to hang on, even when the rock sliced through the meat of her fingers, even when the little beak that felt so good to wrap her thumb and forefinger around on the way up crashed through the skin beneath her chin the second time her feet scraped air.

Blood gushed from the wound, an upside-down fountain staining her chest. It stung like hell. She could do nothing about it.

When she hovered about five feet from the ground, her hands

cramped, releasing their grip. Her fall left her with a bruised tail-bone and mud stains on her heels and elbows. Her whole body panged and pinged with wild synapses, like a mad scientist was poking at her nerves with an electrified rod. Some part of her still pumped out adrenaline while she gulped air to calm her bleating heart.

But another part of her tingled with euphoria, as she lay back and gazed up at the granite column towering overhead. *I climbed that*. And she did it with nothing but her own muscles.

A trail of red dribbled down the rock. The only proof she could have offered.

When the sun lowered behind the rock, she finally pushed herself up. Her legs quivered beneath her. Luke's phone rested facedown a short distance from the wall. The screen had cracked so badly that shards fell away when she lifted it. The metal housing on the back bore deep divots and scratches, as if something had sunk fangs into it. The charging port bent into a grimace. She did not attempt to press the power button.

―――――――

Dylan stepped through the trees and Sylvia gasped, her notebook sliding off her lap into the mud. Like the final girl in a horror film, Dylan limped into camp. The knees of her pants were ripped and fraying, as though a long-clawed monster had slashed them. Dirt marred every inch of her, swaths of it on her thighs, knees, elbows, and even a few clumps clinging to her hair. Blood dripped from her chin, splattering her neck and the front of her shirt, warm and sticky. It looked like her throat had been slashed with a machete or oversized chef's knife from the camp kitchen, and Sylvia's eyes moved to the space behind her, as if waiting for a masked killer to appear and finish the job.

Adrenaline propelled Dylan forward, her heart pumping blood to her engorged muscles and out the wound under her chin.

"Oh my god," Sylvia said. "What happened to you?"

"An accident," she said, moving her jaw as little as possible.

"Are you okay?" Luke asked, snapping his gaze back from the trees.

"I'll be fine," Dylan said. "I just—I tripped and hit a rock. On the ground."

"Here, let me help you get cleaned up," Sylvia said, leading Dylan toward the firepit.

The alcohol wipe came back a bright red, and Dylan refolded it before wiping more blood off her neck. The astringent sting cooled her. Once there was a hefty pile of stained sheets on the ground, Dylan lifted her head while Sylvia inspected the wound.

"You must have hit a big rock," Sylvia said. "It's still bleeding. It could probably use a stitch—I think I have some superglue, if you're okay with that."

"Glue me up," Dylan said, soreness inking into her as her muscles finally cooled down.

Sylvia wiped Dylan's chin once more with an alcohol pad and placed a small line of glue inside the cut, pinching the skin together until it dried.

Inside her tent, Dylan slid out of the bloodied shirt, the fabric sticking to her skin. A Rorschach blob of red remained imprinted on her chest, a mark she did not bother to erase before shoving her arms through the sleeves of another top. Later that night, she would toss the ruined shirt into the campfire, the fibers growing black, melting and spitting out stinking smoke. Too late would she realize she was destroying her only trophy, her blood-soaked triumph. As the flames licked it, she would itch to save it, to risk third-degree burns on her palm to keep the only proof she'd ever have that she climbed that route—and made it back down. Mostly intact.

"So what happened?" Sylvia asked when Dylan returned to the fire. "I don't believe that you just fell."

"I did," Dylan said. She handed back the useless brick of Sylvia's phone. "I mean, that was how I scraped my chin. I guess I got carried away looking for signal. I walked through a lot of brush and vines. They must have ripped up my pants."

"Did you find anything?"

The mossy-colored copper still flashed into Dylan's head. The relic had already been drowned in her sea of adrenaline and fear. An image wormed its way into her mind, of the still standing upright, gleaming with newly welded buttons along the side. A fire tickled its underside, and a ceramic jug collected the clear liquid that dripped from the end of the coil. Jars and jugs and bottles of the stuff stretched in front of her. The back of her throat burned with the taste of grain alcohol, bitter and sharp. She spat into the dirt, trying to rid herself of the sour taste, but how could she excise a ghost from her tongue?

"Any signal?" Sylvia prodded.

"No," she said. Her free climb would be a secret she kept tucked inside of herself. Nobody would ever believe that she had free soloed a high-ranking route—a 5.14a if she were rating it—and downclimbed its sixty feet, too. Hardly any climber could do that, let alone with no shoes or preparation. No one had been there to record it. Nobody had even been there to witness. Sylvia hadn't written it down in her notebook, and she never would.

Dylan didn't want to add to Sylvia's burden, to erode her sanity any more than was necessary. When she wasn't writing or fussing over Luke, Sylvia picked at the skin curving around her nails, pulling a cuticle until it bled. She seemed at her wits' end over her new role as nurse.

"How are you feeling, Luke?" Dylan asked.

"About the same," he said. "Aspirin is helping my head a little bit."

Sylvia finishing unwrapping Luke's ankle bandage, made from a long-sleeved shirt she'd ripped into a strip. Both women grimaced at the sight: his foot was a swollen, purple mass, a balloon with toes. The bruise edged up his leg, little tendrils like dark veins. Though it displayed all the signs of infection, they could not find any site where the skin had split, where little armies of bacteria could have breached the hull. Still, Sylvia swabbed an alcohol pad around his ankle before she wrapped it up with a new bandage.

Maybe Dylan didn't tell Sylvia and Luke because they wouldn't believe her. Maybe because she didn't want to hear the gasps, the chastising, didn't want them to put into words what she already knew, that she should not have risked her life doing that. Or maybe because it felt like church to her.

MARCH 11, 2019
4:15 P.M.

The trees wobbled and swayed, the bowl of the valley swinging like a pendulum across Luke's vision. He swallowed to keep down his bile—he'd only managed to eat half a bowl of oatmeal, and if he vomited, the acidity would scrape his throat raw. One drumstick pounded a tempo against his temple and the other tapped a steady rhythm between his eyes. The aspirin was wearing off.

Dylan sat next to him, a clean slate—*Clean from what?* He couldn't remember anymore—and placed her hand on his thigh, the good one, the one not tied up.

"How are you feeling?" she asked.

"My head hurts," he said between clamped teeth. He covered her hand with his unbound one, tried to smile. "Been better."

They appeared again, just behind the first row of trees.

Luke pinned them in place with his gaze. He didn't blink until his eyes were dried-out husks, lest they move out of place, lest they start toward him.

"Luke?" Dylan asked. She shook his shoulder, a back-and-forth motion that made the group dance, there among the trees, but Luke would not turn his head. He swallowed the rising contents of his stomach and squeezed her hand tight.

"He's been doing this on and off all day," Sylvia said. "I think it's getting worse. I've been writing down the times—it was pretty sporadic at first, but it's happening more often. Sometimes it sounds like he's whispering something, but I can never figure out what. And by the time he comes out of it, he says he doesn't remember."

He did remember, but he didn't want to speak it aloud. Didn't want to worry the rest of the group more. Didn't want more proof of his receding sanity.

Dylan's fingers tightened around his. He would not break his stare.

"A couple of times he called for Slade," Sylvia said. "Once he even tried to get up and go into the trees. I guess he thought he saw Slade and was trying to go get him."

Slade had been there, and Luke had tried to go to him—he remembered that much, had scrapped any recollections from the past five hours to hold on to that one, a token to keep for the future.

He had seen Slade. His dog sat panting, just inside the trees.

But it had not been Slade.

Not really.

It was some sort of trick—of his mind or of this place, that much was fuzzy.

But, now, in the trees, *they* stood, like a mirage. Both there and not there. A woman with a stained dress and a bloody mouth. A man in soaking-wet clothes, fire licking his pant legs, flames that never grew, never climbed farther up the wool. Two men with dark holes where their eyes should be. Teenagers with hollow faces, pleading eyes.

Luke wasn't sure if they were a product of his broken head or something else. Something in his gut told him to pin them in place, to watch them closely—or else.

Standing at the edge of the group was a man in a slate-gray coat stained with ash and buttons gleaming bright as the teeth in his hungry grin.

OCTOBER 1861

The river pulsed in front of them.

They'd had to pull back from the battle at Camp Wildcat. General Zollicoffer had told his next in command to hold their current position while he and a group of soldiers pressed into the wilderness, due north, skirting the camp they'd just retreated from, Union prisoners in tow. If only his men had arrived a day before, they would have outnumbered the Union soldiers three to one. But a road so muddy that the wet sludge reached their wagon axles had delayed them, had allowed enough time for reinforcements to rear their ugly heads.

But he'd gotten what he needed: seven shivering, bone-thin boys in Union colors, linked together by a length of rope coiled around their waists and wrists.

They'd snuck past the enemy's camp without even a chirp from the prisoners, boys too young to want to risk sacrificing themselves, boys who'd always gotten their way if they'd just been obedient.

Now, the boys and their captors stood at the edge of the swollen Rockcastle River. The moon, just short of full, crested into the night while the general's soldiers tied each of the boys to a horse like luggage, hoping to avoid the water's hungry waves. This human chain, like clothespins on a line, dove into the river. They crossed and the Confederates cut the boys free.

Not even the general knew where they were going. He tramped his men and horses through the Kentucky wilderness, searching for a secluded spot. He'd know it when he found it. His men followed behind their leader, the horses shimmying through the looming tree trunks, their hooves squishing the mud. The general, at the head of the pack, stopped in the bowl of a valley—the only space they'd encountered free of massive trunks—and dismounted.

This was the place he'd been looking for.

A deep, strong voice in the general's ear, one that did not belong to him, told him so. A little hand tugged at his cuff, urging him forward. With gunpowder, he drew a large circle on the floor of the valley. His instructions were clear: the Union boys moved into the center. He lit the ring and flames burst up, as tall as a man. The fire gobbled the prisoners' ragged pant legs and soon their skin and flesh as well. The hushed incantation, a dark prayer for the Confederacy's success, uttered from the general's lips, was drowned by their screams.

But the earth hadn't yet had its fill.

The flames spread, tickling the ground until they grabbed at the ankles of the Confederate soldiers, too, who hadn't enough time or sense to remount their horses before their crazed hooves disappeared into the trees.

Soon their screams, too, reached the empty limbs of the trees, and by the next morning the only remnant of the night's events was a thin circle of ash.

MARCH 11, 2019

4:45 P.M.

Clay focused on the ruts and puddles of the muddy trail. The trees repeated and stitched together like an optical illusion, the leaves duplicating. If he pointed his head down, ignoring the crazy trees, he wouldn't vomit or risk becoming so disoriented that he'd fall on his face. The trail repeated as well, but the constant brown of the packed dirt smoothed over the replications. The world didn't spin around him if he just stared at the ground.

Still, it made him dizzy—like one of those carnival tunnels where a neon tube spun around a platform, but your brain thought you were moving, so you listed to one side, which Clay did as he followed the trail. When he lifted his head, trying to track whether he'd made progress, whether the trail curled ahead or whether he'd finally reached the end, he had to stand still for a moment and close his eyes, his body swaying with vertigo.

He must have had too many swigs of the moonshine. The bottle sloshed at his side, the glass bruising his hip. He sucked down water from his pack to dilute the alcohol in his stomach.

"Fuck this place," he whispered, waiting for the sensation to pass.

Clay swiveled his head over his shoulder. Each time he did, the same view greeted him. The last horse in the caravan never seemed to grow smaller. The horse's clopping shoes bounced down the trail, its hooves slapping the mud, but Clay had the insane thought that they were stamping in place, as if the animal was on some sort of invisible treadmill.

The woman still held her limp baby—sometimes he could hear her cooing to it, her whisper both soft and sharp. Even as Clay traveled away from her, her face grew clearer. The dark ring around her mouth was slick blood, a horrific parody of clown makeup. There was no mistaking it now. She licked away the blood as far as her tongue could reach.

Fuck it. He took another swig of the alcohol, bitter and sharp. If he was going to hallucinate—Was it the moonshine or exhaustion? Dehydration?—he might as well be drunk. At least then the tightness in his chest would melt and his endless stream of thoughts would dissolve into static.

Every muscle in his body ached, from the soles of his feet to the locked muscles of his jaw.

The congregation's hymn rang out, the same tune over and over and over.

How many fucking verses does this song have? Clay wondered, pushing his hands over his ears.

When he turned around again, the woman's face hovered over the baby's. She lifted it and stared straight at Clay, a fresh halo of blood around her mouth. She grinned, her yellow teeth stained anew. Something fleshy had wedged itself between them, and Clay's stomach heaved.

Beside her on the trail, a dog—a gray and black long-furred thing that Clay thought didn't look too different from

Slade—pulled meat from bone, sinews snapping in its jaws, wet and dark as the woman's. Clay snapped his head back around. He didn't want to know what the dog chewed on. In the brief flash he had caught, he thought it resembled a human leg, cut off at the knee. One end had flopped as the dog pulled at the muscle, like an ankle joint. Clif bar inched up Clay's esophagus—he was sure there had been toenails—and he stumbled to the side of the trail to vomit.

The hymn continued, a soundtrack to his retching:

> *See him set forth before your eyes,*
> *That precious, bleeding sacrifice;*
> *His offered benefits embrace,*
> *And freely now be saved by grace.*

Something small and fast darted out from between the trees and landed in the center of his barf, splattering it across Clay's shoes. A weapon of some sort—An arrow? A dart? One end was covered in feathers. He spat, the bitter taste of vomit coating his teeth, and sucked water from his pack, swishing the tepid liquid around his mouth. He crouched to examine the thing, to touch it. To see if it was really there.

A static jolt zinged through his finger when he got close. The thing emitted an electric hum, low and steady. The screen on the GPS in his other hand dissolved into salt and pepper before the battery blazed hot, and Clay dropped it into the dirt, the melting plastic oozing like lava.

"What the fuck, what the fuck," he muttered between ragged breaths.

He pulled back his finger, not daring to touch the weapon, as if it would electrocute him and he'd drop dead, right then and there, on that endless trail with a dog munching on a leg and a woman with a dead baby and a bloody grin. He could just barely hear her cackle, a discordant minor to the hymn's major melody. At that moment, she was licking the new blood from her lips, and a shudder vibrated over his skin.

"I want to go home," he whined, pressing his palms against his eyes. Something deep within him nagged at him to claw them out—at least then he wouldn't have to see the leg, the blood, the impossible caravan. He took a deep gulp from the bottle at his side, the astringent sting blocking out every other sensation.

He just needed to make it to the car. Then he could drive away from this place forever. He'd send authorities back out to rescue the others. Fuck his dissertation. Fuck whatever this place was.

Beside him, several more arrows thwacked into the ground, knocked thick strips of bark from the trees. One grazed his shoulder, ripping a straight, fraying line through his jacket all the way down to his skin, and he felt a little jolt of electricity pass through his body. Before he could register the pain he started running, still staring at the ground, trying to keep his head from spinning at the glitching scenery. But at this speed, even the ground looked like several images layered on top of one another. He again vomited—this time a yellow, bubbly sludge that eroded his throat. He cleaned his mouth with more of the moonshine.

He sat, leaning against a tree, spitting up more stomach acid and sucking down oxygen in loud, heaving gulps. Tears singed the corners of his eyes. His little jog down the trail had not moved him any farther from the horse or the dog or the woman. A scream boiled out of his throat.

His brain could no longer manifest explanations for what he

was experiencing. The caravan was not a historical reenactment, not some group of cosplayers so strict they ignored modern-world anomalies. They certainly had no way of making horses walk in place—and why and how the fuck were the trees pixelated? How had the caboose not disappeared by now? Why would an old-timey actress have fake blood? What was the dog eating?

Something fucked-up was happening. Something out of this world.

He turned away from the dog, who was starting on the toes, a long, stained bone jutting out the end of the dog's muzzle, now covered in caked, bloody earth. Clay shielded his gaze with a flat hand like a horse blinder and stared at his shoelace, creating a picture memory to erase everything else. The little plastic tip frayed and peeled away from the lace woven with blue and brown threads. The lace threaded down the front of his boot, the bottom strip pulled taut, caked in mud. He could blind his sight, but he could not close his ears to the dull sounds of the dog's teeth scraping against the bone.

He took another drink from the bottle.

"—think Clay has reached the road yet?"

The voice rang through the trees, clear even over the squelching of the dog's jaws.

"I don't—" a second voice said. "I hope so."

Dylan and Sylvia.

How could that be? How could their voices be so close? He'd been hiking for hours, in a single direction, away from camp. His head pounded. Had the trail turned him around, made him backtrack? Could it really run so close to camp? But if that was the case, how had he not discovered the path earlier? Maybe their voices just carried well in the weird way that sound travels through the woods, like how you could hear whether a party had already taken your spot at the Gorge long before you got close enough to see them.

But, no, that wasn't possible. He had not heard them until this moment. They must be nearby.

He thunked his head against a tree, trying to jostle his brain back to reality. He must be hearing things now. He had to be. He must be drunk and dehydrated to the point of delusion. He put the straw from his pack into his mouth and gulped from the bladder until he sucked in air. But the others' voices still rose from the valley to his ears.

"—looking at?"

"I don't know. I don't—"

In the snippets he could hear between the sounds of the cara van, they talked about Luke as if he weren't there. Had he died? Clay's heart sank. But no, he decided, their voices would be higher, the words strung together into a single sound. Dylan, surely, would be wailing or crying. Luke must just be getting worse. He'd been alert in the morning, but with their limited supplies and medicine, he must have taken a turn.

If Clay had known that the salivating earth was twisting itself to lead him back to the group, that it was straining to keep them together, he might have instead pushed into the trees on the opposite side of the trail, where the voices didn't quite reach.

But his stomach grumbled, empty of even its acid but sloshing with alcohol, and the muscles in his feet throbbed, and Dylan and Sylvia were right there, and it would be getting dark soon. He hadn't packed a flashlight. Hadn't thought he'd fucking need one. He didn't even have the ruined GPS to guide him anymore. If he continued, he'd be wandering blind.

The insistent, enduring, slobbery sound of the dog chewing flesh shoved like a needle through his ear. It pierced his brain. He needed to leave.

He moved to the edge of the trail and stepped into the trees. From here, Dylan, Luke, and Sylvia appeared in the valley below him, tiny like dolls, like faraway actors on a stage.

"Dylan!" he yelled, cupping his hands around his mouth. "Sylvia! Luke! Hey!"

Like the woman, they did not react. They did not even perk their ears or stop midsentence. How could he hear their conversation from up here but they could not hear his screams?

He needed to know whether he was crazy. He needed someone else to bear witness to the trail, to the madness of the woman and her dog. Maybe he was suffering from dehydration, from exhaustion, maybe he was plain drunk and needed someone else to guide them down the trail to civilization. *It has to lead somewhere*, he thought. *That's what trails do. They have heads that people enter and leave. They* go *somewhere*. The trail would be their way out, if only Dylan or Sylvia would hear him, if one of them would scrabble up and follow it. They could leave this insane place, wherever they were.

They could escape whatever sinister thing lay in the backwoods of Kentucky.

He screamed again, tearing his throat apart, daring to push only a couple feet more into the trees, lest he lose the trail again. Still, Dylan and Sylvia did not budge. He edged three steps closer. Standing at the top of the ridge, Clay shouted one more time, and Luke pivoted his head upward, his gaze intense but with no signs of recognition. Like he was staring at something between them.

Clay grumbled. He would have to go to them. He dug inside

his pack, searching for something to serve as breadcrumbs. In a side pocket, he uncovered a dirt-stained roll of canvas tape, some remnant of an old first-aid kit, the adhesive meant for skin. But it would have to do. He taped teeth-ripped strips into oversized Xs on a straight line of trees connecting the trail to the bottom of the valley.

The trail has to lead somewhere.

Luke's eyes widened when Clay appeared in the bowl, finishing his last tape mark, the slash on his shoulder a dark, angry red. Sylvia and Dylan twisted their heads toward Clay, all words dying in their mouths.

Their explorer, their savior, had failed. His presence was proof.

"Hey, no luck I guess?" Dylan said as Clay moved through the trees. She tried to keep the disappointment out of her words. Their third attempt to get help had failed.

"You guys didn't hear me calling to you?" he asked, pointing up the hill. "I was right up there. There's a trail."

"A trail? Are you sure?" Sylvia asked. "I don't remember a trail from when we came in."

"Maybe we missed it or were moving parallel to it," Clay said, defensiveness souring his words.

"I don't think there's a trail," Sylvia replied. "I researched maps and there's no trail map or any hiking in this area."

"So you think I'm just making it the fuck up?" Clay hissed. "I just hallucinated a fucking trail? It's right up there. I marked the way back to it. We can all go see for ourselves."

"Someone has to stay with Luke," Dylan said, squeezing his sweat-soaked hand. He stared into the trees, into the space Clay had just passed through.

"I can stay," Sylvia said.

Dylan and Clay hiked out of the valley, following his little breadcrumb trail of Xs. Her arms pimpled with goosebumps when they crossed into the trees, right where Luke was staring—a cold spot. As they climbed the hill, every other tree bore a bright, clean mark. The white of the tape practically glowed in the dusk.

"What happened to your shoulder?" Dylan asked. Feathers fluttered out of a rip in his down jacket.

"You wouldn't believe me if I told you," Clay said stonily.

Dylan didn't respond. A heaviness descended into her stomach, hard like a rock.

"I think when we get to the trail, we should turn right," Clay said.

"But wasn't the road south of where we are?" Dylan asked, concerned. Her stomach turned again as they climbed, all the trees blurring together, spinning her insides to mush. "Right would be north, farther into the woods."

"I don't think so," Clay said.

"Should we even try to get back to the car? It's going to get dark soon." She wasn't sure she wanted to be alone out here with him for long. She'd never felt unsafe with Clay, but something was off with him tonight.

"You want to get Luke to a hospital, right? We need to get to the trail and go right, back to the car."

But they never got to choose left or right. The sky pricked with purple and orange by the time they reached the last mark. The lopsided X seemed to burn into the bark of the tree. It stood surrounded by close-set neighbors. There was no trail to be found—not even a gap or a clearing.

"There's nothing here," she said, clicking on a flashlight, spinning its light around.

"They must have fallen off," Clay said. "This medical tape isn't very sticky. It must be just a little farther."

Clay's breadcrumbs had ended too soon, as if someone had followed behind him and plucked off the makeshift trail markers and pocketed them. Or Clay had imagined the whole thing— Dylan wasn't sure which option was worse.

"Clay, it's getting dark. I don't think there's a trail. Are you sure you found a trail? Was it maybe a deer path?"

"It was a fucking trail," Clay snapped. He scratched through the underbrush, searching for more Xs. Leaves exploded around him. "And it was right here. I know the difference between a trail and a fucking deer path."

"Clay—"

"It has to be here," he said, scurrying farther into the trees. "I am not fucking crazy. I need you to believe me, to see this."

There was something wrong with Clay. With this place.

Something must have happened while he was gone.

The scream bubbled up through his lungs and out his mouth, a shrill, guttural, inhuman noise that bounced between the trees. Tears slid down his face. He punched a tree and filled his nails with bark, ripping the useless marker away.

"Fuck," Dylan whispered. What the hell had happened to him?

"It has to be here," he repeated, dropping to his knees.

He rummaged through the leaves and the brush, thorned vines scratching his hands as he swept leaves away, looking for the clean white lines of tape among them as if leaves had fallen strategically to obscure the fallen markers. He sat in a patch of thorns, thumping his head against a trunk, babbling.

"It was here. I swear. There was a trail and I saw a huge group of people but they didn't listen to me. It was like they couldn't hear me, like they were—like they were not really there. Or they were ignoring me. At the end there was this woman and a fucking dog. The dog looked like it was eating someone's leg. And the woman—"

"Clay, we need to go back," Dylan said. She didn't want to be alone with him.

She stood helpless behind him. Her flashlight pinned Clay like a spotlight, center stage in his own madness. When he started to pry pieces of bark from the trees, she squeezed his shoulder, and he let her lead him back to camp like a child.

Something had partied last night.

Dylan, the first to emerge from their tents, froze in place, her stomach rumbling and screaming. Sylvia followed, her jaw dropping as she took in the ruins of their camp. Empty granola bar wrappers twinkled in the rising sunlight, crinkled in the low wind that scraped the bottom of the valley, kicking up like glitter in a snow globe. The lid to the cooler had not only been removed but, somehow, shredded—curls of white plastic rose like a cowlick from its remains. It had spilled its beer can guts into a puddle created by the melted ice. When Dylan righted it, she discovered a perfect hole in its side, the edges smooth. Like something had stamped right through it.

The bear canisters had not done their job—the lids remained screwed in place, but something had scratched through the metal. Upon first glance, Dylan thought they'd exploded from the inside, as though some local hunters who'd happened upon their campsite had loaded them with cherry bombs as a prank. But chalky flash powder did not line the edges of the openings, where uneven crimps of metal folded out from the center like razor-sharp teeth. And wouldn't the blast have woken them? After so many restless nights, somehow the night their campsite was ransacked was the one they'd all slept like rocks. Surely anything with enough force to rip apart metal and thick plastic would not tiptoe, would not set its paws down precise and gentle.

The only object that appeared to be untouched was the five-gallon jug of water.

Sylvia ducked back into her tent and pulled a trash bag from her backpack. She and Dylan silently picked up empty wrappers and cans and ruined supplies, piling anything still usable by the firepit.

"What the fuck?" Clay growled.

Dylan and Sylvia froze, then twisted back to face him. He trembled as he exited his tent, whether with despair or rage Dylan could not determine.

"It's okay," Sylvia said, her tone one of forced calm. "We're cleaning it up."

"We're fucking trapped here and now we're out of food," he said. Dylan wasn't sure what had burst inside of him, but he wasn't the same since returning the day before.

His anger sent a ripple through the camp, a shiver twitching over Dylan's skin. She didn't know how to respond. She didn't know why the expeditions to reach the car had failed, but surely they weren't trapped.

Right?

She and Sylvia turned to face each other, sending each other the same, silent question: *What is this place?*

Clay erupted through the campsite like a storm, kicking up dirt, spitting acid rain from his mouth.

"What the fuck is going on?" he said, panting. He paced and

growled like a wild beast. "What could have possibly done this? What could have ripped through the metal without waking us?"

"I don't know," Dylan said. "Calm down, Clay. We'll figure it out. It'll be okay."

"This is impossible," he continued, his words slurring together. He kicked the canister, and it emitted a twangy scream. "Someone must have left the lid cracked."

"The lid is still screwed on," Sylvia replied.

"It doesn't make sense!"

Dylan froze, her muscles tense, like a deer staring down the barrel of a hunter's gun. One wrong move and it might explode. She'd never seen Clay like this.

"You don't believe me," he said. "About any of it. You don't believe I found a trail at all. You think I'm making it up."

The women looked at each other, each hoping the other would respond. What could Dylan say to him? There was no trail.

"You think I'm lying, that I'm crazy, and you're making fun of me. I know what I saw. I found a trail, and I saw a woman eating her own baby."

"Something weird is going on here," Dylan said. She felt around in her pockets, wishing she'd tucked her knife inside. Clay was her friend. He wasn't dangerous. But still, the urge made her fingers twitch.

"Maybe spores are in the air," Sylvia suggested. "Or our food got contaminated? Maybe something in the wood we've been burning, like the sap. The GPS seeming to malfunction, you seeing things—"

"Oh, so you think I have some sort of brain damage too?" he yelled. "Just like Luke?"

"What are you talking about?" Dylan said. "Something is

going on, but we don't know what it is. Getting worked up won't help anyone."

"You think I'm stupid," he continued. "You think I'm crazy and that it's my fault we're all stuck here. There's no way out."

"We don't think that," Dylan said. "We'll figure something out together."

"We're trapped," he said. "You all agreed to come here. I didn't force you."

"No one said you did," Sylvia said. "We all wanted to come. Nobody expected this to happen."

"Now we don't have any food left, and I bet that's somehow my fault, too," Clay said.

"How would this be your fault?" Dylan replied. "Something got into it while we were asleep. It's nobody's fault."

"Where is everything? You cleaned everything up before I could check to see if there was anything we could save."

"Clay," Dylan said, "we saved any scraps that we found. They're in a pile over there, but there's not much left. We wouldn't throw out anything useable."

He snatched the trash bag from Dylan's hands, stretching the white plastic between his fingers, wedging a nail to tear a hole in the side. Like a wild racoon, he scavenged through the bag, throwing empty beer cans across the camp, flinging greasy, metallic wrappers and wet, mushy banana pulp, which landed with a plop and a splatter at Dylan's feet. He inspected the corners of foil pouches, his fingertip returning with a coating of gristle or dried hairs of chicken jerky. He reminded Dylan of a starving coyote, some beast at once both pitiful and terrifying. She stood quiet, her mouth gaping, making no movements lest he turn his insanity upon her. Did he bring drugs here with him? Was he high or drunk right now?

"How could you let this happen?" he muttered, pushing another wrapper inside out, no scrap of foil or zippered bag or plastic shard from a Tupperware container left unchecked. The pile of salvaged food did not grow larger, but still Clay dipped his paws into the trash, searching, leaving little pieces of white plastic garbage-bag confetti, relittering the campsite like the bear or whatever monster had torn through it the night before.

Once he reached the bottom of the bag, he even examined the canister, his fingertips gliding along the ripped metal, as though he could figure out what could have possibly torn it open by touch.

"It doesn't make sense," he repeated, dropping into the dirt.

Dylan tiptoed around his crumpled body, itching to hold her knife.

When she unzipped the tent to retrieve her blade, Luke erupted in screams.

MARCH 12, 2019
9:16 A.M.

The ghost party stood around a table covered with a moth-eaten tablecloth.

Rotten food was piled on top of it. The ghosts dug their hands into it, mold crusted beneath their fingernails, and shoved the sludge into their mouths—banana mush, pulped moldy bread, and rotten, reeking strips of jerky. Flies flitted around their feast, jumping away from the reeking compost pile when the ghosts went back for more handfuls, landing on their open eyes, darting into their gaping, chewing mouths, feeding on the rotten, juicy splatters on their arms.

Luke stared, eyes gaping. The man in the gray uniform caught his gaze and licked his teeth, as if testing their sharpness. He and most of the others—the woman, the teenagers—stepped back into the trees. But one man, bloodied like a butcher, stepped forward, sliding a fingertip along the blade of a rusty hatchet.

Luke swallowed, the knot in his throat bobbing in place, and he couldn't breathe, because it wasn't rust on the blade.

It was blood.

MARCH 12, 2019
9:34 A.M.

The tent was a dizzying orb of bright orange when Dylan entered, the color sending daggers through her skull, a hunger-induced headache forming right behind her eyes. Her pulse beat around it.

A putrid smell smacked her in the face, and she would have vomited if she'd had anything in her stomach. She wondered whether the stench was coming from Luke's damaged leg.

"Are you okay?" she asked. "Did you hit your bad ankle on something?

"No, I—" His eyes refocused to Dylan.

"Why did you scream?"

"Uh, yeah," he said. "I must have shifted my weight wrong."

"How's your leg?" she asked, fishing the pink-handled knife out of her backpack and slipping it into her pocket.

"Feels swollen," he said. "My head feels a little better, though."

"I think there's some pain meds left in the first aid kit," Dylan said. "I need some too. Let me help you out."

She pulled the makeshift crutch off the ground outside the

tent, the bound-up sticks looking more like a witchy omen than a medical aid. She stuck her hands beneath Luke's armpits and pulled, guiding his fragile body up and through the opening of the tent, into the spring sun—but the air still reeked, the rotten stench lingering, attaching itself to the hairs inside her nostrils. His leg must be really bad. Was it decomposing? Did he break the skin?

She became aware of a strange humming noise. Once she pulled Luke entirely out of the tent, the buzzing grew louder. She helped him balance on his good foot and the shoddy crutch, never daring to put his whole weight on it lest it snap, but now the twigs flexed beneath the duct tape as he leaned away from her, back toward the tent.

"Dylan—" he said, his eyes wide, his gaze fixed on the ground.

Dylan looked down. The ground between the tent and the tree line pulsed, vibrating and humming like a living carpet. A blanket of flies lay at her feet. They twitched and crawled over each other, fucking, making maggots. Dylan stumbled right into the dark, writhing mass.

"Oh my god!" she screamed.

The swarm flew up, tangling their twitchy legs in her hair, screeching in her ears, flitting onto her arms and knees and elbows, crawling down the back of her neck into her T-shirt. She danced, a jerky, interpretative twirl, legs kicking and spasming, arms swatting at her face and batting at her ears and fanning the hem of her shirt. The pain of each smack lingered, the smashed bodies seeping redness into her skin. The bugs' infinite legs scrambled against her, parting the soft, baby hairs along her spine and arms. Her synapses shorted, too many sensations all at once, disgusted shivers pulsing along her spine.

Luke could only stand at arm's length and watch with his two working limbs and a gaping mouth.

One fly swam through the air, a serpentine maneuver, and landed on the mountain of Dylan's nose. It jumped around her scratching fingers, crawling across her cheek.

Heading for her eye.

She shut her eyes and it battled against her eyelashes. It wiggled, trying to burrow, trying to separate the lids so it could stick its feet against the soft white of her eye. She smacked her hand, hard, over her eye. When she removed the fleshy eyepatch, a splotchy, gooey mess of guts and metallic wings stuck to her eyelid, already cold.

She pitched forward, toward Luke, exhaling sharply through her nostrils to shove out a fly that had wedged itself into the one opening she couldn't close. Her lips were a thin line, her jaw clamped shut. Her teeth ached. If she released her scream, it would only be an invitation, an open door. She didn't want to know what flies tasted like, didn't want to feel their flittering wings tickle her throat or their feet dance on her tongue or their incessant buzzing vibrate her teeth.

She slapped her hands against herself again and again. Welts began to rise along her skin, graves for the mashed corpses. The sharp, flat sound of her strikes ripped across the valley. Each thick, juicy body that exploded beneath her palm was one less to crawl its way toward her face. Some had become trapped in the tangled web of her hair. Some buzzed in orbit around her head, waiting for an opportunity to strike. Some, suffering snapped or torn wings, crawled across her torso.

It felt like whole decades had passed before the flies were either dead or gone, before she scooped the last twitching creature from her ear, guts settling beneath her fingernail. A transparent, glossy wing wedged between the nail and the meat of her finger. She completed her dance with a crumpled bow, falling to the ground in exhaustion. Sticky corpses dried against her skin, like chicken pox, hundreds of spots along her arms and legs, dripping down her forehead to her neck. Resting her hands on her knees, she gulped air, finally able to part her lips.

"What the *fuck*?" was the question that escaped.

———————

For the second time in two days, Dylan manifested at the edge of the campfire with the look of a lone survivor. When she said there had been swarming flies, Sylvia could only hand her a rag and point to the water jug.

That's when Dylan discovered their fate, found the pinhole and the puddle pooling beneath the water canister. It had been leaking into the dirt beneath it, a small but steady trickle. As if whatever had decimated the food had poked the bottom of the vessel with a small nail and careful concentration. There were only dregs left inside. Dylan cursed—quiet enough that Clay wouldn't hear—and flipped the canister so that the last bit of potable water could not escape.

Sylvia helped Luke into a seat, unwrapping his bandages, while Dylan dabbed the rag into the puddle, deciding that dirty water was better than bug juice. She scraped the wet rag over her skin, wincing, the fly guts sloughing off, leaving bruises beneath.

Dylan returned to Luke as Sylvia pulled the last loop of fabric off his leg. Even the dingy, dirt-stained bandages were a stark contrast to the dark hue of his skin beneath. Dylan inhaled a sharp breath, sucking in a stench like weeks-old putrid eggs steeped in garlic. After just two days, the purple bruises had a twinge of green, the flesh of Luke's ankle bulging as if there was a baseball of pus beneath the surface of his taut skin. And, worse, the discoloration was spreading. Green-purple veins crawled up his leg like poisonous vines. Like blood poisoning, Dylan thought, but—though the skin looked tight and ready to burst— she and Sylvia could still find no scrapes or scabs or lacerations, nowhere bacteria could have entered.

"Am I going to lose my leg?" Luke whimpered.

"We'll get you to a hospital soon," Sylvia replied.

Everything was going to shit. Tears, hot and sharp, welled in Dylan's eyes. She covered her face and let them fall, let herself mourn her now-surely-dead career, her pitiful boyfriend, her grumbling stomach. But she had to keep it together—she couldn't let herself despair, leaving Sylvia to babysit three broken heads. She wiped her eyes and got back to work.

While Clay continued his ravenous clawing, now working his way through a second trash bag, the women scooped muddy water into a pot and boiled it, using it to heat a rag to try to soothe Luke's swelling. He swallowed three rust-colored pain pills and two tablespoons of their remaining drinkable water.

"How are you feeling?" Dylan asked him.

"My head hurts again," he said. "So does my leg."

"You keep looking off into the trees," Dylan said. "What do you see? Do you remember?"

He did not respond. He dropped his head, his face pointed toward his lap. Dylan wasn't sure which was more alarming—his foggy head or his rotting leg.

"Yesterday you were mumbling about something," she continued. "I think you said something about a gray suit. Do you remember anything about that?"

No response.

"Luke?"

She lifted his chin with her hand, and his eyes locked on to something over her shoulder. He gently pulled her hand away.

"I'm okay," he said, sliding his eyes back to hers. "I'll be okay."

"Have you slept at all since the accident?" Dylan asked, wringing out the hot compress, rewetting it, and draping it over the swollen baseball that used to be his ankle. "I could hear you last night. It was like you were trying to say something, but it just came out as garbled nonsense."

"Just pain, I guess," he replied. "It's hard to get comfortable when it hurts to move and you're sleeping on the ground."

"Last night you were making some noise, and when I turned over, you were just sitting up, staring straight ahead. This happened a few times." What she didn't mention was that each time she found Luke sitting up, a little tapping finger had woken her. For her own sanity, she pretended it had been Luke's finger, even though the sensation moved as she shifted her body in the still-zipped sleeping bag, sometimes touching her tailbone, sometimes her thigh, her vertebrae. Tickling.

"We're worried about you," Sylvia said. "We need to get you out of here."

"I know," Luke said. "But what are we going to do? Every time we leave, we end up back here. And Clay lost the GPS."

The rock glittered in the morning sun, raising goosebumps along Dylan's arms. She turned her back toward it.

"We'll figure something out," Dylan said.

Clay huffed past them, heading toward the tents. Sylvia

sighed, opened a new garbage bag, and began to clean up the campsite a second time.

Dylan's head dropped into her hands. A sound like paper chafing against itself rubbed against her ear. Luke was scratching the index fingernail of his good hand against his bound arm, his gaze locked onto *something* in the distance. The moment she lifted her head and discovered this was the moment his raw skin broke, erupting with deep red lava that dripped down his arm. The blood coated his finger, but this didn't stop Luke from digging his nail deeper into his skin.

For a moment, Dylan couldn't move or act, transfixed. It was as if Luke's nerves had been shut off and his automation would continue until he scraped through muscle, all the way down to the bone.

"Luke? What are you doing?"

He twitched in his seat. His whole body jerked and spasmed.

"Luke?" Dylan shook him. He might be having a seizure, and she had no idea what to do. His finger wagged through the air, still trying to reach the skin.

She waved her hand in front of his eyes. His pupils did not move, like he was having a staring contest with a ghost. He didn't even blink. She guided his hand away like the arm of a record player.

"What's wrong?" Sylvia asked, coming around the firepit.

"Luke's arm," Dylan said. "He's scratching at it and he won't stop."

"It looks like he just scratched open an old scrape," Sylvia said.

"Luke? Are you okay?" Dylan asked.

His eyes finally refocused to Dylan. "Sorry," he said. "I zoned out." She swabbed the wound with alcohol and began wrapping it with gauze.

Dylan clicked her phone open, turning off airplane mode, waiting for a signal to appear out of thin air. There wasn't any signal, there was never going to be, but still, she resumed airplane mode to preserve the battery, as if there was a chance.

Behind her, the rock still pulsed. Some insane part of her burned to go back to the routes, to scale them, to ditch her mangled boyfriend. Even after her free solo adventure had nearly left her as dead and cracked as Luke's phone, even after it gouged her chin so that pain rocketed through her face every time she spoke, she had to squeeze her nails into her palms to stop herself from pulling on her climbing shoes, abandoning Luke, and heading to the wall. Her muscles tensed into knots that she knew could only be resolved by climbing, by touching the rock.

It wasn't supposed to be like this. She was supposed to hike three miles into the woods outside a small town, set some routes, and become a legend. Obtain all she'd been working toward, years of wearing bare her tendons, slapping her sweat and blood—literally—against rock. It wasn't supposed to end after just two days, with a broken rope and a broken boyfriend. But she never imagined they'd be trapped here. Why couldn't they reach the road?

Luke's prying finger wiggled between the layers of wrapping, his blood spouting to the surface like a spring and soaking into the white bandage.

MARCH 12, 2019

11:40 A.M.

The head of the zipper on the tent ripped free of the teeth when Clay yanked it down. There must be some food left. There fucking had to be. The others must have stashed some in their packs before he woke up—as a sick joke, as payback for his leading them all here, to this place where his sleep greeted him with nightmares in which he lay facedown, pinned to the wet ground, his back raw as if flayed, the skin singed, with figures in slate gray chanting around him, blurred by fire. This place where his eyes flitted open, his body paralyzed in the pitch dark, the chanting so quiet he couldn't be sure if it was real or a remnant of his dream.

There was no way that they were trapped here with only a single serving of food for four people.

He tipped the bottle of moonshine against his lips, the harsh liquor sliding down his throat. The burn felt good. It staved off the lingering headache that threatened to explode if he didn't take a swig.

He ripped through Dylan's and Luke's packs, unrolling each shirt and pair of pants, shaking them as if hidden foil packet meals and granola bars would come tumbling out. Dylan's knife was nowhere to be found. She must be carrying it on her, hiding it. Couldn't the blade have done the trick—wouldn't it be sharp enough to slice through the metal? He tore through the rest of their belongings, kneeling on a mountain of T-shirts and jeans and scrunched sleeping bags and half-deflated mats.

Had he been thinking clearly, he might have wondered why his campmates—his *friends*—would possibly be motivated to eat all of the food and make it look like an animal had scavenged through their campsite. But a voice—indistinguishable from his inner voice—snipped that type of thinking away, folded it, placed it in a far back corner of his brain. It conjured tales, whispered them into his ears—*They did it because you led them here. They did it because they hate you. They planned it from the start.*

He growled and punched the soft pile of clothing. He wanted to rip the orange polyester of the tent between his fists, break the long poles over his thighs.

Instead, he swallowed more poison.

Finding only a single granola bar in a side pocket of Luke's backpack, he stomped over to Sylvia's tent. He repeated his inspection, pulling her clothing out of her pack into an exploded heap. Inside a pair of jeans, he discovered two more granola bars. An apple rolled across the floor of the tent. He shoved these morsels inside his jacket. As he reached his grubby paws into the bottom of a bag, he spied Sylvia's notebooks stacked in the corner of the tent, the ones she'd been scribbling in to document their entire trip. All his research, contained inside the spiraled pages.

He released the bag and swiped the notebook on the top of the stack, flipping through it—slowly at first, and then faster.

The pages were stark white. Blank. Every single one. There wasn't so much as a scribble where she'd tested her pens. He flipped through each and every notebook in the stack, tossing the empty journals over his shoulder as he went. All of them were the same.

Had Sylvia torn out and burned the pages? Had she been pretending to take notes all this time—just scratching a capped pen along the paper?

What the fuck.

He knew he should have been keeping a closer eye on her. He'd known her for so long that he trusted her, assumed she was as invested in the study as he was.

But she'd led them in circles the first night that they tried to escape. She'd tried to convince Clay and everyone else that he was going crazy. She must have destroyed all of their food supplies.

And she'd sabotaged his research from the start. Now, even if they made it out of here alive, he wouldn't have anything to show for it. But it didn't matter, because they were trapped.

Clay screamed, a primal, guttural roar, his remaining sanity collapsing into the blank spaces of his mind.

———

The apple tumbled from the pocket of Clay's jacket, bouncing in the mud. As he stalked back toward the firepit, his steps swaying and unsteady, the sole of his shoe crushed the fruit into mucky pulp. The notebook in his hands flapped like a bird scrambling to take flight. The low growl escaping his lips bubbled into the soundless air.

"What the fuck is this?" he slurred.

The question sliced the one Dylan had been asking Luke in half, froze Sylvia in place, her hand still holding the roll of fabric she had been using to wrap Luke's leg.

"What's up, Clay?" Sylvia replied, her voice cautious.

"Was that a fucking smirk?"

"Clay, you're worrying me. Are you okay? You sound drunk. And no offense, but you kind of reek of alcohol."

"Do you think this is a joke?"

"Do I think what is a joke?"

"This," he said. He slapped the notebook into the squelching mud, the pages falling open to display the clean slate. "Are you fucking with me?"

"Clay, chill out," Dylan said, her voice sharp.

"I don't know what you mean," Sylvia replied. "Don't throw it in the mud, please. I won't be able to read it later."

"Read what? There's nothing written in it." He plucked the notebook from the ground and fanned the pages in front of Sylvia's face. "They're all like this. All blank!"

He dropped the notebook onto her lap. She opened it, scanning the pages before turning back to the front cover.

"Clay, are you okay?" she asked. "I don't understand what you mean. It's not blank. None of them are."

"Don't fucking play games," Clay said, his breath ragged and words stilted. "You never even took any notes, did you?"

"I don't understand. I've been keeping detailed notes—even about the things you saw—the trail, the woman, the dog. You saw me writing. It's all right here!"

She held the open notebook up to him, her fingers scanning a crisp white sheet.

"You guys see it, too, right?" she said, turning the page toward Dylan and Luke.

"Yeah, I see it," Dylan said. "The page is full."

Luke was drifting again.

"Sorry," Clay said to Sylvia, his tone suddenly shifting, as if someone had turned the dial of his anger all the way to the lowest level.

They were all in on it. The scheming bitches. He couldn't let them know he'd caught on. "You're right. I must have looked at one of the notebooks you hadn't used yet and overreacted. I'm stressed out after yesterday—and worried about Luke. Can you help me figure out what's safe to forage while Dylan keeps an eye on Luke? We need to find something to eat soon or we'll be fucked."

"Um," Sylvia said. "Why don't you take a moment to calm down first."

"Sure," Clay said.

"Dylan, can you help me find something we can use to put food in?" Sylvia asked.

"Sure," she replied. "Clay, will you be okay with Luke for a sec?"

"Of course," he replied.

He sat across the firepit with a drooling Luke while Dylan and Sylvia huddled together near the tents, muttering in low voices.

"Are you sure you're okay?" Sylvia asked, returning to the firepit with a dry bag.

"Of course," Clay said. "I'm sorry I overreacted. Let's go forage."

"Don't go too far," Dylan warned. "Shout if you need anything, okay?" She shot Sylvia a worried look. Sylvia mouthed, *I'll be okay.*

Clay feigned composure, letting his rage boil beneath his skin, as he and Sylvia walked toward the tree line with the notebook tucked under his arm.

"Is everything okay?" Sylvia asked once they were out of earshot.

"Yeah," Clay said. "I just wanted to talk about a game plan for getting Luke out of here and what we can do to salvage the research."

His pulse thumped against his temple. He continued walking, and she trailed like a dog as they followed the stream around the pillar of rock.

"Let's focus on finding food while we think through a plan to get help," Sylvia said. "We need to find a source of clean water, maybe send someone else out again to try to get to the road. Or at least find a spot where we can get a signal to call for help."

Clay knew in his bones there was no way out of this place.

He stopped short, and the notebook spilled from his arm, its wings bending beneath it, pages soaking in mud. She bent to pick it up.

"Why are the notebooks blank?" he asked.

"Clay, you're scaring me," Sylvia said, taking a step back. "They aren't blank—I don't know what you're talking about."

"Don't lie to me," Clay hissed. "It didn't just magically all disappear, did it?" The pressure inside his body boiled. His pulse screamed in his ears so loudly he could hardly hear Sylvia's replies.

"I'm not lying," she said. "All I can say is what I know—I took copious notes. They are all right here. Look, there's something weird going on here, and I think maybe—"

"I knew I should have picked someone else," Clay growled. His voice boomed through the trees, bouncing from trunk to trunk. "I thought you were my friend."

"I am," Sylvia replied.

"You probably blame me for all of this, for Luke being injured, for us being stuck here."

"I don't, Clay. Calm down—nobody thinks that."

"You all think it's my fault that we're here, trapped in this fucked-up place," he snarled. His hands formed into tight fists. "You know we're never getting out of here, don't you? There's no way out. But you all agreed to go. I didn't force anyone to come. How was I supposed to know what would happen? What this place is?"

"Clay, what are you talking about?" Sylvia asked. She hugged the notebook, lifting it to her chin like a shield.

"That woman and her dog. There was something wrong with them. I think they were from another time."

"That's not possible," she replied. Her eyes darted around. "You were probably hallucinating from stress or dehydration. Have you been drinking?"

"I know what I fucking saw! I saw a trail, and I saw a huge group pass by, ending with a woman and that fucking flesh-eating dog. Every single night, I've been having hideous nightmares. That's normal to you?"

"No," she admitted. "That is odd. But I'm not fucking with you, I swear. I don't know what's going on, but maybe there's some sort of poisonous fungus whose spores travel through the air in the spring, and we're all just inhaling them and having weird reactions. I've seen lots of odd species around camp and in the woods. Species that shouldn't be in Kentucky. There has to be an explanation."

"There isn't one," he replied. They danced, there in the trees, Clay stepping toward her, his foot claiming the space hers had occupied while she stepped back. "That's a shit excuse and you know it. And I know what else—all of you think this is one big fucking joke! You're all making fun of me! Why else would you pretend to write out all those notes? What else did you do? Did you fail to record all the work we did, too? Fuck with the camera or remove the SD card?"

"Clay—" She stepped back again, her back smacking into a tree. Clay stopped inches from her, could feel the heat and stink of her breath.

"Why did you do it, Sylvia?" he asked between clamped teeth, his hands pinching the meat of her arms, his nails biting skin. "Just to mock me? To prevent me from getting my PhD? So you could come back later and steal my idea?"

"Clay, please," she said, squealing. His hands slithered up to her shoulders. "Let's go back to camp and we can figure things out. We need to find a way out of here."

"I keep telling you," he said. "There's no way out of here."

His fingers crawled, reaching her neck.

She slapped them away, slamming the notebook into Clay's stomach, hard. She tore through the forest, her feet kicking up a confetti of leaf litter. Clay stomped after her. The mud squelched beneath his boots. A low growl rumbled from deep inside him, vibrating up through his lungs and between each of his clenched teeth.

Ahead, Sylvia darted, nimble as a rabbit, deeper into the trees. In her panic she ran blindly, away from camp, away from the only other living humans in these woods who could hear her if she screamed, if she made any noise other than huffs of exertion, a steady staccato beat beneath Clay's snarling.

The hunger of that place rumbled beneath the soil, rocking

the earth under her feet, and it pushed a vine up out of itself, a perfect hook for her boot. She tumbled, face slapping into muck, her forearm smashing into a sharp rock that erupted out of the ground at the moment of impact. Blood gushed down her skin. She rolled over, her other hand clutching the wound, slick already.

And then Clay was on top of her.

He hugged his thighs tight against her torso, spanning her from rib cage to pelvis. His hands wrapped around her neck, fingertips crushing the little bones of her spine, her thick tendons jumping against his palms. She writhed as if he were performing an exorcism, as if his hands were coated with holy water instead of stagnant sweat. Her blood-coated hand found his squeezing fingers, branding them bright red, too slippery to grip. Her hand slapped and slid, the blood splashing little iron freckles onto both of their faces. Her mouth opened, spat a hollow croak.

The hot fire filling Clay's entire body expanded in a sudden burst, and his fingers tightened around her neck. The rock crushing his chest released slowly, lifting away like a balloon, the harder he squeezed. Sylvia's eyes bulged from her sockets like a carnival toy. Her bloodied hand smacked against his face, leaving a near-perfect print, a final, futile gesture before the exorcism was complete, before she stopped squirming. The rag doll clamped inside Clay's hands went limp—still as the towering wall of granite behind them.

Clay could finally breathe. He sucked in deep lungfuls of oxygen. The tense ache in his muscles smoothed like melted butter. He sat back, his ass falling onto her knees.

Beneath him, Sylvia's mouth gaped, displaying a perfect row of bottom teeth. Her eyes bulged—glassy, useless marbles. A red spider bloomed on the skin of her throat—the imprint of his own hands. Her arms splayed at her sides like bird wings stripped of their feathers. Her hair was caked with mud.

Clay cocked his head like a puppy. His vision pulled into focus, the red haze subsiding as if drawn out of his veins by a syringe. It took several minutes before her body came into complete focus, before reality settled. As the anger rushed out of him, he turned meek.

He swiveled his head as he heard a crunching sound—had Dylan come to investigate? Had she seen what he'd done? He backtracked, checking behind nearby tree trunks in case she was hiding. He eventually caught sight of her back at camp, sitting next to Luke in the same spot he'd left her. If he perked his ears, he could even hear her voice. He thought he heard his name between garbled scraps of dialogue. No doubt she and Luke were talking shit.

She would ask after Sylvia. She might even leave Luke to go searching. It would be hard to miss that a fourth of the team had vanished.

The bottle of moonshine burned against his skin, tucked inside his waistband, and he took a deep glug, gathering strength for what he had to do.

He shoveled the litter of the forest onto Sylvia's body—leaves, twigs, wet slops of dirt he scooped up like ice cream and plopped on top of her. He piled whatever he could find until a mound of loam concealed Sylvia's body.

Clay had taken a single step back toward camp when his lips twitched, and the skin of his cheek was pulled beneath the web of Sylvia's dried, caked blood.

"Fuck," he whispered.

He ripped a square of jersey from his T-shirt and knelt by the creek, using the soaked cloth to wipe his face and hands, rubbing the red around. In the glass of his phone, he checked whether he'd rubbed enough of the blood away to disguise it as rosy exertion.

As he approached the campsite, the whispers about him grew louder. The words twisted, smudged and elongated, pulled like taffy. When he stepped out from the trees, standing behind the tents, the comments overlapped, stacked on top of one another until he slapped his hands over his ears. Then the silence of the valley resumed.

Luke, as usual, stared off into the trees, his eyes as glossy and empty as the ones Clay had just covered with two waxy leaves. Dylan's head pointed in the opposite direction, toward the wall.

Behind him, while he folded the bloody square into his pocket and padded back into camp, the ground beneath Sylvia's body roiled like tumultuous waves, ravenous, already picking the flesh from her bones like fried chicken, sucking it down into the rancid earth. It gobbled at her, shredding the meat, slurping her splashing blood. The knobby bones of her spine gleamed, now exposed.

Below, the earth continued its feast.

MARCH 12, 2019
1:05 P.M.

"Where's Sylvia?" Dylan asked, her heart sinking.

Clay stepped out from between the trees—alone—a dry twig crunching under his boot.

"Is he okay?" he responded, nodding toward Luke.

"Keeps going in and out. It's happening a little more frequently. He fucked up his bandage—oh, shit," she said, pulling his free hand away from it again. Fresh blood flicked off of his nail. "He won't stop scratching at it. I was hoping Sylvia would know what to do. Where is she?"

"He looks bad," Clay said.

And he did. Even in the past two hours, the swollen discoloration had crawled farther up his leg, now more than halfway to his knee. Dylan stared at it, holding her breath, trying to catch it expanding. The compromised bandage on his arm lapped up blood. Dylan's knuckles were white from trying to keep his wagging finger away.

"Yes, he does. I fucking know," she said, her chest suddenly heavy and burning. Luke's hand slithered out of hers, and she snatched it again before it reached its destination. "That's why I need to talk to Sylvia. Because she's the only one with any medical training in this group."

"It seemed like he was doing okay earlier."

"He seemed okay a little while ago. He stopped scratching, but maybe twenty or thirty minutes ago, he picked it back up. And he's been out of it since then."

Luke seemed totally oblivious that they were talking about him, right in front of him.

"Where is she?" Dylan demanded. Her anxious leg bounced underneath her.

Clay did not respond.

"You walked off into the woods together. Where did she go? What happened?"

His shoulders tensed up to his ears, like they were being pulled by marionette strings. He stared off in the direction where they had disappeared. Why was he being so cagey?

A pit opened up in Dylan's stomach. She hadn't liked the thought of Sylvia and Clay going off alone. Something inside her coiled and knotted, a tangled skein of doom, when they moved out of sight. She wished she could have gone too, but someone had to stay with Luke. Still, she never imagined that anything more than a screaming match might happen. But now Sylvia was gone.

"We were talking about the research and then we started talking about the GPS," Clay said. "She accused me of breaking it on purpose and dropping it when I went out alone. She said she was going to go try to get help. She left to try to get back to the car."

"That doesn't seem like her," Dylan replied. "Leaving without a plan?"

"I tried to stop her," he stammered. "I told her she'd get lost without a GPS, but she said she was going to just keep walking until she got a cell signal."

"How did you get so dirty?"

His head dropped as if this, too, were a mystery, his hands nearly gloved with Kentucky clay. Dark circles stained the knees of his jeans. Something congealed sat at the receding line of his hair.

"I tried to run after her, to stop her," he replied. "But—uh—I tripped on a vine and fell."

"Are you okay? Is that blood on your shirt?"

Sweat dotted his face. A bead ran down, cutting through the rusty dirt on his cheek. Dylan squinted at him, pulled her lips into her mouth to chew on them. He was acting weird. She'd known him for years, and he'd never acted like this before, never been this nervous to tell her something. The gaps between his replies made her think he was lying. So where was Sylvia?

Dylan rewound the past hour of her memory. Had she heard anything that could have been screaming, mistaken for something else? That space in her mind was filled with stock-still silence. Not even the sound of Clay and Sylvia stamping through the brush had dented her recollection—just calm, suffocating, strangling silence.

"Oh, uh," Clay said, his chin to his chest, studying the splatters and streaks on his shirt before scanning his hands as if they had at that moment sprouted from his wrists. "I guess I must have cut myself at some point and not noticed. Probably when I fell."

The woods behind the curve of the rock seemed to shiver. What had Clay done? What was he hiding? Her sanity did not want to put the pieces together, to trek into the woods and uncover what she might find, to believe her longtime friend was capable of something so terrible. And she couldn't leave Luke alone with Clay or get lost herself.

Dylan's fingers found the hilt of the knife in her pocket. Would she be able to use it if she needed to? And if she stood, would she be able to resist the pull of the wall? Or would she climb to the top, teetering on shaking hands and feet, before she snapped out of the haze?

She didn't know what to think. She rubbed her temple, another headache forming.

Luke's wagging finger moved right back into place, like a magnet. Dylan feared he would eventually tear long, noodle-y strands of muscle and tendons away from the twin bones of his forearm if left to his own devices. This time Clay pulled Luke's hand away, stooping between them, and Dylan could smell the rotten, stagnant stank of Clay's sweat, with a metallic scent stirred in. She swallowed the acid burning up her throat as Clay sat across from them.

Dylan needed to stay calm. Wait until she had all the facts and figures. Maybe he was telling the truth, even if it sounded ludicrous. He'd never lied to her before. Maybe he was simply nervous on Sylvia's behalf.

A silhouette seemed to move through the trees, just far enough away that it could be their missing friend, but it vanished into the deeper woods. It could be a deer. It could be nothing at all.

For the rest of the day, they played a demented version of house around the campfire, Clay straightening up the campsite and

Dylan tending to Luke. She rested one hand on the knife in her pocket, the smooth metal calming—regulating her pulse, though she couldn't say why it settled her. The hilt grew slick in her palm.

Nobody mentioned Sylvia again, as if it had always been just the three of them who trekked down into the valley. Dylan and Clay hardly spoke, and Luke was too far gone for words at this point. The snaps of the fire, like cracking bones, were sound enough.

When the sky darkened and the air bit through any warmth the fire might have provided, Dylan led Luke to their tent. In the slow, hobbling journey there, she craned her head back toward Clay, a vision of fireballs dancing in her head, a worry that he might be too scatterbrained to put the fire out when he went to bed and it would crawl to the trees. Another fear wormed in: that he might spread it himself, starting with their tent, melted polyester raining down and gluing to their faces.

Inside the tent she pulled a thick woolen sock over Luke's curious fingers and then roped it against his chest, both arms now bound as if in a straitjacket. His forefinger continued to twitch underneath the thick fabric, a blood-seeking missile.

She hardly slept. Her muscles remained taut, tense knots. Any time she dozed, she dreamed, sharp and clear, of a faceless figure. Unzipping the tent. Killing her, each instance different: strangling her with the coils of the dirty, broken rope; prying the knife from her sleep-dumb fingers and plunging the short blade into her chest or stomach or neck; pressing a balled-up North Face jacket over her gawping mouth. And while the figure did his slaying, Luke sat, staring directly at nothing, drool pooling at the hinge of his jaw.

Luke whispered all night, rocking in the same position for

hours, his quiet muttering punctuated by the occasional louder whimper. If it had not been for the unusual stark silence, the normal sounds of the forest would have drowned him out. But there were no owls hooting in this place, no whistling wind, no night-time crickets. And so, the moments when Luke went statue-still, even his fingers stiff, and held his breath as if a predator were just outside the fabric barrier became even more jarring. Dylan's breath caught in her throat. Her skin prickled and itched as if thousands of centipedes were crawling across every inch of it.

The pair shared that insomniac, claustrophobic space for hours upon hours, nothing more than the thin sheet of tent barricading them from the horrors of the woods, the things Dylan could only imagine but, somehow, it seemed Luke knew intimately.

Only when the sun filtered through the polyester, the tent glowing orange like a lantern—morning at last—did Luke relax his shoulders.

As if all the creepy crawly terrible things disappeared with the dawn—for a little while.

MARCH 13, 2019

7:37 A.M.

Clay's eyes were tinted red around the iris. He fiddled with a book of matches at the firepit, sliding his bottle out of view as the others exited their tent. Three little matches sat in the dirt at his feet, spent, their heads blackened dust. Dylan pulled out a little pin from the hilt of her knife, struck it, and sparked a fire in the dry kindling he'd collected.

"Where did you find water?" she asked, nearly tripping over the full kettle. She helped Luke sit.

Clay motioned behind him. "There's a creek. Didn't you see it when we came in?"

"Yeah, but—did you bring a water filter?"

"Won't boiling it kill any bacteria?"

"I guess," she said. "I don't know what that weird red shit in it is though. We could see if—"

"See if what?"

"I was going to say, we could see if Sylvia knew, but she's gone. I hope she's okay."

"Me too. There's a little bit of coffee left," he said, an olive branch.

"I'll take some," Luke said. Mornings seemed to be when he was at his most lucid.

"I found it in my backpack this morning," Clay continued. "It was in some canister I had forgotten about. It might be old."

"I'm sure it will taste amazing," Dylan said, the fire jumping, lapping up oak. But her tone did not match her words.

Sylvia's empty tent and her pack sat between his tent and Dylan's like a blemish. Clay tried to forget her, but his body was a reminder of what he'd done—the tendons and muscles in his fingers screamed from overuse.

Deep silence permeated the camp, broken only by the low gurgling of water dancing in the kettle and Luke's fingernails against cotton, followed by the scratchy noise of dry grounds dropping into a tin cup and the hiss of hot water.

"We need to find food," Dylan said.

"We need to leave," Clay responded.

"We can't leave," Dylan said. "Luke can't leave. He can barely walk."

The gangrene bruise now licked at Luke's kneecap, his foot a ball too swollen for his shoes, stretching the limits even of his dirty sock.

"Besides, weren't you saying yesterday that we *can't* leave?" Dylan continued.

"I was just freaked out yesterday," Clay replied. "That's ridiculous. Of course there's a way to leave." He knew this wasn't true, but he didn't want to believe it.

"Do you know anything about foraging?" he asked Dylan.

"Only a little," she said, blowing on the hot coffee. "I know some things to avoid, but we'll have to be careful. I think Sylvia said there was a lot of weird stuff. A lot of poisonous stuff."

"Luke, will you be okay by yourself?" Clay asked.

"I should be," he said. "Don't stray too far."

———————

After they gulped their coffee—a bitter, hot pill—and left the grounds in the cups to reuse, Clay led Dylan into the trees, toward the creek and away from the corpse he'd buried yesterday. He cleared Sylvia from his mind, wiped away the red welts he'd left on her neck, her bulging eyes. He focused on the cold air against his throat, on his breath pooling in translucent clouds. They brushed the dead debris of the forest floor away with their toes, hoping to uncover some new growth, something green. Something edible, something they recognized.

Poking out from beneath a log were more of the false fungus toes, purple-gray and sporting black toenails, and for a moment Clay's organs spasmed and clenched, and he panicked, thinking he'd gotten turned around and brought Dylan right to Sylvia's grave. He kicked them. They popped away from the log, soft and spongy as if rotten.

"There's something over here," Dylan said. She was crouching by a small bush with dark, reddish-purple berries. "These could be poison. I don't know what they are."

"It's all we've found. We can figure it out later."

They plucked them and filled a pocket of the backpack, the juiciest popping like pimples, spilling sticky, dark tar onto their fingers.

After the bush stood naked, they padded farther into the woods. Every few steps, Dylan stuck her hand in her pocket, the one she'd slipped her knife into before they left camp.

She had to know. She had to be planning something. He'd

need to keep an eye on her. Clay snuck a sip of moonshine from the bottle while her back was turned.

A patch of dandelions poked their heads out from the brush. The soft yellow petals stuck to the berry pulp coating their fingers, feathers on tar. They squirreled each decapitated flower head into the backpack. The forest bore other bounty: a mulberry tree with hard, white berries; a squirrel's nest of acorns; early violets and clover. Still, they'd only found a small meal's worth for three grown adults.

They pressed even farther into the woods, straying from Luke, who could have pulled his arm off in the hour or so they'd been searching, who could have cooked his own leg in the fire while he contemplated the fucking forest. The trees duplicated again, like a computerized glitch, and the yellow dandelion head Clay had just plucked reappeared on its neck. Clay's body had finally acclimated to the dizzying effect, the alcohol making everything blurry at the edges, his head no longer fighting it with a migraine. Now he was simply grateful for the regenerating food source.

A shrill, sustained screech bounced between the silent trunks.

"I think that's Luke," Dylan said, a bouquet of violet and gold spilling from her palm. She bolted in the direction of the scream.

Clay followed after her, stooping to retrieve the flowers first. They'd need all the food they could gather.

———————

Clay approached the campsite. Though the scream had died, Luke's mouth was still wide open. He sat stock-still, eyes round and bulging. Like Sylvia's had been after Clay squeezed.

The prying hand was tangled in the stretch of rope Dylan had used to tie it up the previous night. The blue cord looped around his wrist, cutting off the circulation to his hand. It sliced a sharp line into the space where his neck met his shoulder, and Dylan rushed to rescue him from the web, brandishing her knife.

For a brief moment, Clay wondered if they should just put him out of his misery. Let the rope do the work. Or the knife.

Clay uncorked the bottle. A sharp, acetone scent escaped the neck.

"Fuck this place," he said. He sipped, recorked, holstered the bottle once more.

Once blood returned to Luke's pale fingers, Clay and Dylan spread out their foraged haul on a small tarp meant to keep the rope clean. They formed little neat rows, surveying the small bounty. The berries, bruised, leaked their sticky juice. It made the gummy energy bars they had run out of look like a fucking four course meal.

"How do we eat this stuff?" Clay asked.

"I don't know," Dylan said. "I've heard of dandelion tea, but I'm not sure if you blanch it or just steep it or whether we can eat any of it raw. I really wish Sylvia hadn't run off. We could have used her plant knowledge."

"I guess we don't have a choice," Clay said, and, as if following a stage cue, his stomach growled, the acid bubbling inside of him, begging for something to digest.

"I haven't eaten much more than a few bites of a Clif bar in almost a day," Dylan said.

"This trip really went to shit."

They chewed bitter dandelion greens, raw. They steamed clovers, crushed the unripe mulberries into a tart paste. More boiled creek water, strained through the densest fabric in their packs, soaked into the used coffee grounds. They saved the bright dandelion heads for tea, waiting for the moment when the coffee grounds could expend no more flavor.

While Dylan tipped the mashed mulberries into Luke's mouth, the white paste dripping like rabid foam, Clay tipped the neck of the moonshine bottle over his mug. The clear liquid glugged into the coffee, some sort of oily film swimming at the surface.

He never wondered how the bottle continued to spill liquor into his cup when it should have long ago been emptied, even of the dregs.

FALL 1924

The brothers planted the corn in straight rows, dropping each little kernel into the soil, dark and fertile and wet. Throughout the summer, they'd sneak into the clearing in the woods by the edge of their farms to chart the growth, yanking out weeds with grime-streaked hands, thinning out the stalks so each one could suck enough nutrients from the soil, could bleed it dry.

In the early August heat, they carefully peeled back the green husks. Red seeped into the white of the kernels—but they were not ready yet. The heirloom bloody butcher could only come off the stalks when the color had pervaded each little knob, the whole ear a dark red.

So the pair didn't notice that the hue was slightly too dark when they clipped them a couple of weeks later, that each little tooth of a kernel was a little too soft.

The harvest took three days of stolen time—spare moments while the sun rose or when their wives would cook dinner. When the older brother twisted off one of the final ears, it popped in his hands. Beneath the husk ran the juices—a deep, staining redness thick as tar. It smelled rotten, and he chucked it away into the forest—not all of the harvest could be perfect or good.

They ground the corn by hand, heated it with malt and yeast, put it through the copper coils of their still, hidden in that valley in the woods, until it ran clear on the other end. The white dog funneled into the green glass. They corked the bottles and sold them, returning to the bare stalks in the woods to stash the cash and celebrate with their own bottle. When they uncorked it, the sharp scent pierced their nostrils, and they toasted to a job well done and sucked it back. A fiery ball followed a line inside each of them, scorching their tongues, their esophaguses, dropping into their stomachs, sizzling the acid there.

They sipped. The warming burn edged into their muscles, wormed its way up to their eyes. The gray haze that swelled at the corners of their sight they took for sleepiness. The more they drank, stealing sips in their morning coffee, great glugs before stuffing themselves between starched sheets at night, the more the bottle beckoned.

But their stock was thinning.

Soon they were down to the last bottle.

In the last moments, when their vision went entirely dark and their eyes burned as if boiling in their skulls, their tongues remained parched. They reached for the bottle at the same time, for the final dregs. His throat yearning, the younger brandished a knife and plunged it into the flesh of his brother, feeling the resistance of skin and bone until his prize was won.

He took a deep gulp from the bottom, choking down the last drops, before he scratched his eyes out with his own dirt-lined nails.

MARCH 13, 2019
11:57 A.M.

The valley swayed in front of Clay, as if the log he sat on were floating in a vast ocean. The edges of his vision were coated in gray.

"My leg hurts," Luke moaned. "Is there any more aspirin?"

The bandages wrapped around his foot seemed ready to snap, like a rubber band ball. The cuff of his pant leg clamped around his skin, seemingly extruding the swollen, engorged flesh, so tight Dylan couldn't get a single finger between the fabric and skin to roll it up. She pulled out her knife.

"Luke," she said, "I need to cut off your pant leg. Your leg is too swollen. I need you to be still while I do this so I don't accidentally hurt you. Ready?"

"Yes," he said. His face drained of blood, pale as a corpse.

She flipped open the blade and went to work. At the first scratch of the cutting edge, the fabric exploded, like a cattail spilling its seed. Dylan peeled the fabric back, inch by inch, uncovering the extent of the damage, a reality Clay's stomach could have lived without. For a moment, Clay thought the blade was covered in yellowy pus, as if Dylan had sliced through skin.

Purple covered Luke's ankle and calf, the skin stretched and shiny, bloated and stinking. Dylan continued cutting while Clay gagged, thinking he might vomit. She continued to uncover more purple until it petered out just a few inches over his kneecap, where his veins stood out like Sharpie lines, little highways pushing out of the rotten forest.

"Oh my god," she said.

Clay gagged and slapped his hand over his mouth.

An unchewed bit of wilted, slimy clover plopped onto the swollen skin from Luke's gaping jaw. The gauze on his arm glistened, wet with fresh blood. His finger tapped between the layers, a frantic pace as if he were sending out a message with Morse code. His teeth chattered around the rest of the mushy greens in his mouth.

"Luke?" Dylan waved her fingers in front of his face, his eyes blinking back to her. "Do you see something?"

"Huh?"

"How does your leg feel now?"

"Better. Cold."

"Did you pack any loose pants?"

"I think so."

She left to ransack their tent, leaving Clay alone with Luke, whose eyes darted across the line of trees. Clay slipped the bottle from his waistband and took a deep glug. He couldn't get through this sober. The alcohol scorched his tongue and sloshed down to his stomach, spreading warmth through his body. Even the soreness in his hands was gone, yesterday's activity a blur.

He took one more sip before holstering the bottle. The hazy halo at the periphery of his vision expanded.

Dylan stepped out of her tent, her foot squelching in the mud.

"Clay!" she called. "Come here!"

"What is it?" he said, stumbling to the tent as if his legs had fallen asleep.

"Did you do that?"

"Do what?"

"That," she said, pointing.

She stood beside the flayed corpse of a squirrel. The skin of its belly unfolded from its putrid guts, a mess of slick, shiny purple and matte white bone, sharp corners edging the peeled skin as if someone had left in the middle of a high-school dissection. Precise, clean cuts. Something white sprouted at the edges of its fur. Clay leaned closer. They were little crystals of ice. *Defrosted* was the word that crossed the highways of his mind.

"What the fuck," he said, covering his mouth. The alcohol churned up with the dregs of stale coffee. "No, I didn't fucking do that. I've been with you guys this whole time."

"Someone did that," she said. "An animal didn't do that. It's too clean. And how is it iced? It's like it froze to death." It was the first animal they'd encountered since they had arrived—well, besides the flesh-eating dog and whatever Luke said he'd seen in the trees—and it had been pulled inside out.

"I don't fucking know," Clay muttered. "What do you think happened?"

"I don't know," she said, scanning the trees. "It didn't get this cold last night. We have to get out of here. What if there's someone else in the woods?"

"We can't get out of here," Clay said. Everything swayed, blurry. He focused on the zipper head at the top of Dylan's jacket, hoping it would ground him, would keep his stomach from remembering the squirrel guts on the ground.

"What do you mean?" she said. "Because the GPS is broken?"

"The GPS is *gone*. I just mean—we can't leave. We tried twice and just ended up back here both times."

"Well, Sylvia left, right? She went to go get help and didn't get looped back."

Clay didn't respond. He avoided her eyes, looking at his shoes.

"That's what you said yesterday, right?" Dylan prodded. "Sylvia ran off to get help?"

"I don't know, but—yeah, she ran away. To get help."

Dylan squinted, stuck her hand in her pocket.

The squirrel lay between them, and they stared at it as if it would spring to life and scurry away.

"Should we eat it?" Clay asked.

"I don't know," Dylan replied. "I guess—it's meat. Do you think it's rotten?"

Their answer arrived when they attempted to pick it up and bring it to the fire. Hands shielded by a trash bag, Clay wrapped his fingers around it, the flesh and guts cold and soft behind the thin plastic. It lifted all in one piece, a flat mass of congealed organs and sinew, as if it had been sitting in a freezer for an entire winter and then left to thaw. A round, purple organ plopped away from it into the dirt.

Dylan gagged. She swallowed it down, but Clay's disposition failed, and he dropped the thing and ran to the tree line to vomit, sputtering up foamy puke polka-dotted by clover and forest greens.

The bitter aftertaste of Clay's vomit coated his teeth, left a film across his tongue. He leaned and spat.

"I'd rather starve than eat that thing," he croaked.

"Are you okay?" Dylan asked behind him.

"Yeah, I'm fine," he replied, feeling another wave roiling in his stomach. "I'll be fine. You can go back and deal with Luke."

After she padded away, he pulled the bottle from his waistband. He swished the sharp corn liquor around his mouth, the harsh drink rinsing the vomit. He spat it out and took another swig, this one following his throat down to his empty stomach.

———————

On the edge of the campsite were more corpses. Clay had wandered away, no longer able to stand Luke, the way he'd stop midsentence to have a staring contest with thin air.

There were dark brown rats as big as Clay's foot with inch-long cuts across their necks, gummy with old blood. No, *frozen* blood. Thawing blood. Headless birds, feathers stuck inside the stumps of their necks. One had its wings extended, as if its head had simply evaporated midflight and its body had plummeted to the ground. Once, looking up into the canopy, he discovered two talons wrapped around a branch, attached to nothing.

The more he drank, the less these sights turned his stomach. They became a morbid curiosity. Was there some demented hunter running around the woods, dropping off things from a deep freezer? Dylan had been right, the slices and dices appeared too neat for an animal. And why would an animal leave its meal behind? Maybe there was a feral band of cats leaving one another gifts. But how had they been frozen? It made no sense. The alcohol sizzled at the back of his throat, and he coughed through the chuckle meeting it.

Maybe he wasn't wrong about the demented hunter—something was stalking him. Twigs snapped behind him, the sound echoing into the forest canopy. If he turned, the earth swaying with each movement, the sound turned with him, a delicate dance of prey and predator. The noise rang out, step by step, slicing through the thick silence.

"Fuck this," he said aloud, kicking a rat. Its body exploded in a cloud of sticky blood, gelatinous organs, and crunching bones. Into the trees he screamed, "Why not just kill me now? Get it over with!"

He positioned the bottle between himself and the sunlight. Half empty. He'd need more than the few shots left to get through this hell, and he kicked at the leaves, hoping to find another bottle hiding beneath the loam. He scanned for that familiar glint of sun on dirt-streaked glass, bringing the bottle to his lips over and over. The warmth of it spread through his cheeks, his nose an unfeeling knob at the end of his face.

By the time the sun dipped below the tree line and he stumbled back to camp, his face resembled a tomato, his eyes tinged with the juice. The blurring at the periphery of his vision edged in, consuming the foliage in a gray cloud.

"Where did you go?" Dylan asked, her hair a blurry haze around her face. Had it always looked like that?

"What?" he replied. "Where go?"

"Yeah, you just got up and went into the trees. Were you looking for something?"

"Am I not fucking allowed to get up?" he replied, heat rising into his cheeks. His feet tangled in the legs of the camping chair. "Wasn't looking. Found more fucking dead animals, though."

"What?" Every feature on her face warped, as if her skin was melting.

"Lots of 'em," he continued. His whole body itched, the

liquor sloshing like a roiling ocean in his stomach. All he wanted was to free the bottle, sitting hot and smooth against his skin, and drink. If he drank himself to death, it would be a mercy. "Same as the squirrel. All looked like they were carefully murdered, necks slit and shit, heads cut off. Frozen, too. Like some psycho playing pranks. Fucking with us."

"Do you think there's someone else here?" she asked. In the haze, her body doubled, vibrated across the fire. "Like, maybe some locals saw us come in and they've got cell phone disrupters or something and that's why our phones won't work? Maybe they destroyed all the food while we were sleeping. But how would we have not noticed them? And just—why?"

"Dunno." Clay hiccupped. "Why the fuck would someone else come here?"

"Are you drunk?"

"N-no," Clay replied, swallowing acidic bile.

"Did you bring bourbon or something?" Dylan asked. Her eyes moved too quickly inside her skull, the irises blurring as they bounced around, searching his hands and pockets for a flask.

"I'm not fucking drunk, okay?" Clay roared.

"Jesus, sorry."

She poured creek water through the fabric sieve and set the kettle over the embers to boil. Clay's ears perked for any sound, footsteps or rustling brush or villainous laughter, the whizz and whirr of some electronic gizmo that might explain why their phones wouldn't work.

Clay knew these things did not exist. There was no blocker device, no pranking teenagers hiding behind the thick trunks. That could not possibly explain how they were trapped, how they had moved in a straight line and ended right back where they began, how the trees reproduced into a pixelated distortion like badly rendered CGI the farther they went into the woods. Still, he listened, hoping logic would override what they'd witnessed with their own eyes.

Dylan dropped the decapitated heads of the dandelions into the tin mugs, the coffee old and spent. The flowers swirled in the water. Clay didn't have the stomach to drink the tea—it looked exactly like piss, and smelled like it, too, had the pisser eaten a fuck ton of asparagus. Dylan took a few tepid sips of hers, but spat it out. They ate more of the bitter greens.

They did precisely nothing of use while the sun pooled above them, moving across the sky. Dylan tried to calm Luke, pulled his twitching hand away from his bloody arm a hundred more times. Clay closed his eyes, dropped his head into his hands. The earth moved around him. He was adrift.

——— —— ——

When the sun started to dip below the trees, Clay's stupor finally faded, the cold spring air again nibbling at his face, his nose regaining feeling. For the second time that day, the acid in his stomach churned, boiled up through his esophagus and into his mouth. He bolted. He made it fewer than ten long steps from his seat before bright greens spewed from between his lips, and he hunched in place to spit out the rest. When he brought the still-half-full bottle to his lips to cleanse his mouth this time, he didn't bother trying to hide it.

When he lifted his head, wiping away spittle with the back of his wrist, his mouth dropped open.

In the dimming light the woman from the trail stood just beyond the first row of trees. Staring. Clay's knees buckled and he fell back onto his ass, his jeans soaking up the mud.

"Oh, fuck," he said, cradling his head in his hands, shutting his eyes tight. "No, this is not happening. It's not real. You're just drunk."

He listened for the inevitable approaching footsteps, the ones that would snap branches before snapping bones, breaking off his arm as if it were dry and brittle as a limb on a dead tree and throwing it to the ground to feed her dog. The silence extended for one single eternity. When he finally opened his eyes, the sun hung just over the tower of rock, a late afternoon wink before the sky would purple. The woman stood there still. Had she moved closer? It was as though the earth had shifted, had pulled the trees closer to where he sat, had folded a piece in on itself. The woman did not blink. Her face gazed back at him in clear focus, the trees around her blurry, a halo of nothing beyond their fuzzy leaves.

Her lips were raw and chapped, but clean. Red freckles spread across her face, the tiniest pinpricks dotting the bridge of her nose and growing larger and longer as they reached her chin. He followed the clear line of blood to her shoulder, where a long wooden hilt hovered, a hatchet blade buried deep in her collar. A waterfall of blood gushed around it, looping like a GIF. Her lips spread, cracking with new blood, revealing yellow, mossy teeth. She smiled with those teeth while she pulled the blade from her shoulder, her left arm shifting down, nearly severing from her body in the act.

"What the fuck, what the fuck," he whispered.

Clay's transfixion ended the moment she took her first step in his direction. Only then did his feet pedal against the wet ground, his hands scrambling. He managed to get to his feet and screeched all the way back to camp, more bile rising in his throat.

"What's going on?" Dylan asked, eyes wide with alarm. She held Luke's hand—the one with the forever wagging finger.

"Do you see her?" Clay asked, gulping air and forming words around heaving breaths. "Is she following me?"

Hands on his knees, he craned his head around, peering behind him but also above and below his body, as if the woman might have gained the power of flight or dug a tunnel beneath him. He tensed the muscles in his legs, ready to run.

"See who?" Dylan replied, standing and dropping Luke's hand. "Did you see someone?"

"That woman," he said. He sucked in air. She didn't appear to have followed, to have left the comfort of the trees. He could no longer see her. "The one I saw on the trail. She had a hatchet. In her shoulder."

"A hatchet?" Dylan asked. "Are you okay?"

"You can see her?" Luke asked.

"What the fuck are you guys talking about?" Dylan said. From her pocket, she removed her knife and unfolded the tiny, two-inch blade. She pressed her other hand against her gurgling stomach and stared, as if waiting for the hatchet-wielding woman to appear out of thin air between the trees. But nothing happened.

While they waited, poised for battle, all of their energy pointed toward the tree line, Luke screamed. The harsh sound pricked Clay's eardrums and left a static hum in its wake. He and Dylan jumped, turning their feet toward the unmistakable vision that had made Luke shriek: a dinner party in the trees, a whole host of mismatched characters staring back at them.

There was a man with a clipped mustache in a singed,

slate-gray uniform dotted with medals and gleaming, golden-threaded star patches. Others in similar garb stood behind him, holding old rifles with blades at the powder-streaked tips, round spots of melted flesh on their faces. The woman with her hatchet and severed, spurting arm stood next to a man also splattered with blood, his hands sized perfectly for the hilt of her blade. Two men hoisted bottles identical to the one burning into Clay's hip, raising them in a toast, deep holes where their eyes should have been. A group of teens with torn and tattered neon windbreakers leered at them.

Clay staggered back, knocking his shoulder into Dylan, who stood with her knife out in front of her, a pitiful warning. Luke's mouth maintained the shape of his scream, but no more air escaped.

"Fuck," Clay said. "Fuck, fuck, fuck, what the fuck is that?"

The party in the trees stood around a long table, empty plates and glassware in front of each guest. *Was there always that gap in the trees?* Clay wondered. He focused on the geometry of the table, all of the joints and lathe work that must have gone into its construction, as if studying it closely enough would cause it to fade away. It seemed like it was built to fit exactly into that gap in the trees while somehow not fitting at all. When he stared at one corner to study the joinery, the opposing corners faded, became translucent, tree trunks poking straight through the smooth cherry top. The illusion only ever faltered at the corner of his sight, where the gray nothingness crept in farther and farther, leaving him with only a pinhole by which to see.

But every speck of his will-powered focus could not blur or mask the oozing smiles the dinner party suddenly revealed, sharp teeth dripping with saliva.

Or was it blood?

His body tried to run once more. With her free hand, Dylan caught his arm, her strong climbing fingers pinching his skin in a vise, and his body twisted until his ass ate mud.

"You can see them too?" Luke asked.

"The fuckin' spooky dinner party?" Clay blurted. "Fuck yes."

"Yes, we can see them," Dylan said, her voice quavering.

"So it's not just in my head," Luke replied.

The dinner party remained standing, hungry-eyed but still as statues until one of them, the man in the slate gray, fingered a knife on the table. Considering it. The three living campers stood stock-still, vibrating with goosebumps. A standoff.

"I thought I was just imagining all of this," Luke whispered. "I thought I was just going crazy. I couldn't speak when I was looking at them."

"What the fuck do we do?" Clay asked, so low he could hardly even hear himself.

As if in answer, the dinner party picked up their utensils, ready to eat.

MARCH 13, 2019

6:02 P.M.

The short, clean blade shivered in Dylan's hand.

In the trees, the party didn't move. Though they gripped their rusty knives and bent forks, they did not come rushing to secure their meal. Instead, they kept their yellow smiles pasted to their faces, teeth bared like cornered dogs, and stepped backward into the darkening shade of the trees. Disappearing one by one.

Sweat slicked across the hilt of Dylan's knife, and even if she'd had the opportunity to swipe it at one of the deadly intruders, she'd more than likely drop it. She switched it to her other hand, releasing Clay, and wiped the sweat onto her pants. This time, Clay stayed put, frozen in place as if movement was how the people in the trees tracked them. He muttered something under his breath.

The sky turned a bright red, the sun having sunk behind the tower of rock an hour before. Darkness crept into the spaces between the trees, breeding shadows there, the valley like a bowl holding the last of the light. Behind the campers, the fire crackled, breaking a huge log in half, spitting orange and red sparks that tickled the back of Dylan's elbows, the crunching carbon the only sound besides their shallow breath. In the accumulating shadows, she saw flashing glints. Eyes? Teeth? Her crazed imagination?

Dylan stood poised and waiting for a surprise attack of sharp nails and teeth and rusty blades digging into her flesh, too many all at once, her knife knocked from her hand. She switched hands again, wiping away new sweat. Her arms raised goosebumps as if anticipating the gray hands that would clutch them and pull her backward, her feet scraping through the mud as she disappeared into the forest. Her ears perked for crunching leaves, rustling brush, growling—anything beyond her own ragged breathing. But the woods remained still.

Another crack in the firepit behind them shot a flash of heat against her back. Sweat dewed on the nape of her neck. Luke was the first to move, to pivot his head toward the fire. Dylan's and Clay's shoulders unhitched, and they, too, relieved their backs of the heat.

Before them, the fire had spread. Around the firepit, a ring of flames burned a clean circle on the ground. This was no random sizzle. Flames, high as their knees, licked around the ring—as if one of the people in the trees had poured kerosene beneath it.

"Holy shit," Clay said. "What the fuck?"

"We need to leave," Dylan whispered. The flaming ring had to be connected—somehow—to the people in the trees. She scanned for an exit. "We need to get away from the fire. It's going to spread. We have to go into the woods."

She wasn't sure which would be worse—being burned alive or being devoured by ghosts. But the fire was more pressing; she'd deal with the ghosts when they attacked. If they were even real.

"We can't fucking leave," Clay replied. "There's no way to

leave."

"We have to try. Help me with Luke."

They each took a side and lugged Luke, moving slow, toward the trees, toward the spot they remembered entering from. The sky had already shifted, too quick, to purple and then a deep, starless, moonless navy. The tiny dot of Dylan's flashlight—a cheap thing built into the end of her pocketknife—poked a pinhole into the dark curtain behind the trees, their bark slick with sap. Reflected flames danced inside the sticky sweetness. Then flames stopped licking and started biting, the ring blurring at the edges as it began to spread.

"We're going to die here," Luke said.

No one responded to this truth.

Dylan and Clay filled the space between the trees with grunts and curses, the party stopping every other minute to suck in oxygen and shake out their tense, knotted limbs. With every five-legged step, their monstrous silhouette nearly toppled, thorny vines clipping boots, saplings thumping into shins, Luke's bulbous leg catching around a skinny trunk, forcing all of them to pivot and shift. The stink of the rotten meat ballooning beneath his skin pierced Dylan's nostrils, eating through the rank sweat puddling beneath their arms and their bitter dandelion breath. When Luke placed weight on his good foot, Dylan prayed to God or Satan or whatever force remained in this hellish place that it would land, solid, and that that ankle wouldn't bend and twist and snap too. Dylan's stomach boiled inside her, the exertion gobbling the foraged meal, percolating up.

She dropped her portion of Luke's weight and vomited. She heaved empty air and fell, her feet sliding in the barf. What the fuck were they doing? They couldn't outrun the flames, not with

Luke to carry. Even now, the growing wall of heat behind them singed the tiny hairs on her exposed skin. For a split second, she considered running into the flames, letting them consume her. Put her out of her misery.

"We're moving too slow," Clay said, breaking her spiral of despair.

"I'll scout ahead," Dylan said, spitting into the dirt. She scraped her dirty boot against a tree, a trail marker of her own slime. "I'll see if I can find the car or a road or something."

"Or a trail," Clay whispered, just loud enough for her ears.

"I don't think we should split up," Luke replied.

"I don't think so either," Clay said. "It's never helped us before. Plus, you've got the only flashlight. We'd be completely in the dark."

"I won't go too far," she said. "I'll move just a little bit farther ahead than you guys. If I see anything, I can warn you and we can turn around."

Dylan strode ahead. The flashlight on the end of her knife neared pointlessness, illuminating half of a leaf or one miniscule knot on a tree. She swung it side to side, the circle slicing through the forest. The monsters could appear at any moment, sudden and close.

She cursed herself for not taking three extra seconds to grab the big flashlight from their tent. Behind her, Clay and Luke trudged along—two steps, one hop, repeat—still slow as hell. If the ghostly party did track by sound, they were surely goners. While Dylan's feet landed soft, her companions crashed through the brush, grinding out curses under their breath and cracking twigs—doing everything short of shouting, "We're over here, come and get us!"

Clay and Luke kicked up so much noise and commotion that she almost missed it—the moment one swing of her flashlight caught the ghosts' hungry, dark-eyed faces, the pendulum swinging away again before the image registered, imprinting on her brain. She forgot to breathe. When she scanned back, trying to catch them in the light again, they had disappeared.

"Fuck," she said, sweat pouring out of her palms again. She shook the beam wildly, trying to form a composite picture, trying to catch the path of the ghostly figures.

"We need to go a different way!" she yelled, her breath returning, ragged and shallow.

When she turned back toward Clay and Luke, the swinging light caught on metal, a glint of a wire. Whatever it was was half buried in a deep hollow. She carefully picked her way down the short incline and plucked the thing out of the mud.

Her breath caught in her throat. It was a spiral notebook. Sylvia's notebook. She flipped it open. Every page was filled, the ink running, the paper stained with mud. What was it doing out here? Had Sylvia dropped it on her way out of the forest? Something wasn't right.

Transfixed by the notebook in her hands, she crashed right into an obstacle—like a log but too soft—and her feet twisted below her. She toppled over it, her feet up in the air.

Her knife slipped out of her hand, the blade somehow unfolding, stabbing leaves and brush and not her own skin, thank fuck. The barrel of light connected to it illuminated waves of leaves as it rolled away, before finally settling on a white leather shoe, the toe box sticking up, inches from her face. The heel disappeared into a low mound of loam.

Everything moved in slow motion as Dylan wrapped her

fingers around the still-wet hilt, rolling her knees beneath her and crouching into a low, scrunched ball.

Luke and Clay still toiled behind her, Clay's question hanging in the air: "Did you say something?"

The light at the end of her blade snaked up the mound. With a shaking hand, Dylan pushed away the detritus. Beyond the shoe was a too-thin leg encased in denim, connecting to a T-shirt that nearly lay flat. The tiny beam could not illuminate everything at once, so Dylan patched this corpse together like a puzzle, her flashlight providing a single piece at a time: a deep bloodstain on a cotton sock; a gold rivet set into denim; a gaunt cheek caving into the skeleton, dotted with pale freckles. Wide, glassy eyes had deflated into their sockets, one still pointing up toward the bony tree canopy, the iris of the other pointing right at her. Dehydrated lips peeled back to reveal pearly teeth, even their roots exposed by receding gums, the pink gummy and hard like jerky. From the neck spurted blood, an endless stream of it, more than this husk of a person could possibly hold. A puddle formed beneath a neon windbreaker, too much for even the earth to swallow.

"What the fuck," she whispered. Her stomach churned.

She started to stand, to gather her weight onto her feet to bolt, but her hand hit more cold skin as she reached out to steady herself. She flung her beam around to reveal another dead person, blood flowing from their thin, desiccated wrists. The little orb of light rested on the teenager's palm. The creek of blood spilled down their hand, filling in the wrinkles, the lifeline etched across the skin. A leaf was stuck to the blood, like a little boat. Dylan stood, trying to ignore the hot wetness soaking into the knees of her pants, her bottom, her hands, every part of her that had touched ground.

An aborted scream caught in her throat. The light jumped around on the ground, revealing more and more bodies, five in total at the edges of the hollow, circling her like a barrier. Each one poured blood from their wrists or neck or the backs of their knees or the insides of their thighs, anywhere arteries ran close to the surface. Too much blood. Like a waterfall. Her boots splashed in it, the red that rose around her ankles like a flood, sputtering and spitting up bubbles, as if the earth itself were boiling.

As if it were sucking the blood down into itself, slurping and lapping.

The dinky light swung, searching for dry land, for a gap between the bodies she could crawl through. The beam scanned these unrecognizable bodies, the faces still youthful even with the skin pulled back against bone, all of them dressed in what looked like weird 1980s ski-lodge cosplay—a dead-and-breakfast club sprawled at her feet. A copper scent filled her nostrils, like she stood on a mound of pennies. Her pulse slapped at her wrist, along her neck, all those places from which their blood poured like a fountain, like the blood inside her ached to join in.

Still searching for an exit, Dylan waded as the puddle became a lake, the blood scalding as it tipped over the lip of her boots, soaking into her socks like hot oil sizzling around bacon. The moment she decided she had no choice but to crunch the corpses' forearms beneath her boots was the same moment the orb of her flashlight fell upon a sixth body. The scream vibrating inside of her did not come boiling out until the light pointed there, directly upon Sylvia's face.

Dylan wouldn't have recognized her except for the University of Kentucky sweatshirt hanging limply around her corpse. What remained of her skin was tinted a purplish green, putrid already, falling away from her bones like well-cooked ribs. Her hair spread like a halo behind her, dyed crimson with blood. Dylan scanned the flashlight beam down, stopping at the spot where her own shoe had knocked loose the flesh on Sylvia's calf as she fell, leaving a clear indentation beneath her friend's jeans.

Had Sylvia really gone missing just a day ago?

How the fuck was any of this possible?

A rotting stench, stark and acrid like a thousand overboiled eggs, rose from the bodies with sudden force, stirred into the bitter metallic scent of the lake of blood. Dylan retched, spitting clear bile into the still-rising pool. Now it reached halfway up her calf, wicking into the fibers of her pants, little tendrils of it climbing toward her knee. Her boots were like buckets, her socks like sponges. Blisters grew on the delicate skin of her feet, little welts filling with fluid as the hot blood cooked her. Even as the blood rushed in a fast current, threatening to topple her again, Dylan stayed frozen, her synapses firing blanks.

How could Sylvia's flesh have melted from her bones overnight?

Who were the other bodies?

What was this place?

Dylan kept her flashlight pointed at Sylvia, passing it over the length of what was left of her body. The underside had melted away from her skeleton, revealing a rib cage full of swelling, rotten organs before her body, too, was drowning in the blood that rose like a filling bathtub, the remaining green flesh on her front floating like an Ophelia who'd languished for months.

Only when the red covered the tip of Sylvia's freckled nose, only when it crested her own knees, did Dylan move. She waded through the roiling liquid, hot and thick. It was impossible to determine whether the snapping beneath her boots was stick or bone.

She reached the shore, her feet angled upward, and fought to escape. One foot bit into a chunk of soaked mud, sliding down and pulling her entire left leg with it. The blood lapped at her thigh as if fighting to pull her under, to do to her whatever it had done to Sylvia. She yelped, a shrill, piercing noise. With one final heave, her hands squishing wet earth, she pushed herself up and out, and rolled onto semihard ground.

The lake ebbed, receded out of the beam of her flashlight.

"What's going on?" Luke yelled, a faceless voice in the dark.

Dylan pivoted the light behind her, unable to stand. Clay and Luke shuffled toward her, breath extinguished from their lungs, legs and limbs fighting against the forest.

"She—" A sob snaked up her throat. Sweat mixed with tears. Suddenly her entire body ached. The blood in her clothes was already congealing, sticky like molasses.

"Are you okay?" Clay asked. "What happened? Did you get hurt—is that your blood?"

"I'm okay," she said, her throat sore, her voice husky, her tears flowing as freely as the blood had behind her. In her struggle, the blisters on her feet had popped and the blood still sloshing in her boots stuck sharp teeth into the raw polka dots of skin.

At the end of her blade, the flashlight faltered, flickered out. Darkness surrounded them; not even light from the fire burning through their campsite reached them any longer.

Had she pressed the button while shifting her grip? While trying to find a single dry patch of callused skin to hold on to it? She clicked it again and again. It stayed dead. The darkness pressed against her chest like a vise.

"What did you see?" Luke asked. "Are they ahead of us?"

"I saw—" she began. Sylvia's face floated before her again, hot blood collecting in the lashes of her wide-open eyes. She opened her blade and pointed it to where she thought Clay might be. "What the fuck did you do to her?"

"What are you talking about?" he replied. She shifted her aim toward his voice.

"You know what the fuck I'm talking about. Sylvia."

She clicked the button once more, pointing it toward the blood sauna. The orb finally appeared, faint and dim. But in its perfect circle was the remainder of Sylvia's face, streaks of red dripping away like sweat.

Clay's arms fell slack at his side. All of Luke's weight crumpled to the ground.

"Shit," Clay said.

EARLY SUMMER 1982

There was never anything to fucking do in Livingston—unless you could drive out of Livingston.

Mark and his friends had become intimate with the boredom. They'd been kicked out of the tiny grocery store for loitering, followed around the hardware store too closely to achieve mischief, and had never been let in the small, mom-and-pop boutique stores that lined Main Street—not that they'd want to peruse dusty racks of felt hats and moth-scented vintage clothes anyway. They were tired of watching MTV in dusty basements on corduroy-lined couches.

But there was one pocket of Livingston they hadn't explored, one place whose mention sent tickles across their skin, even now at age fifteen. The woods that stood behind Main. They'd heard countless ghost tales about them from older siblings, from childless and wifeless uncles, always punctuated by a chuckle. But there must be some kernel of truth in them—why else would their parents seem to squirm and change the subject if they asked about camping or hiking back there?

The same vague stories rattled around in their heads as they wrapped a case of beer in a blanket and strapped it to the back of Tom's bike, as they dropped their metal frames in a heap just inside the trees and hiked away from town: *You know the woods behind the post office? They're filled with ghosts, ones that want to eat little kids. You go in there, and you'll never come back the same. If you come back at all. One of my old high school buddies went in there, trying to catch a deer, thought it'd be a good place for hunting. When he came out, he'd lost his gun and his hair had turned white, and he never talked about what happened in there.*

But they were so fucking bored. So, fuck it, they trekked into the haunted woods to get drunk. Being scared would be better than being bored. It was the first weekend of summer vacation, and their moms were already tearing their hair out at their constant presence, shooing them outside and telling them to find something to do. They were just following directions.

They found a cozy little hollow among the trees and sat against trunks and on rotten logs. Sipping the bitter Bud, they exchanged ghost tales, as many as they knew, until they ran out.

"This sucks," Mark said. He drained his can, crumpling it beneath his shoe like a squashed beetle, and kicked it into the trees to rust. The early June sun had finally set behind the trees, the air a humid fog. "There's nothing in these woods but bugs."

"Maybe the ghosts need to be called," Jimmy said, tossing his empty onto the ground. "Like a séance. Maybe they don't just show up all the time."

"A séance?" Susie asked. She and Tom exchanged looks in the same obvious way they'd exchanged saliva behind the school during homeroom. They hadn't signed up for actually conjuring ghosts. They'd just wanted to drink and sneak away to make out in the dark, carve their initials into a tree. Tom's knife had become sticky with dark sap.

"Hell yeah," Julia said. "Let's do it."

"We don't have anything to do it with," Mark said. "Don't you need a Ouija board or something?"

"We have this," Jimmy said, clicking on the gas lantern. "You just need fire, right?"

"Come on, guys," Susie said. "Let's not."

"It's not like it's real or anything," Jimmy said. Then, in a spooky voice, he intoned: "We call upon the spirits that reside in the forest. If you can hear us, give us a sign."

The group tensed, tuning their ears to any sudden noise, any hushed whispers that might float through the trees. Clouds descended, obscuring the sky, and a deep darkness pervaded every recess, every gap between the trunks. Everything disappeared except what remained inside the circle of light from the lantern. The light seemed to glimmer, to catch some sort of metal, little flecks in the dirt.

But nothing happened. They sipped their beers, dropped the cans, released their shoulders. How could they have been stupid enough to believe in ghosts?

Disappointed, Jimmy plucked up the handle of the lantern. The metal seared into his skin, flaming heat raising a stiff welt across his palm, and his fingers released. The glass shattered, spilling shards across dirt, the now-released flames licking up any organic matter. Neat tendrils of fire followed a clean circle as if drawn with lighter fluid.

"What the fuck," Mark said, tipping over the edge of the rotten log he'd been sitting on.

The darkness inside the trees grew eyes.

Susie screamed first, her nearly full can of Budweiser plopping onto the ground, a little geyser of beer spurting from the top. The eyes grew faces, grew bodies, until they stepped into the firelight, forming a circle around the buzzed teenagers. Before any of them could speak, before they could ask who the fuck all these people were, before they could catch all the little ghostly details—the darkened eyes of the men, the hatchet so oversized it seemed ready to chop an ancient tree down, the unmoving bundle in the woman's arms, and the gleaming, dripping smile on the man with the coat with charred edges—the ghosts went to work.

They stabbed their nails into the empties, ripping them into shards, which they used to slice against the skin of the teenagers, wrists and necks and any other exposed arteries gushing into the dirt, filling it, blood pouring out of their bodies until it swam to the edges of the flame-lined ring.

The town would call it a suicide pact, would block off the woods with yellow tape, and parents would keep close tabs on their remaining children, letting them go nowhere without a grown-up in sight. All crazed summer adventures halted immediately.

They would not have guessed that as these five teenagers lost consciousness, as their blood spilled into the hungry earth, the ghosts had licked the bloodied edges of the shards, disappearing only once the lake of blood had extinguished the flames in the circle, one by one.

MARCH 13, 2019
7:54 P.M.

"Fuck," Clay said.

"I thought you said she went to get help," Dylan said.

"She did," Clay insisted.

Sylvia's skin had taken on a dark hue, a deep, eggplant purple. The back of her skull, the white bone, created a divot in the dirt. A chunk of cheek plopped away from her face, sinking into the wet earth like gelatin. Clay swallowed moonshine-laden bile.

He could still feel Sylvia's smooth skin between his palms. The red welts he'd left there had disappeared beneath the rot. The space where his long fingers squeezed had been entirely consumed, showing bits of spine. It was hard for him to get the full picture. Was Dylan's flashlight dimming or had the haziness surrounding his vision crept inward?

"I—uh, I guess something must have happened after she left," he lied.

"Bullshit."

"Clay, what the fuck!" Luke screamed, using every working limb to scoot as far away as he could manage.

"I'm telling the truth, I swear," Clay said. He blinked,

squinted, his waning vision still pinpointed on Sylvia.

"We're not even that far from the campsite," Dylan said. "If something happened after she ran away, you would have seen it—heard it. So what are you hiding?"

"Maybe that woman did it," Clay replied. "The one I saw on the trail. Or all those people we saw in the trees."

"We would have heard her," Dylan said. "Wouldn't she have screamed?"

"I don't know," Clay said. His face flushed. How had her body deteriorated this much overnight? He couldn't have done that. "Clearly something fucked-up is happening here. Please, I'm telling you the truth. I swear."

"When you and Sylvia left," Luke said, "those people were all still in the trees by the campsite. They didn't disappear until you came back."

"I don't know," Clay said, words sputtering out before he could stop them. "I don't know. I didn't know what I was doing. It was like—like this fucking place was controlling me, like it was pushing all this anger into me. I was in some sort of fog. And when it went away, my hands were around her neck and she was limp."

"So you just fucking left her there?" Dylan spat. "And lied to us about it? I thought you were her friend. I thought you were *my* friend."

"What was I supposed to do?" Clay yelled.

"Not fucking kill her!" Luke screamed.

Dylan pointed her blade at Clay, some celestial light glinting off the tip. It was the only thing he could see. His vision had become a pinhole, gray nothing haloed around the sharp blade. The bottle dug into his hip, the liquid sloshing and burning against his thigh, as though the flames had boiled it. The raised etchings on the bottle branded the skin at his waist.

"I thought I knew you," Dylan said, helping Luke up from the ground. "I thought we were friends. We're going this way, and you better not fucking follow us. Get lost."

Dylan and Luke lumbered away into the trees, leaving Clay alone with Sylvia's body, with the proof of his deed. He retched, the scent of iron and copper tickling his nostrils. He sat in the dark, listening to them struggle away from him, until even their grunts and footsteps through crackling leaves had faded.

His eyes did not adjust to the dark. His pupils widened but took in no light. He held his hand in front of his face, waggled his fingers—nothing. Even in total darkness, he did not need to pat his clothes to find the bottle at his waistband, to slip off the cork and bring the glass to his lips. He sucked deeply from it. The acidic alcohol sloshed over the corners of his mouth.

This fucking place. He wished he'd never flown over this swath of trees. Surely there was an undiscovered rock wall in some other place they could have gone. It would have been better to find nothing at all.

At least the liquor kept him cozy. Against his back, the rough bark of a tree scratched through the fabric of his clothes. Time stretched as he sipped from the bottle, the gray surrounding him seeming to grow thicker. Had he been sitting there for seconds? Minutes, hours?

It didn't fucking matter.

The silence pressed, as dark and heavy as the absence of light, and just as disturbing. If not for the sulfuric scent emitted by Sylvia's body, so pungent he could taste it, he might have hallucinated, might have pictured himself clawing out of the forest, finding the Jeep, and leaving on the open highway. Grabbing a greasy burger from a drive-thru. Hell, even visiting that weird-ass waitress from the run-down diner, just to tell her she was wrong, that there was absolutely nothing in the woods but bugs and leaves and dirt. Instead, he felt like he was in some void that held only rotten air. He stabbed his fingers into the mud, wet earth filling the space beneath his nails, pinching his fingers together, squeezing out a liquid he hoped was rainwater. He even sniffed in Sylvia's stench, deeply, just to have some grounding sensation.

But, all too quickly, his fingers numbed and his nose had memorized the stink. Everything faded into the background. There was only gray nothingness. He might as well have been in outer space.

At the moment when he reached the verge of madness, conjuring more terrors than cozy fast-food fantasies, at the point when he could neither feel nor hear nor smell nor see, when he stuck his tongue out into the cold March air in one last-ditch attempt to activate this sense and tasted not even the smoke from the fire that had raged behind them while they fled, at the point when the moonshine—now down to the dregs—no longer burned but tasted clear as water, he started to hear things. Rustling branches snapping against their siblings. Some sort of human noise. Laughter? Grinding teeth? Sucking in drool?

"Who's there? What the fuck is going on?" he called out.

He pitched forward, his back lifting away from the rough bark. An ache blossomed along his spine. A muscle in his thigh cramped when he twisted to turn his ear toward the sound. It was as if the soundscape had startled the rest of his senses back into existence, reset everything to factory settings except for his sight, which remained a blob of gray. The putrid smell of Sylvia again burned the back of his throat, beckoning stomach acid up his esophagus, his equilibrium careening into nausea. A knot of vomit hovered on the back of his tongue.

Behind him, wet sounds, like lapping tongues, created an ugly harmony.

"Hello? Can you fucking respond? Who the fuck is it?"

If his eyes were working, he might have seen what Dylan had—that field of teens from some other era, their blood spilled into the ground, their veins lapping it back up: the memory moving in reverse. He might have noticed their sneakers beginning to twitch, the heels rolling in the dirt. Their fingers scratching, drawing claw marks on the wet ground. Soon, their whole bodies convulsed, shaking into life, the blood from their necks and wrists and thighs slowing to a trickle, and then their wounds closing up entirely. They flopped like fish, and Clay twisted his head around toward this thunderous slapping sound.

"What the fuck!" he screamed. He rubbed his eyes like they were clogged with debris, like he simply needed to remove some sort of darkening lens. He pitched the bottle to his lips—if he was going to die here, he refused to be sober—but it was empty at last.

The slapping noise grew to a crescendo and then stopped, abruptly, as if an invisible conductor had pinched the sound off with his hands. Clay sat still, his fingers fisted into the soil, his eyes glazed. It was not until the teens' mouths opened and emitted a shrill noise that sounded more like a train whistle than a human scream that he scrambled into motion. He pulled himself upright against the tree, his feet gathering his weight, and ran.

The young teenagers opened their eyes. They pushed themselves up from the puddle of their own making, turning their eyes to the fleeing man. They zipped up their jackets, the zippers flowing through dirty triangles of magenta, lime, and cyan. Each held a rusty shard of aluminum. The sharp edges were stained by their own blood, covering up the faded red-and-white Budweiser logos. Their mouths parted into smiles, sharp teeth glistening like bits of quartz.

If Clay could see, he might wonder: what light was there to make them glint?

"Fuck this place," Clay muttered, stumbling. His foot found a gnarled root and his knee crashed into a too-close trunk. He pushed himself upright again and continued lurching away from where he'd heard those horrible sounds, his arms in front of him like a shield to catch incoming trees. Though every atom in his body urged him forward, he could only creep slowly through the forest. His arms, swinging ahead of him, grazed a tree trunk.

"This isn't real," he whispered. "It can't be real."

Not one piece of him believed his mantra.

The teenagers kept pace with Clay, staying exactly six steps behind their prey, their aluminum shanks shining and glowing.

A coiled root pushed out of the earth, waiting to entangle Clay's boot, and he crashed onto the ground, hands catching inevitable, razor-sharp thorns, his skin shaving away from his palm like cheese. A low growl escaped his lips. It wasn't supposed to fucking be like this. It wasn't supposed to end in blank darkness and wet, stinking mud. It was supposed to end in glory, in riches.

He clawed his way to standing, pulling on low-hanging branches and pushing his weight back over his legs. His clothes hung heavy, drenched in the iron-scented wetness that plugged his nostrils. Little flakes of it dried on the palms of his hands. They chipped away when he smacked against trunks.

No. It wouldn't end like this. There had to be a way out.

The kids stalked behind him, the distance between them closing only in those moments when Clay fell and righted himself.

Once more his foot caught a root or a vine and he toppled head over heels, his arms pinwheeling in front of him. His knees cracked against rock, his rib cage emitting a loud slap as it landed, his hands and elbows touching down last. He pushed himself up onto aching, screaming knees, felt around in front of him with bruised and bloodied palms.

He felt solid ground. No mud. No leaves. Little pebbles rolled beneath his hands, a level patch of them like gravel, like the tiny, smooth gray rocks that lined the shoulders of rural highways. He padded his palms farther ahead, darts of pain shooting through his knees. Let them ache. Smooth stone lay ahead, something flat and warm and just rough enough.

Asphalt, he thought. *Paved road. I've made it out. I'm going to be okay.*

He leaned his head down as if to kiss the road. His lips hovered inches above it, and he inhaled deeply, seeking the scent of tar or rubber. It did not cross his mind, as he crouched there feeling but not seeing, that he could meet his end splattered on the grille of an eighteen-wheeler.

A laugh bubbled from deep within him, rocketing out of his mouth. He'd fucking done it. He made it out.

A snarl interrupted his laughter.

Behind him, the teenagers had caught up. They hovered at the edge of the tree line, considering him. In front of him stood the woman from the trail and her dog, her overloaded horse behind her. Long sheets of bedding snapped in the wind, and little trinkets—a child's doll and a rattle—had fallen out of the basket.

The woman nodded at the teens—a minute motion Clay could not discern with his gummed-up eyesight—as if this had all been planned, as if the teenagers had driven him to this spot where the woman and her hellhound waited.

"Hello? Dylan? Luke?" he said, perking his ears. "Is someone there? I need help."

The figures surrounding him, closing in, did not respond. The dog growled.

"Please!" he called. "I can't fucking see anything! I think I've fractured my knees and I'm lost!"

The others moved nearer, their footsteps silent and precise.

"Are we at the road? You have to get me to the fucking hospital!"

You can't leave.

The thought whispered between his ears, and he rolled onto his side, hands covering his face, as a slimy toe knocked against his tailbone. Bony fingers reached into his hair, contracted like a claw machine, and pulled. He reached up, scratching at the deadly grip, trying to yank the fingers out from the tangle of his hair. But they only gripped harder and dragged him down until he lay flat on his back.

He screamed into the gray void.

The heavy fabric of his shirt pulled taut, rising like a tent between the dog's slimy teeth, ripping with a wet squeal. The dog's sharp nails pressed into his stomach like daggers, the beast's weight heavier than he'd anticipated. The paws squeezed the air from his lungs like a tube of toothpaste.

His throat raw, he whispered his useless pleas.

Gnarly, curled fingernails poked through the rest of his clothing, sharp as seam rippers. They peeled his pants from his legs, ripped through the laces on his boots and unraveled his socks in their haste. The feathers from his down jacket tickled his nose as they fell back down like soft snow. Soon the cold night air pockmarked every inch of his skin. His ass rubbed raw against the rough road and goosebumps populated his crotch.

The dog hopped back onto him, and a hot glob of drool dropped onto Clay's naked stomach, searing like lava. His mind reached back to the trail, projecting a little film against the gray for him—the dog ripping flesh from bone, zooming in on the way the skin had snapped like a slingshot the moment it separated from muscle, panning to the flossy tendon stuck between the dog's teeth, a little sliver of white beneath the thick slathers of blood.

The dog's wet, cold nose probed his exposed chest, sniffing for the most delicious portion, while a sharp nail scratched in the other direction down his belly, both parties looking for their favorite fleshy spot to sink into. His hands covered his groin. He tensed in anticipation of the dog's teeth stapling through the layer of chewy fat on his stomach.

"Please don't," Clay sobbed. With the dog's hungry fangs right above his pounding heart, he dared not move. He could feel its hot breath against his chest.

"Please, please. I'm sorry. I'm so fucking sorry. I didn't mean it. I didn't mean to kill her. Please. Shit."

The nose and fingernail retreated, the ripped hem of the woman's skirt grazing the hairs on his legs. He kicked his legs up, ready to roll and run, when the teenagers descended upon him, a tangle of hands and knees, their stinking, rotten breath invading his nostrils. Corpse-cold hands pinned his wrists to the ground, and he twisted his legs and bent his knees to cover his middle before another set of hands pulled his ankles down and held them. Bony knees pressed their weight into his thighs.

A fifth set of hands pushed their flat palm against his chest before carving into his sternum, performing surgery with the rusted beer can. They worked down in a straight line toward his navel. The can caught on the thick leather of his skin, and a squeal escaped his lips along with a chorus of *Fuck, fuck, fuck, fuck*. His blood bubbled up and slid down into the round bottom of the can. It steamed against his skin. At his last set of ribs, the sharp triangle of aluminum broke away, sliding beneath the flap of skin. The hand threw that can behind it and picked up the next one. The clink of the first can onto the asphalt was buried beneath Clay's screams, his own breath pooling above him in angry clouds.

The world was a gray slate of pain, and he writhed against the icy grips on his limbs. He tried sinking down into the road, a deranged thought ricocheting through his mind—if he'd stayed in the trees, he may very well have been able to escape into the earth. Maybe suffocation, being buried alive in mud, the earth sucking the flesh from his body, would have been easier. But instead rough pavement scoured his bare back while ghosts sliced through his epidermis, now onto the third can. They paused at his belly button, stopping only to reposition and cut horizontally, a straight line across his pelvis, a stripe they repeated near his collarbone.

At some point, Clay expected to go numb, to have accrued so much pain that his nerve endings would spare his brain from feeling it. But instead, every scratch tore with fresh agony. Every hot, stinking breath blew shivers against the hairs on his arms. Every stretch of already-torn skin screamed at the invasion of air.

The only parts of him that had numbed were his hands and feet. His throat scratched raw, his screams were extinguished, useless noises that merely inflicted more pain.

He wished it would be over. Surely it must be soon.

The line across his collarbone now completed, the final can clattered to the ground. Clay inhaled a single breath before hands pushed into the gap, unfolding his skin and muscles like a picnic basket.

The hands at his wrists and ankles shuddered. The five stomachs surrounding him growled. His tormentors seemed to puzzle at his exposed rib cage, tapping it with their nails and then licking the blood from their fingers with a slurp. Despite his destroyed, dry throat, Clay tried to scream when they dipped all ten of their hands between his ribs. Then, in matching pairs, the hands pulled in opposite directions, cracking each rib at the same junctures along the sternum and spine as if the set had been connected to rusted-shut hinges. No longer shielded by skin or bone, his organs lay exposed to the air.

Then they feasted.

The woman and dog joined them, knees scooting along Clay's twitching, roiling body as the others made space. They stained their hands with his blood, scooping his slippery insides, slurping his intestines like spaghetti. His torso was a buffet, and as their knees trampled his arms and trapped his legs, as their sloppy chewing continued through the thick gray nothing that clouded his eyes, his last, wild thoughts were of zombie movies, of campy screen tricks—chocolate syrup as a stand-in for blood and peeled fruits for organs—right before the dog dove in, squeezing its teeth around his heart.

MARCH 13, 2019

8:49 P.M.

At one point, Dylan had thought herself strong—she could do ten pull-ups, one right after the other. Hell, just a few days ago she'd sent six brand-new routes in a row and barely felt it. But dragging an awkward, two-hundred-pound body through a forest with spongy, uneven ground wore her out quick. She had no destination or sense of direction other than *away from Clay*. They were just going.

Though the light on her knife had flickered out, her pupils had widened and she could at least distinguish the trees and the spaces between them. With each step, Dylan held her breath, tensing, expecting to stumble into another pile of bodies or puddle of blood—or some fresh horror. Instead, her ankles tangled in a briar patch, little thorns poking holes in her, and she pirouetted into a spiderweb. Losing her balance, she set Luke down as a shrill scream reached them, echoing through the trees.

"What do you think that was?" Luke asked. "Do you think it was Clay?"

"Don't know," Dylan replied, her lungs raw and craving air. Each breath scraped against her throat. "Don't wanna know."

She stretched her arms, lengthening the tendons, wishing there was a moon in the sky so that she could determine whether they'd been moving for hours or minutes. The sweat that had pooled against her, trapped by her jacket, felt frozen in an icy sheet on her prickling skin. The blood caked to her exterior flaked away in rusty flecks. She shivered.

"What's *that*?" Luke asked, pointing with his good hand.

An illumination twinkled through the trees, their trunks stark and clear against it, no longer different shades of darkness.

"Don't know," Dylan said. A knot formed in her throat. "Maybe the cavalry have come searching. Or maybe we got turned around and it's just the fire working its way toward us."

"Do you think we should go see what it is?"

"Probably not," she replied. "But it's either go back toward a known killer or move toward something that only *might* be a killer. Or could be salvation."

After a few more minutes of rest, Dylan heaved Luke up from the ground and swung his arm over her shoulders once more. The orange haze grew, pulsing light through the trees, its heat melting the ice on her skin back into sweat.

"Oh no," Luke said.

"What?"

"Are we back at the campsite? Are we right back at the fire?"

More questions she couldn't answer. She was so damn tired. She sighed and pushed forward with Luke's body in tow.

Just before the trees spilled open, she stopped. Dylan unlatched her boyfriend and leaned him against a tree like a mannequin. The orange light did burst from a fire, but it wasn't the blaze they had escaped—it was inside a pit, contained by large stones. It burned next to a structure, an old-fashioned log cabin.

Right in the middle, where the roof crested, jutted the rock wall, as if it had crashed right on top of the structure or grown out of the earth, slicing the cabin in half.

It was the same rock wall Dylan had climbed just two days before. She recognized the pits and cracks. Chalk from her fingers and black scrapes from the rubber of her shoes smeared across the granite.

Neither the cabin nor the wall seemed to belong where they stood, like an optical illusion. Dylan wondered if she stepped to the right or left whether the back of the structure would appear, whether the angles would align and the vision would right itself, whole and intact. The ground glittered as if it were coated in ice. That, too, must be a weird illusion.

Was this their undoing or would it be their salvation? The thudding inside Dylan's body provided no answer.

The fire gave off just enough light to set the scene, as if it were a high school theater production and not a camping trip to hell. Had darkness not obscured their view, on the other side of the cabin they would have seen the little mounds of dirt marked with wooden crosses—a graveyard of children.

They waited. Dylan held her breath, her eardrums aching from the silence. She crouched, leaning her weight into her knees, while Luke slunk down into the dirt. She pressed her hand against his chest, a signal to wait—as if he could spring out of the trees with his decrepit leg and various slings, as if they had not spent the last few hours trying to traverse a quarter mile through the woods.

The door of the cabin slid open, the drama unfolding like a silent movie, no sound effects or dialogue. A woman exited first, running, carrying a swaddled bundle in her arms. Through the open doorway behind her emerged a burly man. Before she had made it more than a few steps, he slammed a huge boot down onto the long hem of her skirt, the thick fabric holding strong as she pulled away from him. In her frantic struggle, hoping for a freeing rip, she fell forward. The bundle flew from her arms.

A baby rolled out of the swath of fabric.

Eyes open. Little mouth gaping. Still as a doll.

Dylan slapped her free hand over her mouth, trapping the scream in her throat. All of the blood rushed out of her face.

The woman clawed at the ground, kicking her legs, gripping fistfuls of her skirt and yanking. But it still did not tear around the man's heavy boot. Her hands shot toward her waist, trying to rip the skirt away with her nails, trying to snap the taut stitching. But it would not budge.

By the time her finger found a hole in the seam, the man had taken another menacing step across her skirt. She kicked her legs at him, but they became trapped in the folds, in the fabric tomb between his giant feet. The man easily and handily reached down, wrapping his large hands around each of her ankles.

The woman's finger remained caught in the waistband. Her free arm slapped at the ground, hoping to latch onto a root or a weapon or some chunk of dirt big enough to impede movement. When he twisted and pulled on her ankles, she flipped upside down, her face in the suffocating mud.

For a moment, the struggling woman turned her head and found Dylan's gaze. Her eyes bulged as if sending out a silent plea, her mouth filled with dirt. Dylan bit her tongue to keep from screeching. Blood filled the gaps between her teeth.

The man dragged the woman, pulling her in an arc back toward the cabin and then toward the fire. The woman's free hand sank into mud up to her knuckles, leaving five identical trails in her wake. The claw marks raked through the scorched remnants of the circle that had burned across the grass before Dylan and Luke had left camp, blurring the outline. The ash smeared onto the woman's arms and face and hair.

Dylan's legs tingled beneath her. She risked shifting her weight to allow blood flow, risked the earsplitting decibels of a snapping branch that might draw the man's attention. Though the fire blazed some distance away, sweat emptied out of her pores, her bare skin scorching as if she stood right next to the flames.

As if she stood right in the middle, burning alive.

The woman spoke only in piercing shrieks, and the man replied only with deep grunts. There were no words exchanged, no pleading or bargaining. He moved with mechanical purpose but not malice, like this was any other task he needed to complete, same as chopping wood or hauling the deer he'd hunted back to the house. An indifference shuffled into his muscles, as if this was simply some unpleasant task he'd put off for too long.

The man dropped one of the woman's ankles. With his newly freed hand, he retrieved a large blade from his belt.

Luke gasped and Dylan tensed next to him, wondering if the noise had been too loud, even underneath the woman's screams. Her stomach churned. She squeezed the hilt of her knife, waiting for the moment the man turned toward them, stomping toward his new prey.

One-handed, he pulled the woman, still screeching, closer to the fire. Flames danced. Dylan clamped her eyes closed and slapped her hands over them for good measure. There was a dull, wet, thudding sound. And then another—and another. The woman's screaming ricocheted through the trees.

And then it didn't.

The fire hissed, as if consuming something. Through the air wafted a singed scent, a particular burning smell that Dylan didn't want to accept that she knew—a mix of sulfur and charcoal and meat.

Minutes passed. Dylan swallowed bile.

"What's happening?" she whispered to Luke. "I can't look."

"He went back inside," Luke replied. "He hasn't come back out or made any noise."

Dylan unpeeled her hands from her face and her lids from her eyes. The scene would be picturesque and quaint if not for the paths carved into the dirt leading to the fire. She couldn't make her eyes move to the flames, to look directly at what she knew she'd find there. Everything was still.

By reflex, some remaining instinct from the world she'd left not even a week ago, she pulled her phone out of her pocket. The top right corner flashed an angry red low-battery warning at her. Next to that, a little airplane symbol. She clicked that mode off and it was replaced by the empty triangle—no signal.

"What are you doing?" Luke asked. "Any signal?"

"No," she replied. "I'm going to take a photo."

She clicked open the camera, ignoring the battery warning, and pointed it ahead toward the impossible cabin. But inside the screen, the structure had disappeared. The whole scene before them was gone—no cabin, no fire. Just the rock wall, grainy and barely visible.

Try Night Sight, her phone suggested.

"Oh my god," she said.

"What? What do you see?"

"Nothing. Look," she whispered, twisting the screen enough

for Luke to see.

"I don't see anything. It just looks like a black screen. Like you're covering the lens."

"Exactly," she said. The phone shook in her jittery hand. "It's not real. It's not actually there."

"What do you mean? It's right there in front of us. We both saw what happened."

"I know, but it's not showing in my camera. It must be—I don't know—some sort of shared hallucination."

"After all the shit we've just seen? You think this is a hallucination?"

"A hallucination, a ghost, whatever the fuck you want to call it, it's not really there," she said. "I'm going to go check it out." She shifted her weight again, pushing up against her heels. The same magnetism that had pulled her toward the wall, that had propelled her to scale sixty feet of treacherous, slippery granite without rope, now tugged at her again. Like a hand pressed against her back, pushing her forward, a comforting invitation to exit the trees and knock on the cabin door.

"What?" Luke hissed. "Where are you going? Don't leave me here!"

But she had already stepped out into the valley. The fire prickled at the right side of her body, the left side icy and shivering. The flames snapped when she stepped past the firepit, as if they were baiting her, trying to force her to turn and confront what they were eating. She stalked ahead with her phone in front of her face, hoping it might reveal ghostly breadcrumbs that would lead in a direct path out of the valley, up hill and to the car. The screen remained dark. Its lens sucked in nothing but the moonless night. She stood in front of the house as if she had a dinner invitation, breathless with anticipation. The screen did not display the door and its thick, uneven slats of log, scratchy teeth marks from a handsaw etched into it.

She reached her hand out. She rubbed it against the door, the buzzing nerves in her fingers incompatible with the reality on the screen. When she pulled her fingers back, a thin splinter of wood stuck out of her thumb.

She pivoted, twisting toward the direction of their camp. Inside the phone, their tents were pitched in a row, the firepit they'd made covered with the embers of the log they'd burned earlier that day—everything dark and outlined in gray. But when she lowered the phone, they all disappeared.

"What the fuck," she whispered.

Behind her, hinges groaned, and she pivoted again. The man stood in the open door.

Baring his teeth, he reached for his blade.

From his spot in the trees, his limbs aching and throbbing and screaming, Luke shouted in the loudest voice he dared for Dylan to come back. He craned his neck to see around the trunks blocking his view. Dylan had disappeared behind one when she approached the cabin.

"Dylan, come on," he hissed, low and strained. A burst of pain rocketed up his calf as his weight shifted onto his bad leg. "What the fuck are you doing? Let's get out of here."

In answer, Dylan bolted away from the cabin, her long, lean legs pumping toward the other end of the valley. The man trudged out from behind the black silhouettes of the trees that stood in front of Luke's vision like censor bars. Though Dylan sprinted and the man seemed to move in slow motion, he stayed directly behind her, as though she were running in place. Somehow his huge stride cut the distance between them easily. But she remained persistently out of reach—to his lumbering dismay, she was not wearing a long skirt he could trap beneath his boot.

"Holy shit," Luke whispered.

Luke leaned left, still trying to see between the trees when Dylan and the man disappeared into darkness beyond the fire's light. The flames crackled. It was like they had walked off the edge of the map. No grunts rose into the sky, no screams hurtled through the forest, no sounds of snapping or sloshing through the brush reached Luke's ears.

What the fuck was he supposed to do now? Every movement bloomed some new pain that shot through his entire body, immobilizing him.

Still, Luke tried to push himself up. The sensation of one thousand knives pricked into his leg, poking into the filled, bulbous skin like they were slicing into a water balloon. The jabs of pain reached all the way up his thigh, even a stray knife in the crook where his leg connected to his groin. The sensation was still crawling upward. Soon it would be eating at his belly, his chest—his heart. The thought made that organ pause.

He pushed his good hand back against the trunk behind him, trying to balance himself on his working foot at the same time. But his foot slid against the soft ground and the sharp bark shredded his palm.

Still no screams from Dylan, no indication that the pair hadn't simply been swallowed whole by the earth when they moved out of the light of the fire. Luke pitched forward, rolling onto his stomach with a grunt of pain, and crawled. His good arm pulled against roots and thorned brambles while his good foot dug into the clay and pushed, his bad arm and leg dragging, nerves firing warning shots across his entire body.

As he neared the tree line, the full scene came into view. The fire, still digesting its meal, sizzled. The cabin's door stood open like a dropped jaw—a gaping mouth full of shadows.

"Dylan," he called, heaving breaths between each word, "where are you? Can you hear me?"

When no response came, he crawled forward. He remained inside the trees lining the valley, not wanting to stick his vulnerable torso into the light of the fire, offering himself up like a sacrifice. But maybe that would be best. At least he'd be put out of his misery.

Like stepping on a half-crushed, still-twitching bug.

The bandage on his arm frayed and unraveled as it scraped against the brush, catching burrs and vines, probably something poisonous that he'd pay for later. His wrist rolled beneath him. The hitching pain that should have accompanied it was masked by the larger agony screaming from his leg, the knives jabbing in and out, the whole thing consumed by a burning sensation like the fire had spread to his skin, boiling whatever lay beneath the purple surface. He expected, at any moment, that a thorn or sharp rock would catch the bloat of his skin, popping the balloon. He didn't want to find out what would emerge. Something deep inside of him conjured an image of thick, black tar.

Finally, mercifully, his hand clasped around a fallen branch, solid and strong. He wrenched it out of the ground, half of it buried. With a heave, he pushed himself upright, the stick bending slightly under his weight when he fought to get his working foot underneath him. Finally upright, he stumbled toward the cabin, the branch working as a makeshift crutch, the toes of his swollen foot dragging leaves out into the valley.

He worked his way to the other side of the cabin, to the place where Dylan and the man had vanished. He moved more like the man, one clumsy step at a time—a sturdy stamp of the branch and then a hop—and with the same determination. But Luke aimed to save the damsel and not end her, not throw her to the flames that hissed and roared as he approached.

The fire burped. It spat sparks, some flying so close that they singed his neck. Lying across the firepit was a black silhouette, the vague shape of a body, toes pointing up. Singed wisps of white fabric—squares of her skirt bordered in black—littered the ground. The reeking scent of burning hair reached his nostrils, and he might have vomited if there had been anything left in his stomach to expel. When he breathed through his mouth to avoid the scent, he tasted her, a bitter, dry charcoal flavor that lingered at the back of his throat.

"What the fuck is this place," he whispered, forcing himself back into movement.

What the fuck was he doing? How could he possibly help Dylan when he had zero free limbs with which to fight? He stopped and took a deep breath. He had to at least try.

The cabin blurred at the edges, as if it were a mirage, as if a hot layer of air stood between him and the structure. It mesmerized him, drew him closer, until he, too, touched its rough exterior. Solid wood. Even this close, the inside of the cabin was shrouded in darkness, the opening a dense mouth of nothingness. He hesitated. Twisted his head left and right. The scene remained entirely still. He limped inside.

The far side of the cabin was eaten by rock. A table was cut in half by it, two legs holding a flat top that disappeared into the wall. A climber's dream home, he thought, somewhat hysterically—bouldering in the kitchen. A half-finished meal sat on a plate, a thick slab coated in green-gray mold—some sort of rancid meat, dotted with buzzing flies. Like it had been sitting there for ages. His stomach gurgled at the meal, whether in hunger or disgust he was not sure.

Luke scanned the room for a weapon, anything he could use to attack the man, to protect Dylan and himself. Next to the plate of rotten food stood a fork and bent spoon. On a bench lay a knife, the blade small and dull, just a couple of inches long. Nothing compared to the hatchet the man wielded, had buried into the woman's shoulder, the blade hacking through her bone like butter. But this tiny knife would have to do—there was nothing else. Luke stuck it in his waistband.

He stumbled through the door before moving into the darkness on the other side of the cabin. It fell in front of him like a curtain, a hard border between the reach of the fire and the black forest. A single step into the darkness, and his skin prickled with goosebumps, the air here thin and cold, his breath clouding in front of his face. Here the trunks could not be distinguished from the gaps between them, and Luke's crutch knocked against them with a hollow thud.

Every atom willed him to turn around.

"Dylan," he called, "where are you?"

Silence filled the space between his words.

Who am I kidding, he thought, leaning against the thick branch. *I won't be able to catch up.* And even if he could—what was he going to do to stop that man, twice his size? Even if he didn't need this oversized stick to stand, even if his other hand were not strapped to his chest, what could he possibly do with the tiny knife he'd found?

Still, he thought, *what else am I going to do?*

He had to try, he decided. He couldn't just let Dylan be butchered.

So he plunged farther into the darkness, deeper into the trees.

His pupils widened, adjusted, and eventually he could see the trunks and where to move between them. With every step, he scanned for signs of Dylan or the man, for some ripped piece of fabric from Dylan's pants or jacket, small footprints engulfed by massive ones. But there was no sign of them, no sound from their chase, no movement in any direction that passed in his periphery. Behind him, the fire continued to digest its meal, the eerie snapping sound somehow reaching him still.

He shimmied through the forest, each step more unbalanced, teetering over gnarled branches and the sticky, rotten pulp of poisonous fruit. The knives shooting into his swollen leg had penetrated to his bones, and each step brought a new fear that his swollen ankle would shatter. That he'd be left with nothing more than a sack of blood and puss and pain.

"Dylan," he yelled. "Where the fuck did you go?"

Farther ahead, something glinted through the darkness. A little speck of light reflecting off of something shiny. He supposed it must be catching the farthest reaches of the fire somehow; no moon or stars hung in the sky. Maybe it was capturing Dylan's flashlight?

He pushed ahead, following the shimmer. When he'd nearly reached the thing, the mysterious object set in the dark like bait, he hopped his good foot right into the curve of a root. He pitched forward, crashing into the mud. The tip of the little dull knife in his waistband nipped at his flesh. He lay in the dirt—more mud than fabric covering his body now—his teeth clamped shut, shuddering in adrenaline and agony.

He wiped muck from his eyes. They adjusted again, pupils dilating into big round orbs.

In front of him lay a tiny paw edged with gray-black fur.

Slade.

His breath hitched inside of him.

His hand brushed through the fur—stiff and ice-cold. His fingers lingered against the dog's belly, his own breath paused while he waited for that reassuring expansion of Slade's chest. But the body was still. Limp.

The tears welled up, steaming against his cheeks. In that moment, Dylan and the man pursuing her disappeared, truly, into the darkness of the forest, not even a blip in his memory. Now he thought only of his dog, his precious Slade, the pup he'd rescued three years ago from a shelter. The dog who'd followed him from his campus-adjacent apartment back to his parents' house and then to a rental with Dylan. Slade had never missed a crag trip. He'd snooze in the sun, dirt penetrating his undercoat, dusting his wet nose.

But Luke had abandoned him, left him to wander into the maws of these woods, this fucked-up forest that conjured ghosts with blood-eating grins, that pushed you in maddening circles until you collapsed into a heap of muscle stretched like taffy, too tired to run anymore. What had it done to Slade? What terrors had he seen in his last moments?

Luke wailed, the noise slicing through the silence, rising into the muddled sky. He nuzzled his nose into the thing's neck. He rocked back and forth with it, sobbing. Had he pulled himself away, had he studied the face, the patterns of the fur, had his brain not been scrambled with a concussion, he might have noticed that the nose was slightly longer than Slade's. Its hair was shorter, its ears not as perky. He might have realized that the edges of each hair were curiously blurred. He might have puzzled together that this was simply another trick, some clone for him to find. But in that moment, he only knew grief and howling pain, and so he held his not-dog in his arms, pressing his face against the not-ears, his fingers following the familiar instinct to rub little flecks of sleep out of the not-eyes, an action he'd performed countless times before.

Then something jabbed him, poked against his arm, just below the collar that hung around the thing's neck. Something blunt and hard and cold.

Something meant for fingers to wrap around.

A hilt. He screamed, his cry like a slaughtered goat, and squeezed the body against him. *Someone killed Slade*, he thought. *Someone stabbed him.*

It had not been a dumb bear or coyote in need of a meal or a mama deer kicking out to protect her young   it had been some thing with motive, something with intent. Something that knew what it was doing and did it anyway.

He squeezed the hilt in his fist. It felt familiar in his hand. Then his fingers found the evidence.

Along the side, an engraving sunk into the hilt. Letters he'd watched being carved into it with his own Dremel tool.

DYLAN PRESCOTT

A fire bubbled inside him. It pulsed through Luke's stomach and up through his chest. How could she have killed his dog? She knew how much he loved Slade.

Had he been thinking straight, he might have wondered when Dylan would've had the time to plunge her knife into Slade's neck—after all, it had been in her hand when she'd exited stage left, pursued by a bear of a man into darkness. Had she really sprinted so far ahead of this ghost man, his stride the length of ten steps, that she was able to not only find Slade but lure him to her and stab?

These thoughts were tiny specks at the bottom of his grief.

If he had tried pulling the blade out, examined it, he would have discovered the lie.

But his face flushed, his teeth chattered. Hot and blurring, tears flowed down his face, sending up tiny tendrils of steam into the cold night. Snot bubbled in his nostrils. For a moment, the heat of rage overrode the sting of the open wound on his arm, gathering dirt as the bandage unraveled. Even his leg had numbed, and he forgot that the purple was practically tickling his balls now. He squeezed the dog tight, kissing the top of its skull.

"I'm so sorry, Slade," he whispered. "I should have looked for you. I shouldn't have listened to her. I should have done everything I could to find you."

He couldn't make Slade come back. But he could make that bitch pay for what she'd done. He kissed the thing one last time, hugging it to his body. He covered it with a brushing of dirt, yet another shallow grave in the woods. Then he pushed himself back up onto the branch and plunged farther into the forest.

He called out to Dylan, his voice echoing back to him, as if he had not discovered her crime, as if he were still the valiant boyfriend trying to rescue his girlfriend from the big bad man. The tiny blade he'd found in the shack burned at his side, his skin shriveling and searing in its heat.

"Dylan, help me find you!" he yelled. "Tell me where you are. I found a weapon!"

Maybe the ghost had done it for him. Maybe she was already lying dead, mangled and bloody, somewhere in the woods, or maybe the man's colossal hands were already wrapped around her ankles, dragging her toward the fire. Maybe they were around her neck.

Maybe he was the last one left.

MARCH 13, 2019

10:37 P.M.

Dylan's legs pounded beneath her, striking damp footprints into the ground. They moved on autopilot now—the muscles like a rubber band coiling and uncoiling, past the point of soreness or tiredness. Objects in motion, especially those being chased by hatchet-wielding ghost men, tend to remain in motion.

Every few steps, she'd crane her head backward. Sneaking a glimpse. The man stomped behind her. He somehow always hovered an arm's length—or a skirt's length—away, always ready to reach out with his enormous hands and crunch the bones of her ankles inside them.

Her breath hitched, a stitch forming next to her rib cage. The chill in the air threatened to seize her lungs if she didn't stop soon, didn't slow down her greedy heart. When her foot slipped on wet leaves and her body shot forward, her heart got a small break, stopping completely in her chest, restarting only when the other boot landed and pushed away, her body upright and running still. She would not yet fall prey.

But she couldn't keep up this bizarre cat and mouse routine forever. She'd surely already run a full marathon through the woods. How do you outrun someone—some *thing*—that never tired? She'd have to fight him. She'd have to get close enough that he could chop her to pieces. She couldn't keep running forever.

Her knife remained clasped in her hand. The blade was folded, useless, inside its housing. As she weaved between the trees, dodging trunks and low-hanging branches, she worked to open it. It fumbled in her hands while she coordinated her movements, trying to pinch the blunt side of the blade in the little cutout of the hilt. The tip poked its head out, a sharp little beak, but the rest of it remained stuck in the enclosure. Finally, with a wrench of her fingers, the length of the blade snicked free.

Behind her, the man grunted and snapped branches beneath his boots, the wood sounding more and more like skeletons, like brittle breaking bones, and the image of those teenage bodies flashed behind her eyes, then the gut-churning remains of Sylvia. Flesh flopped from Sylvia's rib cage, the image seared across her vision, and in this bloody haze, Dylan's foot found a root, kicking her toe right into the loop of it.

Her body shot forward. As she fell, she gripped the hilt with one hand, not wanting it to go flying into the dark woods. She crashed into the ground, the blade snapping over her thumb.

Blood gushed from her thumb, a lot of it, the digit trapped between the blade and its housing. It pulsed, hot, around her hand, overflowing like a pot of boiling water. Through the new, searing pain in her thumb she managed to unhook her caught ankle, struggle upright, and continue running.

She chanced a look behind her, wary of another root snatching at her ankles, but she had to know. She had to see where the man was, how much ground she had lost in her fumble. *Oh shit*, she thought. *Is he going faster? Or am I slowing down?* He was definitely closer now—his boot immediately replacing the space her foot had just vacated. His grunts sounded clearer, and his swing of the hatchet seemed to miss her by centimeters. She even thought she could smell his decrepit breath, a mouth full of rotten, mossy teeth. Acid crept up her throat.

The knife chomped her thumb like a bear trap, the blade notching her bone. Her blood left the entire thing so slippery she could barely hold on to it, let alone lift the blade out of her flesh while running. Her legs pumped on autopilot, her lungs numb. All of her pain had migrated to this single digit, had been replaced by the waterfall at the end of her hand.

"Fuck," she breathed. "Fuck, fuck, *fuck*."

On the wind she heard something—her name? Some syllables wove underneath the persistent grunting, the hot huffing breath on the back of her neck. She desperately searched for the source. Could it be a rescuer? She picked out the first syllable—*dill*—and tripped again, spilling forward into the dirt. As she struck the ground, the knife bit more deeply into her thumb, close to severing it.

She scrambled on hands and knees, her legs twitching beneath her, but her foot remained hooked into the loop of the root, which seemed to be constricting around her toes, receding into the earth. Still, the pain migrated, split itself between her thumb and twisted ankle.

She could do nothing more than scream.

With two oversized steps, the man straddled her. She finally unhooked her foot and tried to dart out from beneath him, but his fingers wrapped around her ankle, clamping tight, unyielding even as she flailed. With her free foot she kicked at his hand, but he did not even grunt, as if he felt nothing at all. Her kicking foot was a mere annoyance, like a mosquito nibbling at his thigh.

This was it. She'd be murdered by a hatchet-wielding ghost and thrown into a nonexistent fire. Nobody would find her ashes. They'd disappear with everything else. No one would ever know what had happened here. What she'd accomplished before it all went to shit. Her name would disappear. At least she'd spare her family the expense of a funeral with nothing to bury.

No. *Fuck that.*

She began working at the knife eating her thumb, ignoring the rocks and debris clawing at her back, tangling in her hair as the man dragged her through the woods. She pinpointed all of her attention on freeing the blade, sticky and slick with her blood. Her fingers slid away from it. Sharp, stabbing pain rocketed up her arm each time she got close to pinching the blade, to removing its teeth from her thumb.

A glint of orange glowed through the trees. He was dragging her back to the fire.

Then her own name rang through the trees, clear and close, louder.

"Luke?" she yelled in response. "I'm over here! Help!"

"Dylan, I'm coming as fast as I can," the voice replied. "I have a weapon!"

A voice spoke in her head: *What if it's a trick? What if it's another trap?*

"Fuck it," she responded, out loud. "I'm dead either way."

With a roaring scream and a spurt of blood, she finally wrenched the steel blade from her thumb. The gash spat out buckets. She bent at the waist, climbing up her own leg, leaving a trail of wet, red splotches across her pants. Folded in half, her chin banging against her kneecap with each bounce of her bottom across the forest floor, she hacked away at the enormous hunk of flesh that was the man's hand. A line of dark, viscous fluid spilled down her arm, hot and thick as tar.

How many times would she have to stab him for the fingers to release? She kept at it, unsure if any number of cuts would make a difference. He didn't seem to feel pain. Maybe she needed to saw them off, digit by digit.

With each slice of her knife, more of the putrid pus emerged, and Dylan gagged, holding her breath against the foul, musty odor that stung the back of her throat. The fluid soaked into her pants, seeming to melt the acrylic fibers. When it found its way to her nearly decapitated thumb, it burned inside the wound, the pain so intense she nearly dropped her weapon.

She swallowed bile and plunged the knife into his hand one last time and yanked it back out again. He roared, an inhuman wail like a wounded bear, and released her. She convinced her twisted ankle to bear weight and hobbled toward the sound of her name.

"Where are you?" she yelled.

"Over here!"

She pivoted toward the sound. Behind her the apparition followed, stomping in the same steady cadence, both slowed by their respective wounds.

"Luke?" she called. "Keep talking so I can find you!"

After following the auditory breadcrumbs, she nearly crashed elbows first into Luke, who limped along with the help of a large branch. Even broken, resembling a scarecrow more than the man she'd entered the woods with just days ago, the sight of him warmed her, ebbed her pain. She was no longer alone. What the fuck was she thinking, going to explore a ghost cabin with a ghost murderer? She reached for an embrace, arms spread wide, but Luke brushed them away.

"No time," he said, pulling a miniscule carving knife from his waistband, somehow still balanced upright.

Together, they turned on the man bumbling in their direction, his eyes focused on Dylan—whether because she was a woman or because she was the one who'd sliced open his hand, she wasn't sure. They stood ready, each of them shivering, their tiny blades against his hatchet large enough to fell a tree with four swings.

"Stand by with your knife," Dylan whispered. "I'll distract him."

Dylan stepped gingerly to the side, Luke shaded in darkness. The man shuffled to her, all eyes on her. Luke might as well have been invisible. When he reached Dylan, he towered over her small frame, somehow as wide and tall as three grown men. She jabbed her blade, all three inches of it, into his abdomen. The little wound dribbled more tar, inconsequential as a knee scraped against concrete.

With his uninjured hand, he strangled Dylan. His hand was so huge his fingers touched at the back of her neck as he hoisted her into the air. The knife dropped from her hand, stabbing the dirt. Her feet dangled, kicking, while carbon dioxide became trapped in her lungs. She had to be ten feet in the air. Her hands scratched at the green, rotten skin, trying to unpeel it from her larynx.

"Luke—" she spat, a gravely, hoarse noise.

The edges of her vision blurred, spawned fuzzy darkness. This couldn't be the end. Luke would save her.

Seconds later, her body dropped heavily to the dirt, landing on top of her injured ankle, twisting it further.

A long thin, mark had appeared across the ghost's neck. Luke had somehow climbed onto the man's back and reached around with his knife. A cascade of thick, steaming tar poured from the wound, splashing onto their shoes. The stench adhered to the hairs in her nostrils, and she struggled to contain her vomit.

The impossible man tipped forward, his knees buckling beneath him. The impact of his body shook the trees. Their branches rattled overhead, raining down bits of dried bark and dead twigs.

Even in the darkness, Dylan's wide pupils couldn't mistake the image of his body dissolving into the muck.

MARCH 13, 2019

11:57 P.M.

Luke tightened his grip around his knife, the edge somehow already rusted and corroded from the impossible man's tar-blood. He sucked in fresh, cold air, his heart pounding inside his skeleton, pumping around the last dregs of adrenaline. The spot where the man had melted held a dark puddle that they both kept their distance from. At least he, whatever he was—A ghost? An entity?—was gone. In the distance, the woman screamed, the same shrill sound they'd heard when they first encountered the cabin, as if they hadn't killed the man but had merely transported him back there, the deadly scene looping over to the start.

The adrenaline finally ebbed and Luke's rage filtered back in. Dylan's knife in Slade's cold fur. Luke ground his teeth.

Dylan limped to Luke, moving behind a tree to avoid the pool.

"Thank god I heard you," she said. "I twisted my ankle on a root. I don't know how much longer I could have kept running. You saved me."

"Yeah," Luke said, his fingers sweating around the wooden hilt of his knife.

"That was fucking crazy," she said, wrapping her arms

around him, leaning her head on his shoulder. The putrid scent of tar and blood on her made him gag. The knife twitched in his hand. She was so close. He could plunge the thing into her neck in one swift motion. "Let's figure out how to get the fuck out of here."

"Why did you kill Slade?" He had to know.

"What?" she asked, lifting her head. She limped back, out of easy reach. "What are you talking about?"

"I found him. His body."

"Oh my god, Luke. I'm so sorry."

She stepped closer, preparing for another embrace that Luke could not stomach. He preempted her touch by asking, "Then why did you kill him?"

"Luke, I didn't kill Slade," she replied. "I'm really sorry that you found him like that, that you found his body. But it wasn't me."

"I know you did it," he sneered. The wooden hilt burned against his palm. "I found your knife in his neck."

"What are you talking about? My knife is right here."

She held out her empty hand, covered in crusted blood, a small river still pulsing out of her thumb.

"Shit," she said, ripping a strip of fabric from her shirt to wrap around her wound. The makeshift bandage licked up the blood, and she winced and gritted her teeth as she wrapped it.

"You can't find it because it's inside his body," Luke said.

"Luke, I swear, I didn't kill Slade." She limped over to the space where she had grappled with the man, toeing around the edge of the rancid puddle. "I just had my knife a moment ago. I had it just now—you saw me with it! I used it to stab that man, that *thing*."

"Don't lie to me," he said. Leaning his weight on the branch-crutch, he hobbled back toward the shallow grave he'd created for Slade. It was so much closer to the tree line than it should have been, but he didn't spare a thought to that anomaly. The daggers of pain inside his leg had faded, replaced by the taut, burning rage in his chest.

Dylan dropped to her knees, swiping her hands through the brush, as if hoping her fingertips would graze against the cold hilt of her knife. She did not appear to care if they dipped into the rancid puddle, or if she'd smack the meat of her palm right into the open blade.

"You and I both know the knife isn't there. It's in Slade's neck," he said. "I didn't just *see* Slade. I felt him. I held his cold body against mine. Can you even imagine what that's like? To find someone you love dead—*murdered* like that? Cold? Limp?"

"I'm sorry that you found Slade like that," she said, "but you have to listen to me. I don't know what you found or saw, but it wasn't my knife in Slade's neck. It might not have even been Slade."

He brushed dirt away from the body. "Here's the evidence. You probably didn't think I'd ever find him. That I'd feel your name carved into the weapon buried in his fur."

She stared, mouth open, at the cold body. "Luke, that's not Slade," she said.

"Don't you think I'd know my own fucking dog?"

"I don't know where that dog came from, but it's not Slade," she said, her voice pitching higher, the words stringing together in desperation. She really wanted him to believe this bullshit. Trick him into thinking he couldn't recognize the dog he'd raised from a puppy.

"Don't lie to me," he said.

"Luke, look—Slade had that whale-shaped marking along his neck, right? Where is it? It's not on this dog. And the ears are wrong. Slade's were pointy and these are floppy. It's not him!"

The hilt of the knife pressed splinters into his palm. He growled.

"Luke, please," she said. "Whatever that is—there's something wrong with this place. It's making us see things. It could be another one of those *things* for all we know. Another ghost or something! Didn't Clay say he saw a weird dog on the trail? Didn't you see one yourself that first night?"

She backed away from him, from the evidence of her deed, shuffling farther into the trees.

He pushed toward her, not even bothering to skirt around the puddle. The foul substance kicked up, soaking into his pants, into the makeshift gauze hugging his ankle. He barely even felt the burn of it. With one quick slash of his knife, he destroyed the sling holding his other arm hostage. He no longer cared whether it ached. The steel glinted in some ghostly light when he transferred it to this newly freed hand.

His vision became a pinhole, all his energy pulsing and aiming at one thing. He could not rest until he did it. He shambled toward her, faster now that he could better grip the crutch.

She scrambled backward on her hands, her back pushing up against a tree, Luke a double of the ghost they'd just slain. Before he could get close enough to slash at her, to slice a neat line across her neck, she stood and stepped backward, one foot steady and the wounded one timid.

He sliced the knife across thin air, still too fucking far away even at the edge of his reach. He was moving too slowly. He placed the slightest bit of weight on his bad leg, the one now completely swollen and purple and rotting, the one that should have incapacitated him with the pain of a thousand knives at the slightest touch, but it had numbed beneath the waves of rage. He sliced its sling away, too.

"I held him in my arms," he roared. "I thought you loved him too. I never thought you'd hurt him. You killed him that first night, didn't you? You let him out of the tent on purpose!"

"Luke, please," she said.

He lunged at her, the knife swiping inches from her nose. Hot, burning rage rose up through the ground, into his feet with each step, boiling his insides. Dylan's mouth moved, but a sharp buzzing filled his ears, like the swarm of flies had returned and filled the space inside his skull. His entire body thrummed with red tension, each muscle and tendon taut, his breath slow and loud and grunting. His heart beat as if locked inside a vise, and release would only come after he avenged Slade.

Luke moved slowly, but Dylan's ankle was wounded. She bobbed through the trees, favoring her left side. But she could pivot and make sudden turns, zigzagging through the trees while he scraped behind on his makeshift crutch. He couldn't lose her.

Ahead the trees opened. The fire blazed beyond them, the orange flicking wild behind the silhouette of the cabin. She turned in front of him, a hard right into denser woods. Luke grunted and changed his trajectory.

"You can't run forever," he growled.

Her feet did not stop pedaling away, just out of reach, until she reached another clearing in the trees, the trunks thinning like hair. She paused at the sight of those ghoulish teens, the ones that had surrounded Sylvia's corpse, now huddled in a circle, their heads down and bobbing. Each one on their knees, fighting over *something*. Slurping. A scream boiled out of Dylan's throat, and their heads rose, their eyes beady and yellow above their maws matted with muck.

They smiled at Luke, their teeth full of sinew.

He smiled back. He'd give them another meal soon enough.

Another orange glow erupted ahead—more flames, spreading in a line as if following a path of gasoline. Luke grinned. A trap waiting, wide enough that Dylan could not change course to avoid it, could not switch directions before it encircled them, leaving her unable to do anything but face him.

Without a weapon.

"Fuck," she said.

For a moment, Luke thought she might try to cross through the ring of fire, leaving her scalded but not dead. Luke needed her dead. She pressed forward, closer to the flames, considering. The air grew thick as honey, steam rising from the mud, from the ground that had just been frozen. Every pore on his body evaporated sweat, expelling the little water he'd swallowed in the last twenty-four hours. It felt like swimming—drowning. His blood seemed to boil, bubbling against his reddening skin, until he felt he was actually cooking, his muscles browning and stiffening like a flank steak on a grill.

Luke squinted through the smoke, his retinas dry in their sockets. A sulfurous cloud shrouded the face of a figure behind the flames. Light winked against his chest, shimmering gold pinned against slate felt. The figure—the man in the slate-gray uniform—nodded at him, motioned for him to proceed. When the man opened his mouth in a pleasured snarl, the red-orange light reflected off his saliva, his teeth glowing.

Dylan coughed in the smoke, now backing away from the flames.

Luke laughed, the sound thick and distorted. He had her.

"Fuck me," Dylan said, twisting around, following the ring of flames to its inevitable conclusion, to Luke.

Luke grinned. Everything inside of him, every atom of his being compelled him, urged him with screaming fury to complete the task—to avenge his beloved dog. He could not rest until it was done. Everything vibrated, hovered in the margins of his vision: the flames, the dark forest around them, the ringleader standing on the other side of the fire, somehow putting messages inside his head: *Keep moving. Do it.*

He'd been given a clear chance. Dylan stood clutching her ruined thumb to her chest, wobbling on her feet. He laughed at this easy target. Even with his bad leg and sore wrist, this should be quick. He held the only weapon.

"Luke, please," she said.

He growled and lunged the blade at her. But it sliced only through the smoke. She'd jumped out of the way. The pair danced, an unbalanced, interpretive cat and mouse, as if they were performing ballet with weights and chains strapped to their feet. Even in this small arena, she evaded his blade, hopping out of reach.

"Stop running, you bitch," Luke snarled.

The walls of flame pushed inward, licking up the grass and brush in their path. The fire burned their backs, and they both stepped closer, their dance becoming more intimate. Beneath the smoke, he could smell her, the rank scent of blood and sweat and grime and ghostly pus. He stabbed at her once more, the blade catching skin, leaving a dark line of blood at her shoulder.

"I've got you," he said. More glistening teeth appeared behind the flames, urging him on. *Make her bleed.*

The fiery ring grew smaller still—no more wiggle room for her to dodge. Above the shrinking ring stood a knobby branch, and Dylan abandoned the dance and threw her arms at the bark, doing what she did best: climbing.

"That's cute," Luke said, grinning. In one crooked step, he stood under her, wrapping his fingers around her ankle, squeezing and dragging her back down. She kicked at him with her other leg, and he plunged the blade into her calf as far as it would go. She wailed, sharp like the last bleat of a slaughtered goat. Her hands unclenched from the branch, her body flopping into the dirt.

Now she lay prone beneath him, her face against the wet leaves. He could end it quickly, if he picked the right spot for the tiny knife, if he did it before she twisted or fought. Then he could release the tension that choked his breath, that pulled at his tendons like marionette strings. He needed her to die. Only then would everything inside of him relax.

Her neck glistened with sweat, the skin soft and thin. An artery pulsed there, a big one, and he dropped her ankle and bent over her neck, the faint purple beneath. He lowered the knife, sharp and swift.

But instead of the resistance of flesh, it landed in dirt.

She had somehow twisted beneath him, that little bitch, had dodged the blade. Now, her face, smeared with mud, stared at his, teeth gritted and brows clenched. He lowered his weight on her, his forearm against her collar, and plucked the knife out of the ground, poised again to plunge it into her neck. But her hand caught his wrist, her fingers strong and unbudging. They tussled in the dwindling ring, her climbing muscles fighting against his weight.

This was supposed to be the easy part. The blade was so close to her neck. But she had always been the stronger of the two, always pushed harder in the gym and on the walls, could do ten pull-ups for every three he completed. He pressed all of his weight into his hand, into pushing the blade down, but her arm locked in place. Her hand gripped so tight around his wrist that blood pooled on either end. His fingers tingled with numbness.

Now she grinned.

MARCH 14, 2019
1:13 A.M.

Dylan squeezed Luke's wrist until her knuckles went pale, until the pain of it wrinkled her forehead. Until she could feel the cracking of the little cylindrical bones beneath his skin. He still strained to lower the blade. While she crushed the bones in his wrist, she bent her knee, working to wedge her leg between their bodies. All of his focus stayed on his plunging, wilting wrist, and he didn't notice what she'd done until her knee jabbed into the bottom of his rib cage.

Maintaining her killer grip on his wrist, she dug her knee into his chest and lifted him away, enough for her to plant her foot on the middle of his chest. The tendons in her fingers tingled. Every inch of her sagged with exhaustion, her eyelids heavy, her skin sticky and gritty with sweat and dirt. She inhaled, pushing every little bit of energy she had left into her foot, still clenching his wrist, pushing up until her knee locked out, her leg forming a straight line.

A distinct *pop* rang into the air.

It was the sound of tendons tearing and joints misaligning, loud even over the crackling of the fire. Luke released the knife with a cry of pain, and it sliced a fine line across her cheek as it fell. The rusty steel, tacky with tar-blood, burned as it cut, leaving an irritated, splotchy welt. The sting pulsed down her face into her nose and lips, as if it had already infected her.

Now, he lay on the ground, trying to push himself upright on broken wrists, one swollen and one limp, his hands flopping like grounded fish.

The knife lay next to Dylan. She didn't want to get up. Even if she made it past this trial, if she got away from Luke—she knew this meant killing him, but she couldn't bring herself to imagine that, that she could plunge this knife into his flesh enough times and in the right places—even if she made it out of here, she'd still have the fire and the ghosts to contend with, and even after that the fucked-up looping forest, and now probably some unknown bacteria in her wounded cheek that would kill her anyway. But what could she fucking do? Give up this close to the end?

Luke nearly to his feet, she grabbed the knife and held it in front of her—a warning. She didn't intend to return his favor.

"Luke, please," she said, struggling upright. The fire pulsed at her back. "Don't come closer. I don't want to hurt you, but I will if I have to."

His ankle bones cracking and swollen skin darkening, he stumbled toward her, still intending to finish the deed, even without his weapon, even with his mangled hands.

She could only stand in the center of the ring, the blade between her and her boyfriend who wanted to kill her, while he lumbered like a zombie in her direction. The flames licked at her back, and she felt herself shrinking inside her coat. Her knees wobbled under her, her body barely able to stand from dehydration and exertion.

Tears welled in her eyes, the last speck of water in her, blurring her vision, painting her possessed boyfriend in watercolor.

But, somehow, it still wasn't over. Not yet. He still moved toward her, propelled not by the fire but by his own rage, his face sweltering in both.

"How's this supposed to work, Luke?" she asked, her voice cracking. The blade shook in her fingers. "How are you going to win this? I've got the knife. What's your plan? Your hands are too fucked-up to strangle me. You might as well just wait for the fire to take us both."

He showed no signs of recognition, of having heard even a single word of her plea. He moved like something out of control.

The tears that poured from her eyes when she was forced to plunge the blade into him left a hard, cold pain in her chest. A pain that grew when she plunged again, left with no choice but to shed his blood into the hungry earth.

The knife dropped to Dylan's side, dripping with her boyfriend's blood. Below her, Luke lay still, eyes wide and bulging, mouth agape.

"Dylan," he said. His wide eyes found her. No longer possessed. Still bleeding out. He reached up toward her, and she took his useless hand.

"I'm sorry, Luke," she whispered. "I'm so sorry. I should have never agreed to come here. We should have gone to look for Slade."

His hand squeezed hers. Then his eyes became orbs of glass, nothing more.

The ring of fire dwindled around her, the flames extinguishing into a smoky haze that left her coughing, left her huddled close to the ground, soaking in her boyfriend's hot blood and holding his cold hand, waiting for the smoke to rise up into the trees. She folded into herself, pulling her knees to her chest. The tears that emerged dissolved into steam. What had happened? How had she become the final one left here, in this despicable place? How had it come to a point that she had to murder her own boyfriend? Could she have saved him—would one single stab have broken the trance?

She considered the knife next to her, that maybe it would be better to end it now than to fight anymore, than to outrun more ghosts or fire or poison or whatever else this fucked-up valley might hold. Blood and tar gummed the short blade. She knew it would hurt. It would not be quick.

She couldn't do it, she decided. She couldn't let this fucking place win, not in that way. It had had enough victories. It would have to work harder for this last one.

The smoke finally cleared, leaving a ring of scorched earth around her. A charcoal scent lingered, something she'd always associated with friends and climbing, with good times and marshmallows and stars and hot dogs. But she would, for the rest of her life, associate this scent with this place, with Luke's death. The carbon burned the back of her throat like a cigarette.

The air hung quiet—no sound at all, no birds, no wind, no crunching of leaves. No more screams. The dark cold of mid-March returned, seeped into the ground, into her clothes, and she shivered, all of the sweat and fear and blood hardening into pellets of ice along her skin. Her base layer, a thin polyester shirt, fused to her back. She wondered if she would fare better if she stripped down to nothing, if the chill of the night air would be less painful than the trapped ice beneath her jacket. In little clouds, her breath pooled in front of her.

She sat up, leaning against a tree, the sheet of ice cracking against the trunk. She didn't move for what felt like hours. A whole millennium. Her eyes glazed, squeezing out stray tears. She lolled her head against the bark, considering the knife again, waiting for the ghosts or demons or the elements to take her. For the earth to slurp her down whole, to peel her meat off her bones like it had done to Sylvia.

"What are you fucking waiting for!" she screamed.

How had everything gone so wrong? Just five days ago, she thought she was going to be a famous climber with Petzl making her their star, more brands clamoring at the chance to sign her, throwing increasing sums of money at her, plastering her face onto magazine covers and her voice onto podcasts. She was supposed to be the girl who developed a new crag, who conquered the rock first. So how did she end up here, next to the cooling corpse of her boyfriend? How did she end up the final girl, the last one breathing?

Behind her, in the trees, the ghosts gathered. Their yellow eyes glowed in the darkness. They licked their lips, considering Luke's body. They'd had a taste of his blood—already soaked into the hungry earth, into the valley to which they were chained, inexplicably and forever linked. Now they waited for his flesh. After picnicking on Clay's innards, they were nearly full.

Something jittered at her hip, a familiar buzzing that sang a sharp melody. She mistook it for a shiver, barely registering the noise as anything but her own clattering teeth until it happened again. Inside her clothing, her phone screeched. She patted her pocket and pulled it out. She hadn't remembered still having it, let alone shutting off the mode that should have blocked any battery-draining notifications.

The thing continued to vibrate in her hand, text messages and notifications from Instagram stacking up on her screen. But beyond the stylized square icon in the corner, the text was a garbled mess of overlapping letters, dots, and symbols she didn't recognize. Everything a bunch of nonsense. The phone must be glitching—maybe the fire had warped it somehow, or her sweat had snaked its way inside to corrode the computer chips.

She cautiously checked the top corner, holding her breath. One single bar.

She clicked one of the distorted notifications, opening the app. Her heart beat a drumline in her chest. Her hands trembled, and she worried that the movement would shift the receptor out of place, just enough to lose the signal. When the app opened, the screen displayed more of the same: text stacked so many times it created a black bar of babble; pixelated images that would not load further, that were so blurry the colors bled together; more strange symbols, like an alien language.

But it didn't matter. By this point, everything was simple muscle memory for Dylan. She clicked around, knowing exactly which part of the screen would create a new post, would make a story that would disappear within twenty-four hours. She wasn't sure she had even that much time; her final cry for help would surely outlive her.

Even the clock in the corner of the screen was broken, displaying a time that did not exist: 65:67. But it must be night or early morning—the sun hadn't risen yet. At least not here. Maybe outside of this cursed valley, the sun shone and it was a glorious afternoon for the rest of the population in Livingston, Kentucky.

She started a live video.

She wasn't sure anyone would be online, would log on to watch her stream, but something began to populate on the screen where usernames of viewers usually appeared, where comments would pop up. But it was just more of those symbols.

"If there's anyone out there seeing this," she said, "please contact the authorities in Livingston, Kentucky. Something bad has happened—I'm the only one left."

More tears welled, hot, in the corners of her eyes. In the screen, everything was bathed in blurry gray.

"I don't know exactly where we are. I don't know the specific coordinates or anything. Sylvia had those. We had a GPS thing, but it broke. We're back in the woods, down a hill. I think we came in off Route 490. We—I can't find the way out. I twisted my ankle. I need help. Please send help."

Words fell out of her mouth like vomit, as if she needed only to say the correct set of them to get home. She rambled as more crazed symbols accumulated across the bottom of the screen. She clicked the button she knew would flip the camera—it had been pointing at the dark dirt in front of her.

The sight of her own face, even muted in the darkness, stole the sentences from her throat. Dried blood dripped out of the scratch on her cheek, a raised welt. Snot pooled in her nostrils, caked her bottom lip. Even in the darkness, every little capillary inside her eyes was highlighted, redness obscuring the whites. Her hair plastered to her cheeks, curving and branching like veins. Like bare trees.

"Please," she said into the camera lens. "There's something here. Ghosts. I don't know. I know that sounds crazy. Maybe I am crazy. But I swear, there's—"

For the second time, her thoughts died in her mouth. In the

corner of the screen, behind her own face, behind the tree she leaned against, there was another face. One with yellow eyes and dripping teeth.

Holding the phone steady, she twisted her head backward, craning her neck to see around the trunk. She held her breath, not wanting the tiny clouds to conceal the view. She froze, blinking. She waited for her eyes to adjust from the brightness of the screen back to the darkness. But even when her pupils dilated, she found only the trunks of more trees behind her.

Maybe I really am crazy.

But back on the screen, it was there. And it was smiling.

"Do you see that?" she asked, more rambling to fill the feed, a gut-reaction to streaming live. "Do you see that face, right there? Right over my shoulder? In the top right corner?"

She turned her head backward again, swiveling it in slow motion, as if sudden movement would spook the ghost into action. Still, nothing sat in her line of sight but the dark silhouettes of trees. When she moved her head back to the screen, the ghost was right behind her—the man with the slate-gray jacket, regalia like a general. He set his hand on her shoulder. The cold weight of it settled there. The blackened fingertips and gray, rotting knuckles only registered on her screen. The flurry of comments picked up their pace, still unreadable.

She recoiled, her entire body shrinking from his touch, nearly dropping the phone. Pain throbbed through her swelling ankle as she scrambled up and away, limping and much too slow. Dylan held the screen out in front of her, a lens into the other world. Behind her, more of them poured from the trees, descending on Luke. The men with rough cotton shirts and twin voids in the center of their faces plucked out her boyfriend's eyes and popped them into their mouths like gumballs. One of the teens in the windbreakers picked the knife out of the dirt and chopped off his toes, passing each one around the circle.

The man in the slate gray remained behind her, too close, though it looked like his feet were stationary. As if he were floating toward her. In the top corner of the phone, signal bars stacked on top of each other. The jumbled text resolved itself, and at last she could read the comments:

Is this for real?

What's going on?

Where r u?

She should have expected what happened next. At the moment her phone lit up with full signal, the screen went black.

The battery died.

MARCH 14, 2019
7:29 A.M.

Hours later, Dylan still gripped the dead phone in her hand. She'd kept running after it had shut off, slowing to a walk only once she'd spun around and discovered she was alone. Her ankle throbbed beneath her and the layer of ice at her back had melted, again, into stinking sweat and coppery blood. She'd wandered, directionless, through the woods for hours, until she simply dropped where she stood, massaging her ankle, ears perked for any more surprises this place might have in store.

Now, the sky tinted orange. The sun eroded the dark, and for a second, her reflection in the phone's screen made her jump, thinking it had somehow turned back on. Before she could study the purple-gray pools of baggy skin underneath her eyes or the splatter of Luke's blood against her chin or the raised slash across her cheek, she launched the phone as far as she could into the woods. She screeched, a primal release, before the tears returned.

The thin warmth of the new day's sunlight thawed her bones. For a moment, her chest unhitched, her muscles relaxed. Her heart beat at half speed. In all directions, the spaces between the trees filled with light—no more sneaky, crawling things could hide in the night. But she was still trapped here, in this damned valley, and now she was alone. She had done that to herself.

In this moment of stillness, an image of Sylvia surfaced, something Dylan had seen the night before but not processed until now: the back of Sylvia's body, the part that touched the ground, had been gone. The flesh had dissolved somehow. And then the image *moved*. A chunk of flesh from Sylvia's midsection plopped into the dirt and sank down as if the ground were quicksand.

Her ankle twitched, little needles poking the swollen muscle, and then Luke replaced Sylvia in her head, lumbering toward her, dead eyed, like a zombie wanting her brains. Again she felt the little blade plunging into his soft flesh until it hit some tendon or bone that the rusty, dull blade could not counter. Again she saw the recognition return to his face, the Luke she had known and lived with for two years come back. His body fell to the ground again, a slo-mo replay, left there to harden into rigor mortis. Or he would have, perhaps, if the ghosts hadn't come to eat their dessert.

She vomited, spitting up acid that eroded her esophagus. No more foraged food left to expel.

Her hands were stained with his blood—her blood. The blood of countless strangers. She didn't dare look at what lay beyond her waist, what stain remained from that blood pond. She held her hands up to the light, the first time in hours that they were clearly visible. Blood coated them like she'd dipped her hand into a bucket of paint, so complete that only an imprint of the knife's hilt remained unblemished. The red cracked along her knuckles, around her destroyed thumb that burst with pain when she rediscovered it.

Her entire body yearned for sleep, her limbs sore and her head heavy. Her mind ached to rid itself of intrusive thoughts. The brush beneath her seemed soft, and she gave serious consideration to lying down, closing her eyes, and leaving herself to her fate. But the bitter scent of her vomit stung in her nostrils, miming the metallic taste in her mouth. Her stomach grumbled. She wished she had some water, a corner of a granola bar, anything to quiet her body. Where had the creek been? Where was their campsite? Trees stretched in every direction, their limbs carrying spring buds. Through their branches, she spotted the rock face.

She exhaled a sharp breath and pushed herself to her feet. The cylinder of granite burst out of the ground like a geyser, trees surrounding it like a halo. It seemed to be the same distance from her now as when she had first caught a glimpse of it on their way in. She considered turning around, heading away from the wall in a straight line, hoping for the road, making sure the rock always stayed right behind her. But opposite the rock wall was a line of endless trees with pink sky poking through their veiny branches.

"Maybe I've ended up on the back side of the rock face," she said. Behind her could be trees for countless miles. "Fuck it."

She chose the rock, chose to move toward the familiar terror rather than the unknowable one. She'd had enough of the unknowable for the time being. At least at the rock, she'd be at home. She knew what to do with the wall, knew herself when she climbed it. She had full control.

She plodded toward it, her ankle throbbing more and more with each step, the adrenaline waning inside her veins. She wished she would stumble upon the thick branch Luke had been using as a crutch, the thought of his name sending pangs rippling through her chest.

The silence pressed against her ears; even her boots stamping through the leaves did not create a crunch. Twigs split in half but did not snap. Instead, her boots pressed plant matter into the wet ground like moldy slush, like she was walking across a sponge.

"That's odd," she said, breaking the silence. A horrified giggle gurgled from her lips with sudden realization. "There hasn't been any rain since we've been here. Why is the ground muddy?"

Still, she refused to look down, not wanting to determine whether it was truly, simply wet ground or whether it was another puddle of blood. If she had looked beyond the dark red stains that reached her thighs, she would have discovered only plain forest floor. The wet came from beneath. The earth was nearly full, but it still salivated.

Instead, she kept her eyes up, always pointed at the wall ahead, as if it would disappear from view and pop up behind her if she so much as blinked.

She honed in on every pain, every miniscule twinge in her ankle, the stream of blood still pumping from her thumb, the twitch at the corner of her eye, the burning gash along her face. It meant she was still here. And it erased the images, the corpses, that wormed their way into her head. Each time Sylvia's white rib cage or Luke's chewy eyeball presented itself in her mind's eye, she stamped, hard, with her swollen ankle, and one type of pain ate away at the other.

After what seemed like hours, the sun pushing up into the sky all the while, she reached the wall. The electricity of it hummed in her ears, a high frequency she imagined was just for her. She reached toward it, knowing it would consume her. It would demolish all other thoughts. It would be her body and the wall.

But she dropped her hand to her side, her fingernails slicing crescents into her unmarred palm—she knew she would not be able to let go once she touched it. It took all of her willpower to back up, to stay three full feet away from it. She followed the wall. Around the curve lay their campsite, where the tents still stood, three polyester pyramids in a row, visible once more. Their contents lay scattered, as if the tents had exploded. As if someone had been looking for something—or someone. The cabin was gone, the petrified wood foundation they had discovered days ago glinting innocuously in the sunlight.

She gave no response, felt no wide-eyed alarm. She merely picked through the debris for a new set of clothing that was not stained with blood or soaked in muck or sweat. Something clean and untouched. She peeled each layer from herself like a bandage, the fabric practically fused to her skin. She stripped in plain sight, too afraid to discover what might appear if she entered the liminal, concealing space of the tent. But even the fresh pair of clothes could not remove the layer of dried, sticky sweat or the blood on her hands. Nothing to do about that.

"Now what?" she wondered.

The valley lay in deep silence. Nothing moved. No yellow eyes or teeth lingered inside the tree line, no crazed husbands came for their wives, no resurrected teens waited to slice open skin with rusty beer can blades. Black ash spilled out of the firepit and across the grass, the fire that had seemed to light the whole valley ablaze somehow extinguished.

But if she perked her ears, if she closed her eyes and listened, she could hear the passing rush of rubber on asphalt.

Or was that in her head?

She sat at the firepit, on top of a stray sweatshirt on one of the unripped camping chairs. It was one of Luke's, emblazoned with a cheesy-grinning cartoon man with flowing blond hair, from Miguel's, the pizza joint at Red River Gorge where they'd met. The same day she'd sent her first 5.13. The grinning cartoon broke her. Fat tears she couldn't afford to shed spilled from her eyes. Her hands trembled in her lap. She'd probably never see that place again, the place that held so much of her blood and callused skin and sweat. The place where she had found herself.

When her body could not expend another bead of water, the pangs of grief moved to her skeleton, every bone seeming to ache.

The sun lifted in the sky, finally breaking past the tree barrier, and the air warmed. The heat loosened her muscles, countering the dull ache inside of her, a waning cocktail of adrenaline and swollen, sore joints. The light caught something else, a glimmer against glass. A blinding glitter that wouldn't let her ignore it, like a laser pointed directly at her eye socket.

"Fine," she said. "I'll do what you want. I'll go look at this thing. What else am I going to do?"

She followed the glaring breadcrumbs to a phone. It must have been Sylvia's or Clay's, she reckoned, since the screen wasn't destroyed. Clicking it on, she scanned the corner. No bars, and it was password protected. For the hell of it, she clicked the emergency call option, but the call didn't connect. She launched the phone with her unhurt hand, sending it slamming into the rock wall.

She did exactly what the valley wanted. It dragged her close enough to the wall to ensnare her, to send out its invisible tendrils to rope her in. Static spat out a spark that licked her finger when she reached to touch the rock. The spark jolted her, overriding the nagging thought in her head that said, *Do not climb this wall.*

But she touched it, and then it was over. She would climb.

She started up the wall. Taut exhaustion filled every sinew, every muscle, every tendon, all stretched and ready to break. Her ankle throbbed with every movement, every toehold, every time she pushed her weight onto it. Her destroyed thumb left the granite sticky. She didn't flinch when her toes pressed into the very tips of her boots. It felt like home.

The wall was cool and dry. She worked the problem, ascending. She stuck her fingers into a tiny pocket, catching spiderwebs, lucky that the ruined digit was her thumb, not much utilized in climbing. Her feet slipped away from the wall, and she clung with the skin of her fingertips. She would not fall. She would not let herself. She would not let this place win—at least, she would fight it like hell. She'd go out on her terms. The heat from the sun seared her forehead as she neared the top, now within reach. Five inches from topping out, from her body spilling over the lip of the route, she reached up, hooking onto the ledge—an easy jug, a wide, curved handle. No effort at all.

She grinned. It was almost over.

She threw her other hand on the hold, rounded like a ladder rung. She readied her feet. One more high foot hook, and she'd be over the top. She would live. Surely no ghosts would be able to reach her up here. Surely she could signal someone, a passing helicopter—there must be people looking for them by now. She exhaled, celebrated for one single second before hoisting her foot up to the next hold.

From her vantage point, the stretches of Kentucky forest spread out around her, a sea of budding trees. She'd done something other climbers spent their entire careers training for—not once, but twice. And with a swollen ankle and destroyed thumb, with a body empty of food and water. Without even climbing shoes. Even if nobody else would ever know, this fucking valley couldn't take away the fact that she climbed this rock, sent it on her first try with no ropes, no safety. This fucking place took everything from her. Her career, her friends, her boyfriend.

But it couldn't take this.

One last throw of her hand over the top, and her fingers landed in grooves of skin, in someone else's hand. It squeezed hers, a warm, familiar squeeze she'd recognize even in complete darkness.

Luke.

Haloed by the morning sunlight, he somehow stood at the top of the rock, pulling her up and over the edge. How could he be here? Was this another hallucination?

"Let me help you," he said, the voice soft and angelic. "It's almost over."

She squeezed back and pushed up with her toes. He'd been himself in his last moments—maybe he had escaped. Maybe he wasn't dead after all. Maybe he'd made it up before her. He was a decent climber, too.

No.

It didn't make sense.

It was a trick.

Her head crested the ledge of the granite and it became clear. She was never going to make it out alive. This place—whatever it was—had lured her up here. Just wanted to see her try. Make her hope.

Behind Luke's face were all the others: the ghostly dinner party from the trees, the eyeless men, the soldiers, the teenagers in their garish coats, the woman and her dead baby. Even the dog Luke had thought was Slade. Clay and Sylvia were there too.

Flesh hung like ribbons away from Sylvia's bones, half her face missing. Clay's intestines spooled out the front of him, his rib cage opened like a cabinet. No longer in silhouette, Luke was missing his eyes and toes, had blood pouring from his mouth. Two stab wounds in his chest. She'd put them there. The hungry ghosts licked their lips.

Luke—*not Luke, this is not the person I loved*—pulled again, now squeezing so hard her fingers turned white, the bones in her wrist rattling beneath her skin.

She braced her feet against the rock. She would not be pulled over the edge, to the top of the wall, just to be feasted upon. She'd heard Clay's agonized screams ringing through the woods. The aftermath of Sylvia's day-old rotten flesh was seared into her mind. She'd seen Luke's eyes and toes eaten like candies, like delicacies. Fuck that.

When she pushed against the rock with her feet, it cracked. A chunk slid away, broke off the wall entirely, falling with her.

Her hand slipped out of Luke's.

Out of whatever he had become.

There was nothing for her to reach out for, no last-minute, deus-ex-machina thing to grab on to. She would fall to her death. At least it would be on her terms. Maybe she'd escape the fate of her fellow campers, maybe not. But she refused to let this fucking place win.

For a moment, she glimpsed the spot where the chunk had broken away, a moment that stretched and extended. The rock bled. It gushed like a waterfall. As if she'd injured it.

Good, she thought.

She dropped through open air. Starting at the point of injury, the waterfall eroded the pillar around it, cracks extending like lightning across the structure. The entire thing collapsed, swallowed back into the earth. Taking her with it.

In the aftermath, the air hung still. Dust settled.

No more rock.

Only Kentucky sky.

APRIL 2019

Tabitha hadn't heard an update from Clay since he left. No social media posts, no emails, no texts. He'd promised to send word about their findings when they ventured back into town to re-supply, but it'd been weeks and he'd ghosted. Maybe he'd gotten so caught up in the research that the group hadn't left the site yet or had only sent out one person to retrieve more food and supplies. Maybe something went wrong with the study, and he hadn't been able to go or it had been cut short, and he didn't text because he was embarrassed. She mulled over these flimsy excuses. But they didn't fit—something nagged at her, like a hand pulling at her pant leg.

Had she misremembered the date they were leaving? She tried texting him, but never received a reply. He'd gotten caught up in studies before, but he'd never gone this long without some type of response. She searched in her inbox for clues, uncovering an email from February with the coordinates, subject line: WE FOUND SOMETHING!

On a clear day, she flew back over the spot. By now the trees had filled in, green and full, and the plane no longer had the LiDAR machine strapped to its belly to create a map of the scene.

Why had she bothered? What could she possibly see from the sky? But, still, when she reached the destination, the coordinates forming an imaginary X right below her, her heart paused and her breath hitched in her chest. Something was different, and it wasn't simply that the foliage had grown in like hair where before there had been only stark, bare branches, or that the sky was blue instead of the cold, dreary gray it had been on the day they'd discovered the wall.

She couldn't put her finger on the difference. Still, anxiety filled her chest.

She zigged and zagged over the space, twisting the airplane around to pass back over as many times as she could, flying as low as she dared. It was not until hours later, after she had landed, driven home, cooked and eaten her dinner, and stood brushing her teeth that the epiphany sprouted, that she realized she had missed the obvious.

There had been no towering wall of rock in that spot.

The valley had vanished.

She twisted in her sleep, the question on the edge of her mind: which had stretched higher on that February afternoon, the naked trees or the column of rock?

The morning after Tabitha's flight, her eyes dry and red, she called the Livingston police department. She sipped her coffee while the voice on the other end droned on about these missing persons, as if bored by their absence.

"We've been receiving some calls about a missing group of hikers in the area," the voice said, deadpan and bored. "Users from some app or something, Instacart? Instasnap? I don't know about those things. Let me see here. Hold on a second."

The scratchy noise of rustling paper filled the earpiece. Tabitha felt a sinking feeling, like a heavy ball of lead had dropped into her stomach, splashing her coffee, which suddenly tasted bitter, the milk sour. How many missing hikers could there be in the woods near Livingston?

"Ma'am? The calls we got were for someone named Dylan Prescott, who the users said was traveling with her boyfriend, Luke, and they think maybe a couple of other people. Do you recognize that name?"

"I don't," she replied. She slipped her phone away from her face and opened Instagram while the officer babbled about social media and prank calls. She found Dylan's account, the bio reading: *red river gorge. always climbing. Petzl athlete.*

"We really don't have much to go on," the officer said. "I mean, we get all kinds of weird calls. But we're a small department—we can't go searching the woods every time some teenager wants to make a prank call."

"Officer," Tabitha said, swallowing, "I think my friend Clay was with Dylan, the person you've been getting reports about. He went into the woods off Route 490 in mid-March, and I haven't heard from him since."

She offered the coordinates to the officer and hung up. She scrolled down Dylan's feed. The top posts on her account were dark squares, off-brand from the rest of the photos gleaming with smiling faces, harnessed bodies, food, or dogs. She clicked open the first photo, pinching to zoom in. She pieced together grainy outlines of leaves. In the top corner, two white specks stared back at her.

When the Livingston department scouted at the edge of 490, they could not find anything but a skin-and-bones dog with a name tag reading SLADE. The dog had its teeth clamped around a large bone. They did not discover the rust-colored Jeep nestled into the woods, nor did they stumble upon Luke's eyeless face or Sylvia Skeleton or Clay's spilled guts. They couldn't have. Not yet. The place was not finished with them. It was still digesting. It could not yet let the bones of its meal be uncovered. The ground hardened while it grew full on its flesh-and-blood dinner.

The authorities input Tabitha's coordinates into their outdated equipment, which promptly malfunctioned, powered down, or took it upon itself to rearrange the numbers, leading them to a bare patch of woods, unearthing only rotten logs and a proliferation of mushrooms in rings and trees and trees and trees.

A few officers, however, came back with goosebumps and wide eyes, swearing they felt *something* out there in the woods, some weird presence none of them could really describe. Some swore they saw a woman in the distance, hiding behind trees, but she always disappeared when they tried to approach.

After the story of the missing hikers started gaining media attention, bored adventurers said they saw the same woman after venturing into the woods—one managed to catch her on grainy footage that spread like a disease, much to the dismay of the tiny Livingston police department, who worried that their entire force would soon be dedicated to rescuing idiot teenagers from a patch of woods that had sat quietly on the side of 490 for decades.

The video showed a dark silhouette peeking out from behind a tree, the voice of the person filming whispering, asking if anyone else sees it. But as they inched closer, the silhouette transformed into shrubbery. Still, it garnered millions of views and rebuttals, from people debunking it to people claiming the shadowy figure was one of the hikers hiding out in the woods after luring the others there to kill them. Later, the sleep-deprived investigators would replay the footage a thousand times, trying to sharpen the blurry image.

Inside the precinct, the phone rang after each dispatch, like clockwork. The officers lifted the phone, knowing the voice on the other end would belong to Tabitha before she spoke.

"Did you find anything?" she would ask.

"Nothing but trees," they would answer.

While the Livingston police department sent out officers to hunt for the same goose egg, threatening the assignment to anyone complaining of boredom, wasting money and time with their easily tricked GPS technology, the earth feasted. Four months later, Sylvia had almost become her moniker, nearly every last bit of skin, muscle, sinew, and organ sucked down into the earth. Chunks of flesh slid away from her, flopping onto the mud like a slow-roasted rack of ribs. Any trace bruising along her neck became irrelevant—Clay's handiwork would become impossible to discover. His bony hands had not even squeezed hard enough to crack the delicate bones of her larynx or hyoid. By summer, the humid Kentucky heat worked in tandem with the greedy earth, melting away the last few bits of epidermis left on the top ridges of her body, across the bridge of her nose, on her forehead, letting them slide away like an avalanche.

The ghosts tied to that valley had long since had their fill of Clay, his sternum opened like a picnic basket—their first full meal in a long time. Not since they'd sucked the blood from their next-newest companions, forever clad in loud eighties jackets. They'd slurped Clay's intestines like never-ending trails of spaghetti noodles, stabbed their teeth into his organs like they were fresh apples. They licked their fingers clean, their ghostly bellies full and satiated, before they found Luke, his body still warm after being murdered by his own girlfriend. Next to him lay a little gleam of steel, the tiny blade sticking out of the dirt. The perfect instrument for their delicate dessert, for all those little morsels sticking out at the edges. While his girlfriend ran into the night, they carved off his toes and fingers, crunching them like carrots. They divvied the exotic offerings, the ones too good to share: the chewy ears, the juicy eyes. The most coveted they fought over before the general returned and claimed it for his own, taking the knife to carefully carve the tongue away, leaving a straight, precise line by Luke's back molars.

Full to bursting, they merely sighed when Dylan pushed away from the wall. Let the earth take her. Had she pressed farther into the woods instead of returning to the heart of the valley, to her one true home on the wall, she might have escaped, the site and its residents too engorged to notice one more body at the margins.

As the fruitless search wore on, articles about the missing climbers trickled in, a few paragraphs appearing in the local news in Lexington but spreading once Petzl released a statement about Dylan Prescott, about how saddened they were to hear of her disappearance, how they hoped their brand-new sparkly client would resurface. Months passed, and the story reached the national stage, with the AP releasing updates, with countless podcasts theorizing where the missing campers could be. Even NPR and the *New York Times* had published articles about the disappearance, dubbing the area Prescott Pass, after Dylan.

But it wasn't until fans somehow got a hold of leaked crime scene photos months later that anyone latched on to the biggest quirk, something the investigators hadn't even noticed, distracted by skeletons and missing organs and missing persons: there was no wall. They'd never encountered any type of wall, nothing like the structures in Clay's scans, at any point in the investigation. They went there to climb, right? So why hadn't anyone found a wall? Weirder still, a giant gaping hole in the puzzle, was that fans were adamant they'd *seen* the wall in Dylan's few livestreams. Tabitha followed the news relentlessly, flew over the site continually. She couldn't believe no one had found the wall yet—she had seen it with her own eyes. Hadn't she?

Tabitha continued to call the precinct, but now her calls ended in a voicemail, a prerecorded cheery voice promising to return the favor and directing news agencies to their new and harried publicist. By now, the campers' parents and family had pressed the department for answers, and the case had spawned, enfolded more detectives from the Kentucky state police, who streamed biweekly updates on the case, likewise uncovering nothing but thousands of trees. Maybe they should chop them all down.

Confusing the search was the fact that Dylan's account continued to livestream, sending out grainy and dark clips, soundless and lasting only seconds. Yet more pieces of evidence on the heap that added no clarity. Did that mean she was still in the woods? The streams would pop up on occasion even years later, the itch of discovery returning with each one, reviving crazed, sleepless obsession across the nation.

The police would discover nothing until the place slept, until it was satiated. With a full belly and a new group of ghostly victims, it no longer cared if a motorist with a full bladder uncovered the rust-colored Jeep in the trees, if he stumbled and stared at the dirt-streaked sole of Luke's toeless foot. The earth didn't bother to hide Sylvia Skeleton's bones, didn't mind when investigators plucked up each one and placed them into plastic bags.

It had had its fill. Let the authorities and morticians ruminate over Luke and Clay and Sylvia. Dylan's body had already been digested beneath it, already set in a grave. That wretched place wanted the rest of them discovered so the authorities would clean up, returning the spot to pristine wilderness.

Leaving no trace.

ACKNOWLEDGMENTS

This book has been a very long time coming. Truly—so long I don't really remember how everything fell into place. It was conceived during a regular trip to the climbing gym, where I wondered how I could incorporate climbing into a horror story. That seed started to grow after a friend supplied the LiDAR piece of the puzzle on a trip to Red River Gorge—I actually stole his idea directly, with permission, to use it as a method of finding new climbing areas. I remember reading and researching that cold winter in Kentucky's history while sitting on a sunny dock at a family lake house. Discovering that the Livingston woods do actually hold a real, mostly undeveloped rock-climbing spot just off Route 490. I remember the first chapter screaming at me, waking me at 3 a.m., and spilling out into my phone's too-bright screen in the bathroom, much of which still remains in the final draft.

Who's to say how the other pieces fell into place? How I thought up a sentient, evil forest with a history of luring people to it? I suppose that's the magic of writing—and working on the same project for five years.

And now it's in your hands!

There is a very long list of people that led to this book being published—probably much longer than I can remember.

Major thanks and gratitude to Cynthia Pelayo, who was gracious enough to mentor me and help guide me through a crucial edit of this work. Without her guidance, continued friendship, and support, this book would be in a worse place.

Thanks to Lane Heymont, who believed in this book and in me.

To Rebecca Gyllenhaal and the team at Quirk for making it the best it could be and putting it out in the world.

Thanks to Rob, who continues to support my goals and dreams.

To my mother, Martha, for daring to open a niche bookstore with me, and to my father, Mike, for supporting us, even when we want to do crazy things like paint dripping blood on the outside of the building.

To Andrew, who allowed me to borrow his idea for LiDAR for the impetus of this book.

To Jessica, Chris, Angela, Jami, Janna, Yvette, and others who I'm embarrassingly forgetting (if this is you, I'll buy you a donut) who read an early version of this book and provided vital feedback. And to my writing communities, for supporting me and helping me grow.

To Adria, Zach, Amanda, Bonnie, and Clay, who have lent their ears (not literally).

To Reese, for his snuggles.

And to Rye, without whom I probably would have finished this book a lot sooner.